December 7, 1976

The Pompeii Scroll

Novels by Jacqueline La Tourrette

A Matter of Sixpence
The Madonna Creek Witch
The Previous Lady

The Pompeii Scroll

by Jacqueline La Tourrette

Delacorte Press / New York

Manufactured in the United States of America

First printing

Designed by Karen Gurwitz

Library of Congress Cataloging in Publication Data

La Tourrette, Jacqueline, 1926–
The Pompeii scroll.

I. Title.
PZ4.L3547Po   [PS3562.A759] 813'.5'4   74-17018
                ISBN 0-440-06091-5

TO FRANCO G. DI ROSA,
my guide, my interpreter,
more than a friend.

On the 24th of August, at about one in the afternoon, shortly after lunch, my mother observed an unusual cloud of enormous proportion. [From the northern coast of the bay of Naples] it was not possible to tell from what mountain the cloud was issuing, though later we discovered that it was Vesuvius. I cannot give a more accurate description of it than by comparing its shape to that of an umbrella pine, extending into several branches at the top. A gust of air must have blown it aloft, causing it to expand as it dissolved, producing the effect that it was white at one moment and, at another, dark and mottled, as though it carried with it earth and cinders and ashes.

—PLINY THE YOUNGER
*(The only eyewitness account
of the eruption that buried
Pompeii in* A.D. *79)*

Chapter One

The sudden motion in her peripheral vision immobilized her with unaccustomed fear. Her heart stopped for a moment, and her mouth went dry. All day, while searching the honeycomb of broken houses for their artwork, looking for a certain tantalizing smile on a certain kind of ancient crafted face, Joyce had sensed that she was being watched, that something besides that smile had followed her all the way from Greece, and that it was getting closer all the time. She had picked up the vibration in her nerves several weeks ago in the Etruscan tombs at Tarquinia, but until now she had not been really frightened, only more observant. Her pursuer had never materialized; he lurked only in the shadows of her intuition. Today, under the blue sky of Pompeii, she felt that he was nearer, closing in on her, and the sudden appearance of a man on the deserted street twanged her tightly drawn nerves. It was getting late. The excavation was open until sundown, but most of the tourists were gone already, and the ancient street was empty, except for herself and the approaching figure.

Sitting on a blazing stepping-stone in the middle of the Strada dell'Abbondanza with a map of Pompeii spread out on her knees, she watched the man out of the corner of her eye. He was the only moving thing among the mottled, half-reconstructed shops, and he was taking his time. One impulse told her to leave quickly, but another . . . either fear or dogged stubbornness . . . urged her to face the problem now and have it done with. It was better to meet him face-to-face in the hot sunlight than in the dark somewhere, when she was not expecting it. She let her heavy leather handbag slide from her shoulder and entwined her fingers in its strap.

Joyce did not know why she was being followed. When she left Athens they had everything they wanted: they had stolen her statue and practically ruined her reputation. The electronic signaling of her nerves had not begun right away in any case; there had been a lapse of several weeks before she picked it up. Her first thought had been of the police, on some peculiar surveillance of their own, but the Greek police had no authority in Italy. No, this pursuit was something more subtle, and she did not like the feel of it. When the primitive part of her mind began to signal danger, she had even considered a breakdown. What had happened in Greece was enough to push her to the edge, but her mind was still clear and constructive in spite of the pummeling it had taken. If she was having a nervous breakdown, there would be other symptoms. But she knew she would not relax completely until she got on the plane for home tomorrow. The tall man approaching slowly on the rutted cobbles might prevent that, though she wondered why he had chosen this time and this place to come out into the open.

His head was bowed, but he was watching her. If it were not for the crispness of his shirt, he might have been an employee who had just completed a hot day's work. Even at this distance he seemed more Italian than Greek. There was something in his walk, an animal relaxation that still had spring behind it, a suppressed vivacity, that betrayed his nationality. Joyce's Greek friends were more intense: they did not know about "the sweetness of doing nothing." If there was nothing to do they *talked*; and if they were alone they hurried quickly to their destination to be with other people. They did not walk like this man, relaxed, thinking. Her tension began to ease without leaving altogether, but she was still on guard.

When she saw the leather wallet hugging his armpit by a strap, she knew he was a guide and her fingers relaxed on her own handbag. As for the crisp shirt . . . well, she had already noted the fastidiousness of Italians: he had probably gone home during the day to change. He was not here to harm her; he might even provide some help. There was one more place she wanted to inspect before she left for Rome, and she could not find it on the map. More than that, she would welcome companionship while she completed the search.

Avoiding guides was almost a science with her. As an archaeologist she felt she should be able to find her way around any excavation unaided, and she did not like to admit that she had already been lost three times this afternoon in this exhaustive expanse of Pompeii's narrow streets. It was hot, too. Once the ancient city had been situated on an elevation, cooled by fountains and breezes from the sea; today it was a hot, airless hole in which casual visitors could survive only a few hours without discomfort. Joyce had been working there since morning. If the guide offered his assistance, she would engage him. If he just passed by, she would forget the whole thing and go back to the relative safety of her hotel room. It was unlikely that what she was searching for was in that particular place anyway.

He was nearly across the road from her when she felt a vague uneasiness again. If a Roman copy of a Greek statue had come to life, it would have had the same impassive beauty. Her habit of staring unself-consciously at any beautiful object confirmed that. His steps faltered. His eyes, squinting against habitual sunlight, were such a dark green that they seemed almost brown beneath his strongly arched brows. He took in all of her in a glance. With everything else on her mind, she had forgotten that there was this to contend with in Italy, too. She should never have worn her cut-off khaki shorts here, no matter how hot the day. Her legs, stretched out from her perch on the stone, momentarily arrested his attention, and she drew them in discreetly and covered her bare midriff with the map. She wore the only clean shirt she had left, and she had tied it in a knot above the waist because several buttons were missing. Her attire would have been all right for digging in Greece, but it was not suitable here. Her hair was drawn up in a blond knot on top of her head and blowing in wisps about her face. She hoped the severity of style would discourage any overtures. She had no patience with this *"bella signorina"* line that had followed her, like her unknown pursuer, all the way from the north. Joyce was conscious of her dignity. She had to be, because she was only a few years older than most of her students. She was always able to maintain the proper distance, even when she wore a bikini in Greece, but this situation was a little different. This man was not a student. He was not "just a man," either: he was an Italian with an image to maintain.

The guide walked quickly across the street, and she decided to handle him with her usual bluntness. In a businesslike voice, she inquired: *"Dov'è il lupanar . . . uh . . . il bordello, per favore?"*

She had done it again—mixed Latin with her traveler's Italian—but she could tell he understood.

"You're way beyond the brothel," he said in English. "I stopped to warn you to get in out of the sun, signorina. It's gone crazy. A German on my last tour left by ambulance with heatstroke . . . and you aren't wearing a hat."

He was not wearing a hat either, but maybe he considered his thick dark hair adequate protection against the crazy sun.

"I'm used to strong sun," she brushed the warning aside. "I can't find the brothel on the map. You're a guide?"

He inclined his head slightly. "It isn't on that map."

The psychology behind the omission seemed obvious: in order to find the building, you must hire a guide. Even if you could find a house on your own, no custodian was immune to a tip. She had been cheerfully shown all the artwork in the House of the Vettii, but she was not so sure of the brothel.

"Are they still silly about letting women in?" she asked.

He raised his shoulders. "Why should they be nowadays . . . when people make love in the streets like dogs?"

There was an actual tone of displeasure in his voice, and he did not seem interested in showing her the brothel at all. Joyce had never had any dealings with guides but suspected that money would engage even the most reluctant one. Lifting her handbag to her knees, she dug through it for her wallet. Beneath a fist-sized chunk of volcanic rock she had picked up on the Via di Nola, the jumbled contents of her bag were pulled out: her camera, her small tools, the geology pick she had added since Tarquinia, all mixed in with comb, lipstick, toothbrush, and Kleenex. She did not apologize for the inside of her purse. She only did that at airport inspections, but she made a mental note to remove the geology pick before she went to the airport in Rome.

Joyce proffered the guide four thousand-lire notes. "If you'll just show me where it is . . ."

Joyce was sure that what she was looking for was not in

the brothel, but she wanted his company, as far as the gate if possible. It was just a short walk to her hotel from there, and her intuition told her they were still being followed, though the street seemed empty in both directions. The guide puzzled over the contents of her open handbag while he made his decision.

"I'll take you there," he said at last, "but you can't take your purse inside. No pictures."

She had checked her purse in many museums, but she had not encountered the practice in Pompeii before and wondered why they were so particular about the brothel. Still, there were several paintings *in situ* there, and she knew too well the precautions that must be taken around antiquities. Aside from the possibility of theft, with which she had become recently familiar, there was the danger that exploding flashbulbs might damage color. At least she could take her wallet and passport in with her. She was on her feet at once.

The guide offered her a cigarette, and when she declined, he lit one for himself. She had to slow her pace to his, because he continued to stroll rather than walk, but she was not impatient with him. For the first time all day, the high note in her nerves began to recede: she felt secure in his presence.

Joyce only half-listened to his running commentary on the weed-choked shops they passed. He pointed out dim Latin inscriptions on the walls and clearer election notices, protected by awnings and glass. Weary as he was, his whole manner changed when he spoke about the excavation. Joyce realized that he was not reciting by rote. There was genuine enthusiasm in his voice, and she became suddenly conscious of him as a human being.

"This section was near the theaters," he was saying. "It had a bad reputation. It is full of taverns and gaming houses. There's a graffito further along . . . warning people away. . . ."

His voice was deep and exciting, and it occurred to Joyce that she had never known a man with an exciting voice before. Of course, most of her contacts with men had been competitive and professional. She had always had to work harder than they did to be accepted on their level. Except for one brief engagement she was a rather lopsided person. But Keith had not had an exciting voice that she recalled: he was just a very good lecturer.

"Otiosis hic locus non est," she quoted from her reading, ". . . *discede morator*. 'This is no place for loiterers . . . idlers be off!' Maiuri thought an angry householder objected to the noise. . . ."

"You know Latin?" the guide asked with interest. She nodded slightly, without explaining how she happened to know it. She was not anxious to advertise her profession right now. Earlier, she had watched the archaeologist working on the Strada dell'Abbondanza, but she had not communicated with him because she was sure he would know the whole awful story of her arrest in Greece. She might never be able to face her colleagues again.

"The city of Pompeii was a seaport . . . full of sailors. Many languages were spoken here," the guide said, and touched the toe of his loafer to a phallic symbol inscribed on a paving stone. "If you'd followed these, you'd have found the brothel. . . ."

"I was following them," Joyce admitted, "but I stopped to chase a lizard." His eyebrows raised, and she continued, "Nearly everything else was found in the excavations, no matter how small . . . an eggcup and spoon, jewelry . . . but not a single lizard. They're everywhere now."

The idea seemed to disturb him by its newness. He watched a green-backed lizard pumping its throat upon a crumbled wall. "They must have run away," he said thoughtfully. "Animals sense these things. The dogs that were chained . . . how they must have whined!"

The image of the whining dogs made Joyce's surroundings come to sudden life, as they had not done in her single-minded search during the day. Her steps slowed to a halt where the Via Stabia crossed the street they were on and Vesuvius came into view like a huge purple limpet on the horizon, deceptively innocent of the disaster it had caused on that August day in 79 A.D., nearly two thousand years before. Perhaps the animals had sensed the danger while everyone else went about his daily business in ignorance even that the mountain was a volcano.

"Doesn't it worry you?" she asked suddenly. "Wasn't there some activity below Naples a few years ago?"

"At Pozzuoli?" he smiled. "It was nothing. . . ."

Of course it was to his advantage to underplay the incident: it might hurt the tourist trade. But he was studying the volcano without amusement. "It may be in its most dangerous phase," he admitted. "The cone's plugged with basalt from the 1944 eruption. There would be warnings, though . . . people could be evacuated in time." His arm swept the ruins around them. "They have this as an example. . . ."

"It was *this* I was thinking about," Joyce admitted with a tinge of guilt. "Pompeii was a vulgar little town, but it's the best-preserved example of Roman life we have . . . with the exception of Herculaneum. I'd hate to see these cities buried again. . . ."

Unwittingly, she had touched a nerve. "Herculaneum," he said disparagingly. "A few villas . . . everything else buried in rock too solid to excavate. A rich man's paradise . . . like Capri!"

"A library was found there, at least," she said in defense of the more elegant rival site. "Scrolls are as rare as lizards here. All the writing's on the walls. It's like the New York subway. . . ."

"It proves that everyone could read and write," he said evenly, but his face flushed. "Pompeii wasn't covered by a mud flow . . . the ashes that fell here were hot. They carbonized furniture, charred the wooden doors. What chance would scrolls have here? It hasn't been fully excavated yet, though. Scrolls may be found. . . ."

But his voice fell at the prospect, and he did not discuss the subject further. Joyce liked his curious loyalty to Pompeii: she also liked him. So, although she wanted to continue the conversation because it took her mind off other things, she let it drop out of respect for his feelings. From what she knew of the site, she could not give him any encouragement about scrolls ever being found there.

As they turned into a narrow alley clearly marked Vico del Lupanare, she wondered how she could have missed it. The guide indicated a balconied building on their left and extended his hand for her purse. One last weary tour was coming toward them from the opposite end of the alley, and Joyce quickly surrendered the purse so she could have the place to herself for a moment. It did not surprise her that the guide chose to remain outside. He did not seem to take much pride in the brothel, and it was suffocatingly hot in the dim, small corridor. Cubicles, each one about fourteen feet long, with a built-in stone bed at the far wall, led off from the small hall.

Locating the paintings over the doors of the cubicles quickly, she regretted that she had not brought her flashlight. The paintings were in poor condition, except for one that had a piece of glass over it. She had already seen the paintings that had been removed to the secret room of the Naples Museum, and she had not really expected to find anything here: the paintings were too late and too Roman. But because she was thorough and did not want to eliminate any possibility at Pompeii, she studied the paintings carefully in the uncertain light. The artwork was not unskillful. The figures had a serenity about them that was almost Greek as they illustrated the acts of love into which they had been sealed for two millennia.

The dim corridor with its "payment desk" at the end was

stifling. It had an unhappy, hopeless feeling to it. She could imagine the laughter of men and the clink of coins at the payment desk, and she was alerted to what was happening to her. It had not occurred for a long time, and it was always unexpected. She was about to have a glimpse into the past, like those she had had at Troy and Knossos, and she did not think she wanted to stay to see this one. She moved quickly toward the door and exited into the clean, hot sunshine, just as the tour reached the entrance.

Her guide, she was relieved to see, was waiting on the opposite side of the alley. She felt drained. If she had glimpses into the past sometimes, why not into the future, where they would do some good? Her head began to swim, and she felt sick in the pit of her stomach, symptoms so unusual for her that she began to wonder if something was really wrong . . . perhaps it *was* the heat.

The guide, watching her face closely, returned her handbag, and she noticed at once that it was too light in her hand.

What had he taken . . . her camera, one of her expensive tools? She could not accuse him without opening her bag, and her hands were trembling too hard to replace her wallet. Angry, disillusioned, she tried to focus on the handsome, unrepentant face. For the second time in two months she had been robbed. And she had liked him, too. Tears started to her eyes, and he grabbed her by the shoulders.

"I know a shortcut to the gate," he said.

She tried to draw away, but she finally had to hold onto him for support. She was so disoriented that, for a moment, she thought the small lane he was walking her down was in an English village.

"I know a nice cool place," he was saying, from far away, though his arm was tight around her.

A nice cool back room where you can get the money that was not in the bag, she thought unclearly. Well, she would not put up with it again. Her fingers closed weakly around the strap of her handbag. All she needed was time to regain her equilibrium. . . .

Her eyes opened onto a network of interlacing leaves. She was afraid to move: he might still be there. She played dead for several moments, studying the leaves through her eyelashes. Either she had been attacked in a vineyard or left for dead in some kind of arbor. No, they were not grape leaves, she observed, though they were so thick on the vines that she could not see the sky through them. Finally, hearing distant voices and the clink of cutlery, she managed to raise herself on one elbow and nearly fell. She was not lying on the ground as she had imagined; she was on a wooden bench beside a table, and her handbag was just above her on the checkered cloth. The guide was sitting at the table beside her. He tried to force her down again, but she shook his hands off and pulled herself to a sitting position. A damp cloth fell from her forehead.

They were in an outdoor restaurant, canopied by vines, and there were other people at other tables. Her head ached, but she was no longer dizzy.

"Are you all right?" he asked with concern.

She picked up the cool cloth and ran it over her face and the back of her neck. "Did you . . . *carry* . . . me in here?"

"No. You walked . . . but you wouldn't go inside." He indicated the dark interior of the restaurant, where a potted plant by the window looked strangely familiar to Joyce. "Would you like something to drink?"

"Some water . . . please." She wanted to take some aspirin for her throbbing head, and when she reached for her handbag he made no attempt to stop her. He was motioning for the waiter.

The waiter, who was also concerned about her health, looked as familiar to her as the potted plant: he must have served her breakfast that morning. She peered into the dark interior again and realized that the restaurant was adjacent to her hotel. They were right across from the excavation. The guide had not brought her very far.

Nothing was missing from her handbag: even the wallet she had been clutching in her hand was inside. She glanced through it quickly, and her passport, traveler's checks, and money were intact. Studying the guide over the rim of the glass, she put two aspirin on her tongue and swallowed them down with water.

He poured a beer and tipped his chair back. "I took your rock," he said candidly. "I was going to tell you, but then I saw that you were sick. . . ."

"My *rock*?" She stared at him blankly. Then she remembered the chunk of tufa for her collection. She searched her bag again. The large piece of volcanic rock was missing, nothing else. "Why did you do that?"

He took a long sip of beer. "I'm so dry! This has been a terrible day. First, the German on my tour . . . and then. . . ." His eyes met hers, which were waiting expectantly, and he shrugged. "You wouldn't understand."

"Why don't you let me decide that? I've been robbed a lot lately!"

Amusement flickered in his eyes, and he held up his hand to calm her. "I'm sorry if I upset you. If I tell you why I did it, you'll think I'm crazy . . . everyone else does."

"It was premeditated!" Joyce cried. "That's why you made me leave my bag outside. . . ."

"Yes." The green eyes became more serious. "All right, I'll tell you, just to prove I'm not a thief. It wasn't a nice thing to do. You can laugh if you want . . . I think I'd like to see you laugh for a change. Pompeii is important to me, out of all proportion, perhaps. Not just because I make a living here. I could make more money elsewhere in the summer . . . in construction. But you see, my family has worked here from the beginning of the excavations. My grandfather and his father before him . . . for many generations now . . . broke all that rock and ash away with picks and shovels and carried it off in wicker baskets. They were laborers and they worked like mules. I'm proud of what they did. One piece of rock may seem like nothing to you . . . but it took two hundred years to uncover that city. . . ."

She did not feel like laughing; she understood better than he knew. "What's your name?" she asked.

"Casale. Antonio Casale." He handed her a printed card with his name on it, inscribed above "Archaeological Guide and Interpreter," and she turned it thoughtfully in her hands, considering the number of Casales who had worked so faithfully on a single excavation. The whole story of the excavation was here if someone were clever enough to write it. Joyce was not that kind of writer.

"I'm Joyce Lacey," she introduced herself, and began to pull the pins out of her hair to relieve her headache. "It seems I stole *your* rock."

He watched the long sun-streaked hair fall over her shoulders and put his glass on the table. "Dr. Joyce Lacey . . . the archaeologist?" he said with surprise.

"Yes," she murmured. She concentrated awkwardly on the pins in her hand and threw them into her handbag. "Even you know about it. . . ."

"I keep up with the literature. I talk to the archaeologists . . . I have to. I'm a trained guide. I didn't know you were so young, though. What are you doing here?"

"Looking for something. I didn't find it. . . ."

"Maybe I can help. I know the excavation like the back of my hand. . . ."

"I've been looking for a theory . . . or a smile I can incorporate into one. I hoped to find something that would put the statue that was stolen from me in Greece into historical context at least. There was a peculiar smile on the face of that statue that I'm sure I've seen elsewhere.

I've been the length of Italy looking for it, since I couldn't return to Greece. I came here hoping that maybe the Samnites or the Oscans. . . . I got desperate and turned to the Romans. I didn't find anything, of course, so I'm leaving tomorrow."

"Tell me," he said, "what really happened in Greece? I don't believe what I read in the papers. Everything there is as garbled as the story of the volcanic activity at Pozzuoli." He smiled to himself. "When you mentioned that today, I had to hold my tongue. . . ."

"Why?" she asked with curiosity.

He sighed. "To appreciate what happened at Pozzuoli, you have to understand the Neapolitan mind. The only activity there was that of some land developers who wanted to move the people out of their old houses. It would have improved their living conditions, but the people wouldn't go . . . they'd lived there a long time. So . . . someone threw a mess of boiled fish and some lye in the water and yelled '*Vesuvio!*' Mass evacuation!"

"You're . . . joking," Joyce said with awe.

"That's what I heard. They also put Murine in the eyes of yesterday's fish."

"I beg your pardon?"

"It makes the fish look fresher than when they were alive," he smiled, and Joyce found herself laughing for the first time in weeks.

"I think I'll give up archaeology and make a study of the Neapolitans!" she said.

"I wouldn't advise it," he said more seriously. "Do you know the meaning of the word *furbo*?" She shook her head, and he defined it for her. "It means something like 'sly' or 'cunning' . . . only it's more subtle. You know Machiavelli?"

"Yes," she said. "I know Machiavelli. I think I ran into the counterpart of *The Prince* in Greece. . . ."

Antonio waited silently, his hand around his glass. He was not going to press her for details, but he was ready to listen . . . and Joyce was ready to talk. The laughter had been good for her: it had cleared her soul. Though she was still in no position to laugh at her own predicament, she was relaxed enough to discuss it.

"My students and I spent two seasons on an Ionian island that looked like a possible trade route between Greece and Italy," she began. "It didn't even occur to me that anyone besides the government knew we were there. We didn't find much last year . . . a few coins, a little pottery, all Greek. But two months ago we unearthed the small bronze statue. It was *unusual*. It wasn't Greek . . . or Etruscan, either, as far as I could tell. I reported it to Athens at once. We photographed it and crated it . . . and it vanished during the night. Whoever stole it was clever . . . he had what you call *furbo*. The Baggies of pot confused everything. . . ."

"Baggies? Pot?" Antonio frowned. "I don't know these words. . . ."

She tried to explain the terms without emotion. "Cannabis . . . hashish, in this case. Whoever took the statue, put the hash into small plastic bags manufactured in America. When the police discovered them they said my students were smoking . . . but they weren't! They put them all in jail. The police in the Mediterranean are so excited about drugs right now that they can't think of anything else. The search for the statue was forgotten in the furor. . . ."

"It could happen here, too . . . with the police, but not with the carabinieri," Antonio said. "The carabinieri have a special division for antiquities and art theft. Some collectors have no morality. . . ."

"The statue was an ugly, corroded little bronze! Only a museum would have wanted it. Its only value is historical . . . and I don't know its history yet. I didn't get a chance to have it dated. It was old, though . . . very old. Stiff and frontal. And it was smiling the most peculiar, joyous smile. . . ." Sighing with frustration, she brushed her hair back impatiently. "Who'd steal a thing like that?"

Antonio finished off his beer while he thought about it. "Why did you take that piece of tufa from the Scavi today?" he said at last.

"It isn't the same thing! I'm a scientist . . . I'm interested in volcanoes!"

"Were you thinking about volcanoes when you selected that particular rock? It was part of a house, you know. . . ."

"I found it lying on the ground. . . . I didn't use my pick!"

"I know that. . . . I looked at the edges when I saw that pick in your purse. But . . . weren't you thinking of how it would fit into your collection?"

For a moment she was bewildered and indignant; then she had to admit that he was right. "I did select one that size to fit into my collection. I see what you mean . . . collecting just for the sake of it. But nobody knew about the statue! There's only one telephone on the island, and I reported it to Athens myself. . . ."

"How much did you pay your laborers?"

"The standard rate . . . not much. Our funds are limited, and the students do most of the work. It couldn't have been one of my laborers! Angelos and Petros were my friends. They were with me both seasons."

His eyebrows arched, and his face looked weary. "They have families to support. Emergencies arise. They may be honest men . . . but there's always necessity."

"An honest man isn't easily corrupted. I can't accept it . . . anymore than I can accept the idea that my students were smoking pot. I *know* they weren't. I'm allergic to the stuff, and my eyes didn't start watering until the police opened those bags. It was put there by someone who knew what he was doing . . . probably someone with a boat at night. It was stupid of me not to consider the possibility. I was in charge . . . I'm the one to blame."

"No," he said softly. "You shouldn't have to think like a criminal. It's the collectors, the dealers"—his voice fell—"the laborers who, in a moment of weakness, or necessity, sell an antiquity, who should take the blame. One of your laborers . . . or students . . . could have accomplished this thing . . . under someone else's direction."

It was a rationalization she wished she could accept. But she knew that neither she nor the board of trustees at the university would look at it that way. She had been in charge.

"This afternoon you said Pompeii was a 'vulgar little town,' " Antonio's deep voice was saying. "You said there were no scrolls there. No lizards and no scrolls. 'The people only wrote on walls.' "

Welcoming the change of subject—to get her mind off Greece—she sat back with her lemon soda to listen to him.

"Well, it isn't true," he said. "There was a scroll . . . in a vase hidden in a wall. The only one that's ever been found. My great-great-great"—he lost track of the generations—"grandfather found it. His family was sick: he needed money. He sold the vase to a collector . . . and he never forgave himself."

The story aroused Joyce's instinct for detection. "A discovery like that couldn't be kept quiet this long. Why, the collector himself . . ."

"You don't know my family," he smiled sardonically. "The collector didn't even know about the scroll. My great-grandfather didn't know about it until after he'd made the deal for the vase. He found it later, when he was packing the vase for delivery. He knew it was important . . . and that it would crumble if he touched it. So he sealed the mouth of the vase with clay before he gave it to the Englishman. . . ."

His voice had dropped to a detached monotone, and Joyce wondered whether, maybe, he was a little drunk. He had already had several beers in the heat on an empty stomach. He was trying to console her, and she appreciated the effort, but his invention strained her credulity.

"Well," she said, as seriously as possible, "if there was a scroll, the collector probably ruined it himself. Who could resist looking into a sealed vase?"

"There *was* a scroll . . . my great-grandfather made drawings of the vase and where he found it. He wrote everything down. I've thought about it a lot. My whole family's thought about it. It's the dark secret in the closet." He smiled faintly. "If you ever come across a sealed vase in your searches, let me know. . . ."

The day was dimming into dusk. A breeze had risen, shuddering the leaves above them. As patrons began to drift into the restaurant for dinner, Antonio glanced at his watch. "I'm late. She won't like that. . . ."

"Thank you for saving me from the sun," Joyce said, shaking his hand and wondering vaguely who "she" was. "You've been . . . very nice, Antonio."

He held her hand between both of his. "Don't *blame* yourself," he said; then he paused inadequately. "I hope . . . you find your theory. You're far too serious, you know. I'd like to see you smile more. Maybe someday you'll be able to laugh about the statue . . . the way you laughed about the fish."

"I don't think so." Joyce smiled, "I'd have to study Neapolitan *furbo* for that."

"You are a complete innocent!" he laughed. "It's just as well you're leaving tomorrow. You turn your purse over to complete strangers. You stare at people like an admiring little child." The pressure of his fingers increased on hers.

"It's a miracle that more has not been stolen. Much more. *Arrivederla, poveretta.*"

"*Addio,* Antonio," she said wistfully, watching his tall figure move between the tables to the street. Yes, it was just as well she was leaving: the man confused her. Why had he said a thing like that when he was hurrying home so "she" would not be angry? And why on earth had he called her, an independent professional woman, a "poor little thing"? She rather liked it.

Chapter Two

Lightning, accompanied by a roar of thunder, plucked tentatively at the hills toward Sorrento, but it had not yet begun to rain.

Emotions, carefully buried for the past few years, welled up in Joyce. She did not face them or try to explain them; she turned away from them instead and concentrated single-mindedly on the incident in Greece. Her feelings about that had acquired only a single dulling layer during her travels in Italy, and talking about it had cracked that open again, too. Everything came back to her now, connected in some hazy way with the story Antonio had told her about the vase and scroll. Though she had discredited that story, in the quietness of her hotel room it began to fit into some sort of pattern. She began to wonder how many priceless antiquities had made their way around Europe without documentation or knowledge, as her own statue was doing now.

The idea of returning to the university without knowing

more about the whole business of thefts upset Joyce. After all the years of training, the long hours of patching shards of pottery together in the basement of the museum, all the work and study that had excluded almost everything else, she did not know what her future held. She was an Hellenic scholar who could not return to Greece, a specialist without a specialty. And all because of her handbag; or rather, because in one of her infrequent bursts of temper she had used her handbag as a weapon. She had not told Antonio that part of the story. She was too ashamed of the week she spent in jail for hitting the policeman.

They had pushed her too far, though. Faced with irrational injustice, she lashed out in frustration. The loss of the statue had been a brutal enough blow. The accusation against her students was too much on top of it. It was the policeman's thick-skulled attitude when he arrested her students that made her swing her handbag. She had not meant to hit him so hard, but her purse was full of tools and he went down flat. Except for some blood and a mild concussion, the injury was not serious, but they had taken her along to jail with her students.

Indignant noises made by her university through the consulate finally got her out of jail. Her students had already been released a few days before on the evidence of her medical record, which verified her allergy to cannabis. They all cheered her as their heroine when she was released, but it had not been a really gratifying moment. She felt that she had let them down. It had not been dignified to hit the policeman, and though the students were almost her own age, she felt she had been a bad example.

After that, the students fled in all directions, some summoned home by angry parents who saw the article in *Time* magazine, not under Science, but under World News; others chose to stay and wander Europe for the summer, and she had lost track of them. She was the only one who tried to follow up on the statue; maybe that is where she went wrong. Maybe some of the fruitless questions she had asked in Athens had come too near the source, and that was why she was being followed.

What kind of person would want the statue, or any unauthenticated antiquity? If he was a serious collector he would want to know its origin, its history: without that, the statue itself was worthless. She switched on the light by her bed and began to make careful notes in her notebook, trying to remember everything she could about the statue and the circumstances surrounding its disappearance. Of course both laborers were frightened by the police, but her conversation with Antonio made her reassess the facts. Had Angelos been, perhaps, too angelic; had he commiserated too much? And was it only shock that had made Petros withdraw and go as silent as a rock?

Trying to recall its dimensions and detail, she made a scale drawing of the statue. She sketched the figure with its short, disproportionate legs, wondering if it had been a portrait, or if the artist had merely possessed very little skill. The bronze had been pitted by more than its long sojourn in the earth. The original pouring had been faulty, but the face was remarkably clear . . . and it was smiling. Not the remote, enigmatic, almost Buddhistic smile of a Greek Apollo, but one of real happiness. It was a joyful little thing, and its expression was as uncharacteristic of the Greeks as its oddly proportioned legs. She knew what she was hoping, though she had not put it into words in her own mind before, but there was no way to verify it, now. The Etruscans were excellent bronze workers after they had contact with the Greeks and traded with them from Italy, but the statue seemed pre-Hellenic. It could not be Etruscan, unless. . . .

No one really knows much about the Etruscans, she reflected: their language is undeciphered, their origin in doubt. Even specialists are divided in their opinion of whether they were an indigenously Italic people, or had come from Asia Minor. What if the statue had come, not from Italy to the island, but from the other direction . . . from Asia Minor on their way to Italy? They may have used metal, rather badly, before they traded with the Greeks. She sighed. Without the statue she could never hazard such a theory.

But putting everything down on paper helped, somehow: it eased her feeling of guilt. She studied the grinning mouth in her drawing and mimicked its expression: at least it was not superior, but happy. Then, suddenly, she recalled Antonio's saying his ancestor had also committed everything to paper to relieve his overpowering guilt. He said there was a written record and a drawing of the vase his great-grandfather had sold. All at once, and quite incredibly, she believed Antonio's story.

Joyce pressed her hands to her temples to contain the light that burst in her head. She had been so convinced it was a lie that she had only half-listened to the story. Now, she tried to remember everything Antonio had said. The vase was found in a wall, which was peculiar in itself; but if true, it might explain the survival of the scroll the old man had claimed to have seen. And if there was a scroll, what was it doing rolled in a vase, instead of on an open shelf like other Roman papyri? The old man *sealed* the vase with clay to protect it and hide the scroll. And the collector had been an Englishman. . . .

If that vase could be found, intact, it would be the most important discovery since . . . Thera . . . or the Dead Sea Scrolls themselves, perhaps. A single document from Pompeii would have enormous scientific value!

No, the whole thing was crazy: she tried to reject the possibility. The theft had taken place a long time ago. He had not said how long, but it could have been any of Antonio's ancestors over the past two hundred years who had sold the vase. She was reaching again, trying to create a single, jagged ray of hope to hang on to.

But something in her rose to the challenge. Beside the Pompeii Scroll, her statue dwarfed in importance in her mind: the only thing they had in common was that they had both been stolen, fallen into the hands of ruthless collectors. Her intuition began to work overtime again. Just because Antonio's story sounded incredible, it did not mean it was not true. How many people had read the *Iliad* before a German merchant picked it up and took every word for the absolute truth? If Schliemann had not followed his instinct, Troy might never have been discovered. She owed it to science, and to herself, to see Antonio again, to find out if there really were any papers in his family.

How many stolen antiquities had never been recovered, she wondered. The police did not have the personnel to guard every site and follow the dim leads on all the collectors. They did not even have the proper training to do so. The job would take a certain kind of person, trained and good at research, dedicated to the endeavor with every drop of energy. An archaeologist might handle it very well. . . .

When Joyce finally fell into a restless sleep, the events of the day wove themselves into the fabric of her dreams. She and Antonio searched through files and drew up a list of names, which she read with excitement, committing each one to memory. They knew who the collectors were: the rest would be easy. Then they were in a marble hall with a rotunda, which looked like the British Museum, but there was only one object on display: a sealed vase with a green-striped lizard curled around it. Hands began to reach for it from all around her. Feeling the familiar weight of her handbag, she began to swing. The heads of the collectors broke like pottery, and the conviction that she had killed quite a few of them gave her momentary satisfaction, until the horror of the act nearly woke her from sleep. She spent the rest of the night picking up the shards of the collectors and trying to put them together again, but some of the pieces did not fit. . . .

As vivid as the names had been in her dream, she could not remember a single one of them in the morning. This did not surprise her. She was more disturbed by the fact that Antonio had been dressed like a Greek athlete at the card file and that she herself had behaved like a wild woman in dealing with the collectors. She did not try to analyze the dream over coffee: its interpretation was too obvious. She consoled herself with Plato's theory that, in sleep, a tiger walks in every one of us. Her subconscious deserved credit for at least trying to patch up the mess she had made, and she cautioned herself to beware of her own emotions: Antonio was far too attractive.

Daylight had a sterilizing effect on the murky waters of imagination, and the hard roll at breakfast brought her further back to reality by cutting the roof of her mouth. The scroll had been missing for a long time; it was unlikely it was still in existence. If she was going to look for antiquities, her own statue was the more sensible quest, while its trail was still warm, but she would have to start that quest in Greece and she had been told not to return there.

The idea of the scroll still engaged her fancy, though: she was completely intrigued by it. The papyri at Herculaneum had only been copies of the works of a minor Epicurean philosopher, already known. There was always the possibility that a scroll might be the lost work of a major poet or statesman. And at Pompeii there still remained the question of a Christian community living there. The concealment of the vase in the wall pointed to something like the latter, or perhaps the record of some kind of shady financial dealings. Why else would anyone hide the scroll in a wall? And if the Pompeii Scroll had survived for two thousand years in an airtight wall and then been sealed immediately with clay. . . .

She finished her coffee in a gulp. It was almost ten, and the prospect of the scroll was far too interesting to ignore. When she weighed it against the alternative of going back to California to face the trustees at the university, it was almost irresistible. She had to find Antonio again.

Two buses disgorged tourists as she was crossing the street to the excavation, and it took her a few minutes to locate Antonio in the milling crowd. He was there to greet one of the tours, and if he saw her, he showed no sign of recognition: he was too busy getting his group together. She was surprised when he began to address the tourists in French, pointing out the old city wall as he led them up the hill and through the toll booth. Joyce merged with the tour, so she could catch him later, and she understood most of what he said. Her reading knowledge of French was good, but her ear was not properly tuned to the language. When she was studying for her examinations, she had concentrated most of her attention on her Greek, both ancient and modern. Joyce was impressed by Antonio's linguistic ability: his French seemed to be almost as good as his English.

Under his direction it took only two hours to retrace the sites that had taken her all day to find yesterday, and even in French, she learned things she had not read in any book. Joyce was amazed at Antonio's vitality, his interest in everything around him. He was not just giving a tour: he was instructing a class on a subject of consuming interest to him. He pointed out minute details on the painted walls ... tiny, perfect peacocks, cupids, fish ... that she had not even noticed in her self-conducted search. If he was working, he was enjoying every minute of it, and his enthusiasm infected the languid group of people surrounding him. What an instructor he would make in her department, she thought, wondering about his background.

Antonio finished the tour at the Edifice of Eumachia in the Forum, and the people dispersed slowly, many coming forward to ask additional questions. Looking around her, Joyce realized that Pompeii had come to life in her mind. It was no longer a "vulgar little town": it was a new discovery. For hundreds of years the Forum had been the heart of the city, bustling with activity—business and religious. The smooth travertine paving blocks were almost gone now, along with the second-story loggia that had connected the buildings, but she imagined it as it must have been.

Vesuvius would have been invisible from where she now stood; the rich dark growth of umbrella pines and plane trees would have been hidden by the Temple of Jove. No chariots had ever entered this area: it was a gathering place for people only. Antonio had pointed out the rectangular stone blocks that made every ingress to the Forum a dead-end street for vehicles. Twenty thousand people had gone about their daily life here, working, bartering, loving, begging, commenting on the weather, upset by an occasional earthquake, just like at home in California, but without benefit of the warning that their city was about to die. The comparison made her suppress a shudder.

After everyone had gone, they stood alone before the ruined columns of the priestess Eumachia's dedication to the city, and Antonio gave her an uneasy glance. His eyes swept the south of the Forum as though searching for a street down which he could flee. Then he pulled himself together and said politely, "I thought you were leaving today."

She felt a little hurt. He had been friendly enough last evening, but he was very remote today. In an effort to close the distance between them, she moved forward physically.

"I'd like to talk to you, Antonio."

Raising his shoulders slightly, he looked over her head at the tourists entering the Marina road. What was there to say? He was clearly a very busy man. Perhaps she had just caught him at a bad time.

"If you're busy right now, it can wait," she said. "I wanted to discuss what you said in the restaurant last night. . . ."

"What did I say?"

She weighed the question carefully. He could not have forgotten the whole conversation so soon; she would just have to be more specific, though she did not want to mention the scroll with so many people milling around within hearing. She waited until a couple of backpacking students passed before she whispered. "You told me about some papers in your family. I've been thinking about them all night."

His expression did not change. "I don't know what I said last night," he said guardedly. "I was crazy with the heat. I was drinking. . . ."

"You weren't drinking that much!"

His denial of last night's story was its confirmation. He had not been lying last night: he was trying to lie now. To console her, he had told her something he had no right to tell, because he thought she was leaving in the morning. And just as his great-grandfather had sealed the vase, Antonio was now sealing his lips about it.

"Maybe I can help," she said impulsively. "Your family lost something. I've lost something, too. If I can see the papers maybe I can do something about it."

Expelling his breath through his teeth, he glanced frantically at the incoming tourists, who were appearing in droves now.

"Come," he snapped. She followed him down a side street in the direction of the theaters and the unexcavated area, which was fresh and green from last night's rain. He stopped beneath the shade of umbrella pines in the small triangular forum beside the Teatro Grande. "What I said, I shouldn't have told anyone," he admitted. "I thought you were going away. . . ."

"I know that," Joyce said, tempted to reach out and touch his shoulder; but, remembering the warning she had given herself earlier, she kept her hands to herself. "It's a family secret, isn't it? But what if we could *do* something to make it right?"

His gaze met hers and held it: he was reappraising her. "You mean well, I think. But . . . my grandfather won't show the papers to anyone. I've only seen them once myself." He sank down on the ledge, and she joined him there, still meeting him at eye level.

Their eyes met again when he lit a cigarette. His expression was suspicious, businesslike. "What's in it for you?"

"I think the scroll might be very important. I don't like art thieves," she said. "I'd like to get back at them."

"Do you think it could really be found after all this time?"

"I don't even know how much time it's been. I'd have to see the papers to decide that. I wouldn't tell anyone about them. There are things I don't want people to know, too. . . ."

He shook his head. "It isn't me . . . it's Nonno . . . my grandfather. The family's kept the secret for such a long time. He'd never show those papers to anyone. . . ."

She picked at the pitchy, damp, fallen pine needles with her fingers. "Has anyone ever asked him? Has anyone ever offered to help before? I'm not saying I could do anything. I'm only offering to *try*."

He bit his lower lip and did not answer.

"In a way, your family and I are in the same position," she pursued. "We've all been dishonored by the same kind of person, an illegal collector. I'd like to find my statue. And I'd like to see the scroll back where it belongs . . . it could be very important."

"What about the police?"

"Why bring them into it? They have their own problems.

I wouldn't call a policeman unless I was being murdered
. . . and then I'd think about it twice. There are other ways.
First, I have to find out who these collectors are. . . ."

There was a flicker of amusement in his eyes. "You are
very naive. My family would kill me if they knew I'd told
you about the scroll. I've only seen the papers once myself
. . . on my confirmation day. That's the way it's done." He
smiled slightly. "That's when the original sin is passed
down. Nonno keeps them hidden in a box."

"Do you remember anything about the papers? The
dates, the name of the collector?"

"A little: the collector was English, a guest of the envoy
to the court of Naples. . . ."

"The *court* of Naples? That was a long time ago . . .
before the unification. I don't remember that date. . . ."

"It isn't necessary," Antonio said. "The vase was stolen
in 1796. I remember that much. It was in my great-
great . . ."

". . . grandfather's papers! Antonio, I have to see those
papers! Could you . . . borrow them . . . for just a little
while?"

"Steal Nonno's box? Never!"

Joyce dropped the pine needles and rubbed her hand
against her pants. "Well . . . I guess that's it, then. It was a
long, long time ago, anyway," she said, rising slowly.
"Don't worry about anything. I really will be getting on
that plane this time."

She freed the toes of her sandals from the pine needles
that had caught there, and with a gesture of good-bye, she
walked away. The scroll had been an exciting fantasy to
keep her mind off other things, a mad idea that she missed
already. There was no escape from reality, though: it was
time to face up to the fact that all her future held was a
long plane trip and the probable loss of her job.

"Joyce!"

Even before she turned, Antonio had caught up with

her, his face both thoughtful and amused. "No one has offered to help before. I think you're crazy, but I love that old man. I don't want to get his hopes up too high . . . but I'll tell him what's happened. I'll ask if you can look at the papers. Don't leave yet. I'll call you at your hotel later."

When the telephone rang that evening, her heart missed a beat. Fumbling for the receiver, she answered in English, instead of with the usual *"Pronto."*

Antonio's voice was on the other end of the line: "Joyce? Can you come to supper at my house tonight? Nonno wants to meet you. I came home early and I've been talking to him. I think he's interested . . . but he wants to meet you first."

Her voice was hardly audible. "Yes. Yes, I'll come!"

"Good. I'll come for you at seven. And don't bother to dress up. In fact . . . make yourself as unattractive as possible. *Ciao!*"

He hung up before she could get an explanation for the last statement. What did he mean, "make yourself as unattractive as possible"? Then she remembered the "she" of the night before. Antonio did not want any trouble from his wife: southern Italians were notoriously jealous. Joyce thought the whole thing was ridiculous. She would dress as she would to go to anyone's home for dinner. She did not think Antonio had anything to worry about. She shook out the wrinkleproof white pleated dress she carried for such occasions and dug in her duffel bag for the matching pair of shoes.

Even without makeup, her face in the mirror was not "unattractive": it was young, clear-skinned, tan, and her large gray eyes were dark-lashed without mascara. With her hair down, she looked like a pretty twenty-year-old. She decided to put her hair up in a twist, at least: it gave her more dignity that way. Whatever Antonio had gotten himself into, Joyce did not think she would set off a jealous rage. She determined to be extremely pleasant to the woman, and she would not look at Antonio all evening. After all, she only wanted to see the papers.

At exactly seven, Antonio's tall figure appeared in the glass door of the hotel lobby, where Joyce was waiting beside the potted plant. Antonio was dressed, not only properly, but modishly, too, with a jacket over a pale-green jersey that intensified the color of his eyes. But as he approached he was appraising her critically.

"You didn't do what I said," he told her. "I didn't want you to be beautiful. . . ."

"I couldn't come for dinner in dirty dungarees," she defended herself. "What's the matter with you, anyhow?"

His face colored slightly. "I haven't time to explain now. I'm afraid you'll find out for yourself."

"Am I going to see the papers tonight?"

"Maybe. If she doesn't make a scene. . . ."

The Casale house was on the main road from the excavation to the village, and he drove her there in a battered white Fiat that ran without a sound. Whatever its outside condition, the car's interior was in perfect repair, and she wondered if he was responsible for that, too. After he parked the car in front of a cameo shop, where pottery and souvenirs were also displayed in the window, he led her to a side entrance, so they would not have to walk through the shop.

"Nonno makes the cameos," he explained. "He's an artist . . . he'll show you."

For a fleeting moment she wondered if she had been brought here to buy a cameo. She was a little suspicious of the pottery, too. She had seen a lot of Graeco-Roman reproductions all along the street, but the ones in the window of the Casale shop were better than average. She did not like their connection with the story of the vase. Some of her initial doubts returned. The Metropolitan Museum scandal had touched off a rash of pottery reproduction, and she wondered if she was playing the innocent dupe again.

Antonio groped his way into a dark hallway and switched on the light. A delectable garlicky odor filled the hall, so, at least, dinner was in preparation. Two figures, both dressed in black, emerged from the parlor and waited silently for an introduction. Antonio's grandfather was probably not as old as he looked, Joyce decided. Hard work and strong sunlight aged the faces of Mediterranean men early, creating deep lines around the eyes, scoring the skin at the back of the neck. Even if he made cameos now, the old man had once been a laborer. His teeth were stained with nicotine, and his white hair was thinning, but his eyes were sharp and clear as he appraised her. Joyce shook his hand firmly, meeting his dark, hawklike eyes directly, and she felt she had made a good impression because the old man did not release her hand.

"Nonno speaks some English," Antonio said, ". . . but I'll have to interpret for Mama. . . ."

He indicated the other figure standing stiffly in the shadows with her hands folded in front of her black dress. The smile of relief that started on Joyce's lips died when she looked into his mother's strong-featured, tragic face. Joyce immediately understood Antonio's odd instructions about her attire and wished that she had followed them. Signora Casale did not acknowledge the introduction by as much as a nod, which in itself was an open breach of hospitality. Though she was seldom cowed by anyone, the solid wall of hostility presented by Antonio's mother dampened Joyce's spirit, and she could not remember enough small talk in Italian to overcome the woman's apparent aversion to her. Confining her greeting to an inclination of the head, Joyce resolved, once again, to avoid looking at Antonio during the evening, this time out of fear of being poisoned.

The parlor was crowded with old, highly polished furniture, and there was a lace doily on every chair. Old photo-

graphs and religious mementos made a procession across
the mantelpiece, and Joyce spied a Communion picture of
Antonio. A typical Latin parlor, she suspected, not lived
in, reserved for company alone, and she was struck by the
incongruity of a bare pine drafting table, covered with
papers and tools, pushed close to the window. Perhaps
Signor Casale designed his cameos here.

The old man, trying to compensate for his daughter-in-
law's rudeness, indicated the most comfortable chair and
kept up a steady, if ungrammatical, flow of conversation.
"Antonio say you are *dottoressa d'archeologia* . . . it is
great honor. The signora make excellent dinner. You have
appetite?"

"Yes," Joyce smiled uneasily. The signora had exited to
her kitchen without speaking a word. Joyce had a feeling
Antonio would not have much interpreting to do tonight.
He must have sensed it, too, because he followed his
mother out of the room.

The old man indicated the drafting table. "Antonio," he
said proudly. "He is good student. He works very hard . . .
for many years, now. Soon, he will be *ingegnere*. Night
school."

"An engineer?" Joyce asked uncertainly, and Signor
Casale smiled.

"Engineer . . . with rocks," he explained. "Is difficult. So
many *numbers* . . . that do not look like numbers at all.
Antonio wants to make . . . how do you say it?" He
indicated straps around his face. "You know . . . like they
put on the mouth of a bad dog. . . ."

Joyce frowned. "A muzzle?"

"*Sì!* Antonio wants to make a muzzle . . . for Vesuvius!"

Joyce rose and approached the drafting table. "May I?"
she asked, looking at the drawings. Signor Casale shrugged
his permission, and she turned a few thin pages tacked to
the board, finely drawn cross sections of the stratification

of the volcano, with carefully computed figures beside them, and sketches in the margins of scaffolds or ducts of some kind. She saw at a glance that it was not a "muzzle" Antonio was working on, but some way to control pressure or channel eruptions. She was overwhelmed by the magnitude of the project. As she raised another tissue paper-like sheet, Antonio came back into the room.

"I'm sorry," she said. "Your grandfather was telling me about your work. . . ."

"It's nothing . . . yet," he said self-consciously. "Supper's on the table."

The old man escorted Joyce into the dining room, where the table, covered with a finely embroidered white cloth, was set for only three people. Signora Casale was setting the serving dishes down with unnecessarily noisy thumps. Joyce glanced at Antonio with surprise.

"Mama isn't eating with us," he said rather curtly, and she could see he was rather angry at his mother.

"Please tell her the food smells wonderful," Joyce said in a small voice.

There was a short exchange in Italian, only a few words of which Joyce could understand. Signora Casale's last remark ended *"Signora o signorina?"* and Joyce guessed what was coming next.

"Mama wants to know if you're married," Antonio translated with exasperation.

Joyce shook her head and waited for the ensuing conversation to end. This time, Antonio balked at the interpretation. He pushed his hand forward, palm down, in a universal gesture that told his mother plainly to calm down. The signora only repeated her demand more loudly.

"I'm sorry. . . . Mama wants to know why you aren't married." He sighed through his teeth. "Mama thinks it's unnatural for people not to be married."

Signor Casale sniggered, and Joyce had a feeling that

Antonio had greatly modified his mother's comment. She was irritated by the question. It was none of the signora's business that she had broken her engagement because Keith did not want a wife who would be skipping off to remote places several months out of the year to dig holes. She had made her choice, but the subject was still painful.

"Tell her," she said coolly, "that I'm a dedicated scientist who only thinks about her work. . . ."

Antonio's grandfather, who understood most of what was said, clucked his tongue with regret. When the statement was translated, Signora Casale gave an unconvinced grunt, raised her chin, and marched with dignity back into her kitchen. She has presence, Joyce thought, I'll say that for her, but her palms were beginning to perspire.

"My . . . uh . . . daughter," the old man said, unable to think of the proper kinship term in English, "is . . . *formidabile*, eh?" He glanced over his shoulder. "But now we can talk."

By the time the *zuppa di pesce* was consumed, Joyce realized she had done most of the talking. Unlike his daughter-in-law, the old man did not ask direct questions: he just encouraged her along intermittently, and she knew she was being interviewed. There was no mention of the scroll, but she was as open with him as she had been with Antonio.

"I want to find that statue," she concluded. "I'd like to recover whatever objects I can and return them where they belong. I'm not rich, but I do have some time. I feel that the police in Greece botched things pretty badly. . . ."

At mention of the police, the old man stiffened slightly. "No police?" he asked her narrowly.

"Absolutely no police," she reassured him. "No scandal . . ."

Signora Casale returned to remove the dishes and brush the tablecloth with an attitude of dismissal, and Joyce forced a smile.

"The food was excellent," she said in her awkward Italian. "Thank you."

The woman's face did not soften, but she murmured *"Prego"* out of habitual politeness, before she left.

"Okay," his grandfather announced suddenly. "I trust you, *Dottoressa*. You are as Antonio said. It was not stupid of him to tell you this thing." He nodded to Antonio, who quickly pushed his chair back and left the room. Joyce heard him running up the stairs, from the hall. "You are well trained . . . and you are angry with the collectors. That is *good*."

"I can't promise anything," Joyce said, mindful of Antonio's warning about raising false hopes, but she could not keep the excitement out of her own voice. "If I think there's a possibility of finding anything . . . I'll *try*."

"I think you will find it," Signor Casale said. "You have steady eyes, steady hands. And," he smiled, "you are smart. You see right through Antonio's mama."

"She worries about him too much," Joyce said simply, and the old man rolled his eyes to heaven.

"She has tried to make him marry for so long! She prays for him in church. She thinks his life is sinful. She is very innocent," he said softly. "And she is afraid you will seduce him!"

"Oh, for heaven's sake," Joyce murmured, and added out loud, "She can be reassured about that. This is business. . . ."

He gave a wheezing laugh and lit another cigarette. "Young people are never *that* busy. I think it would be nice for both of you."

But Antonio returned to the parlor, and the old man's remark was quickly forgotten. As Antonio put an old metal box down before his grandfather on the table, Joyce wanted to leap at it, but she controlled her impatience. The unveiling of the precious papers would be handled like a ritual; she must show Signor Casale that consideration.

"No one outside the family has seen this," the old man said as he fumbled with the lock. "It has not been open since Antonio was twelve years old. . . ."

Joyce could have *picked* the lock in half the time it took him to insert the key. And once the box was ·open, his hands lingered on the papers, and his face grew sad.

Chapter Three

"They have been secret for so long," Signor Casale said, as though even now he regretted sharing them.

The papers were brown and torn at the edges like wrapping paper, probably the only writing material available to the old laborer nearly two hundred years ago. Then something struck Joyce, and she turned to Antonio.

"Your great-great-great-grandfather . . . how did he learn to read and write?"

"Not very well," he reassured her. "We think he learned his letters just to make a record of this before he died. You'll see."

As the grandfather slowly began to unfold one of the papers with trembling hands, Joyce drew in her breath. She wished he would let her unfold them; she was accustomed to handling things that were delicate and old, and the paper was very dry.

"This is the vase," the old man said, pushing the drawing across the table to her. Antonio rose to look over her shoulder, and she felt his breath on her hair.

The vase was biconical in shape, its lines swelling into two levels and tapering at the top, but it had a wide mouth. The drawing had been darkened with graphite until it appeared almost black, except for a few crisscross lines and dots of decoration that had been left bare on the widest convex surface. It had only one short handle, though the other did not seem to have been broken off. It was not an ordinary Roman vase, nor was it a Greek import. With a sinking feeling, Joyce realized at once where she had seen its type before. But what would an Etruscan cinerary urn from 600 B.C. be doing in a wall in Pompeii nearly a hundred years after Christ?

"He drew well," she commented noncommittally. "But I can't read his printing. Of course, my Italian's pretty bad. . . ."

"He spelled phonetically," Antonio decided after studying the paper. "I've never tried to read it all myself, but we'll have to now."

"All Casales can draw," the old man said. "We don't spell well, though . . . except Antonio."

"We'll have to copy the drawing and translate everything," Joyce said, still frowning over the vase. Why couldn't it have been something more distinctive, with pictures on it, at least? She had seen a hundred urns like this in museums while looking for her statue's smile.

With a few swift lines Antonio reproduced its outline and filled in the detail. "He doesn't give its dimensions . . . only its height," he said, "measured by his own hand. 'The vase was as high as two of my hands,' he says. He spelled *vaso* with a *z*. . . ."

"Never mind the spelling . . . how big were his hands?" Joyce asked, though she already suspected the height of the urn. "Let me see your hands . . . and yours, Signor Casale."

The two men put their hands on the table in front of her. Their conformation was almost identical, except that the old man's were calloused and roughened, and blue veins rose on them like mountains on a plain. She observed the fine bones of Antonio's hands, their narrowness and the length of his fingers. Similar as the hands were, they were not the same size. Signor Casale's were smaller than his grandson's, just as the old man was shorter than Antonio.

"Every generation seems to be getting larger," Joyce considered. "Size is determined more by nutrition than genetics, I think. If we calculated backward. . . ."

"We could use my slide rule," Antonio said, and she thought about it for a moment before rejecting the idea. "Measure your grandfather's hands, Antonio. When he was growing, his diet was probably similar to that of your ancestor. . . ."

"Broad beans and pasta . . . when we could get it," the old man said.

"If we use Nonno's hands, our measurements won't be accurate," Antonio protested. "We'll never know to a centimeter the actual height of the vase. . . ."

"You can measure it when you find it," Signor Casale said, delighted that his old hands could contribute to the search. Antonio smiled and measured the old man's right hand carefully against his plastic drafting ruler.

"Seventeen and two-tenths centimeters," he said, converting it silently, "about fourteen inches high . . . by this kind of measurement."

"That's about right, I think," Joyce said wearily, recording the figures next to the drawing.

"You have seen such a vase?" Signor Casale asked with enthusiasm, and she nodded slowly. She did not like to tell him how many she had seen from Florence to Rome.

"If it's what I think it is, it shouldn't have been this far south at all."

"That is what he says!" the old man cried. "Here, Antonio . . . read this!"

He moved the other sheet of paper across the table. It was covered with childish letters and devoid of punctuation. At the bottom of the page was a small cross-section drawing of the excavation during his time.

" 'The vase was not like any other I saw in the progress of the work,' " Antonio read, " 'or have ever seen again in all my eighty years.' He was eighty years old when he wrote this!"

"Since then, Casales have been honest," the old man commented. "The papers have kept us so."

"Here's the part about the man who bought the vase," Antonio said. " 'On the sixth day of May in 1798 a party of Englishmen came from Napoli to see the excavation . . . the English envoy to the court, his young wife . . . very beautiful' . . . he spells *bellissima 'beilsma'* . . . 'and several other gentlemen. . . .' "

"Does he give the collector's *name?*" Joyce asked, trying futilely to read the paper herself. Antonio held up his hand for silence.

" 'The envoy had been to Pompeii many times. They say he wrote books about volcanoes and liked *Vesuvio* . . . he must have been crazy. He collected old things, and one of the men with him collected them, too. . . .' "

"It must have been Lord Hamilton," Joyce said. "He was a vulcanologist and a collector . . . and the date's about right. He had a complete breakdown when his collection was lost at sea on its way back to England. And the beautiful wife . . ."

"Part of his collection, too?"

"Perhaps . . . but he lost her, too. Antonio, your ancestor actually *saw* Emma Hamilton. . . . What else does he say?"

" 'Early that morning I had come upon a vase in my

digging among the broken stones of a wall. I pointed it out
to one of the gentlemen, whose name was Milard Uilobi.
He told me he was very interested in the vase and he would
give me five hundred lire if I would deliver it to his address
on the Via Falcone in Naples. . . .' Five hundred lire!"
Antonio said with disgust, but his grandfather snorted,
"Even when I was a young man, that was a lot of money.
Men have sold themselves to the devil for less."

"How does he spell the collector's name?" Joyce asked,
undisturbed by the money.

"He tried to spell the English name in Italian," Antonio
said. "It comes out 'Milard Uilobi' . . . Wee . . . LOBE
. . . ee."

"Willowby . . . or Willoughby?" Joyce considered.
"We'll need more than that. The first name's uncommon
enough, though. He must have meant something like Mil-
lard. . . ."

"There's no short *i* in Italian," Antonio said. "*Mee*-lard.
Mee-*lard*. And you said the spelling wasn't important!"

"Antonio, say that again . . . more quickly."

After he repeated the name several times, Joyce jumped
up from her chair. "That's it! And it's reasonable! What
your ancestor heard was 'M'Lord'! If the man was a lord,
we can find him in the *Book of Peers*. It all fits. A gentleman visiting the envoy would very likely be a peer himself. . . ."

"An English lord bought a stolen vase?" Antonio said.
"Well, I guess they've done worse things. . . ."

Joyce hesitated. "There's something you should understand. In this transaction the collector didn't do anything
really illegal. There was no international law governing the
disposition of antiquities then. Lord Willoughby bought a
stolen vase, yes . . . and he knew it was stolen. He even
encouraged its theft. But taking it back to England wasn't
against the law. . . ."

"He was as guilty as our ancestor," Antonio said.

"He made it possible for him to become a thief!" the old man cried.

Joyce nodded sympathetically. "There are several things that bother me about the urn, besides the length of time it's been missing. Signor Casale, we must consider all the negative aspects, too." She looked at Antonio, and he agreed with her. "The urn has been missing for a long time: a lot of things could have happened to it. It could have been resold . . . it might have been lost. There have been wars: it may have been destroyed. . . ."

"Too many things bother you!" the old man cried. "I think it is someplace . . . and you can find it."

"What if the English gentleman bought the urn as a gift for Sir William Hamilton?" she asked. "The Hamilton collection never reached England at all. And . . ."

Signor Casale frowned at her with displeasure. "And?"

"Even if we find it, the possibility of the scroll's being inside is negligible. The scroll is the important thing."

"The vase was sealed," the old man argued. "Read it to her, Antonio. . . ."

Antonio scanned the paper in his hand. " 'Before I delivered the vase, I sealed it with clay because of what I found inside. It looked like a scroll. It was charred on top, and I knew it would go to pieces in my hands if I tried to remove it. Milard Uilobi had only seen the vase in the ground. He was excited about it and called it an urn. He did not know about the scroll. To save some of my honor, I sealed the mouth of the vase to protect the scroll.' "

"He called it an 'urn,' " Joyce said. "He thought the same thing I did. . . ."

"And I," Antonio said. "When I saw the drawing again tonight, I recognized it for what it was, and it gave me more hope than I'd had before. What my ancestor did may have saved the scroll. If it was an Etruscan funerary urn, who would look inside . . . imagining there were human ashes there?"

"If the collector knew that much about Etruscan pottery, he may have known about the gold fibulae that pinned the cloth containing the ashes. He might have gone after that. . . ." Joyce began to feel deflated again. "You know . . . what your ancestor saw might not have been a scroll at all. It could have been part of a bone, a bit of burned cloth. . . ."

But Signor Casale's indignation flared at the suggestion that a Casale had not seen what he thought he saw. "If he said it was a scroll . . . it was a *scroll*! You think, maybe, a man who could draw like that at eighty had something wrong with his eyes?"

"Good eyes and a steady hand go together," Antonio agreed. "And he had experience with such things. He even remarked that the vase was like no other he had seen here. . . ."

"What about the cross-section drawing?" Joyce asked. "I assume you've tried to trace the spot where the vase was found?"

"We have looked for years," the old man said. "I searched . . . and my father before me searched. Even Antonio has tried to find it. . . ."

"We think it must have been an exploratory dig," Antonio said. "It was probably covered with fill again. . . . Nonno thinks it's in the unexcavated area. Two-fifths of Pompeii has not been uncovered. There aren't enough funds."

"My God," she groaned, "we have an Etruscan urn where it doesn't belong, and we don't even know where it was discovered! That's what happens when amateurs go poking around."

"All the 'archaeologists' were amateurs then," Antonio reminded her. "They were only looking for treasure. Joyce

. . . *I* have a theory. While we've been talking I've been thinking. When I saw the drawing, it looked like a *bucchero* urn to me, too. And I think the explanation for its presence here is simple. There were collectors in ancient Pompeii, too. Caligula himself collected Etruscan art. And if Pompeii followed the Roman example, as we know it did . . . why not the emperor's passion for collecting? Rome was ruled by three madmen in the fifty years prior to the eruption: Tiberius, Caligula, and Nero. . . ."

Joyce regarded him with growing respect. "Caligula really collected Etruscan art?"

He nodded.

"Okay," she said with relief. "There *was* an Etruscan urn here . . . and there *was* a scroll inside. We won't find either one of them unless we get down to work!"

The Casales were irrepressible and intelligent: Joyce did not express any more doubts. There were only about a hundred reasons why the urn might not still be in existence; but if it was, she was determined to find it. Her euphoria soared as they copied the papers. What they were doing might be crazy, but it was fun . . . her kind of fun: it engaged her mind completely. She had forgotten how it felt in the past few months. And now, engrossed in the work, she even forgot to worry about the feeling she had that she was being followed.

It was nearly midnight when Antonio held the door of his car open for her to take her back to the hotel. The night was clear, beautiful, with none of the threatening thunder of the one before, and she leaned back in the bucket seat with a sigh.

"I think I gave your grandfather more than hope," she said. "I didn't mean to. . . ."

Antonio smiled. "Maybe at his age hope is a good thing. I've never seen him so happy . . . so excited."

He adjusted the rearview mirror and stared into it steadily, shifting his gaze only occasionally to watch the road. She studied his face in profile, followed the shifting of his thick lashes, and gave another little sigh.

"You're very serious about your studies, aren't you?" she said at last. "You must have been going to night school for a long time."

"Yes, but that's all over, now. I have a grant to do geological studies at the institute this year."

"A geological engineer," she considered. "Why not archaeology . . . with your interest in the excavations?"

"There are too many archaeologists in Italy already. A man must be practical. He must plan his life. There's lots of work for an engineer . . . not just the volcano: that's my private whim. There are floods and avalanches that could be prevented, too. But everything's so bogged down by bureaucracy. Something must be done about that, first."

"That sounds revolutionary," she smiled. "No wonder your mother's concerned about you. . . ."

"Mama lives in the past, Joyce. All she thinks about is marriage . . . and lots of grandchildren. She doesn't understand that things have changed. I won't marry until I have something to offer. When I'm thirty-five—by then, I should be established in my work."

He was about her age now, Joyce calculated automatically: that would be about eight years from now. He certainly did have his life well planned. She remembered what had come of her own plans, but she said nothing to discourage him. Maybe she could still get a job as a curator in a museum somewhere.

Only when his eye movements changed, when he began to concentrate more on the rearview mirror than the road, did the creeping sensation in her own shoulders return. "What is it?" she asked.

"Nothing . . . I think. There's a car back there—it's crazy, but I feel like we're being followed." He laughed at his foolishness. "I felt that way after I left you at the

restaurant last evening, too. It's probably all this talk about
the scroll. A cloak-and-dagger complex. Who'd want to
follow anyone in this village? Nothing ever happens
here. . . ."

Joyce wondered whether she should tell him about it.
She was not alone in sensing someone now: Antonio felt it,
too. She remembered the freedom from the presence last
night in her hotel room. Was it because it had removed
itself, temporarily, to follow Antonio?

If someone had pursued her this far, it was likely that he
would continue to follow her when she left Italy. The
Casales would be safe that way, and she would not have to
warn Antonio. It was more important than ever that she
rid herself of her pursuer now, but only after she had led
him away from the Casales. She made a spur-of-the-
moment decision.

"I think I'll go to England tomorrow and run down the
Willoughbys," she said. "You'll take special care of the box
while I'm gone, won't you? You won't tell anyone about
it?"

"Nonno keeps it well hidden. You know we don't talk
about it. What is it, Joyce . . . are you still in some kind of
trouble?"

"No," she said in a small voice. "I just want to make
sure you don't get into any. . . ."

As they pulled up in front of the dark hotel, she opened
the door of the car before he could get around to open it
for her. She was momentarily embarrassed. The manners
in this country emphasized how independent she had become, and she did not like it much. They stood beside the
car in awkward silence.

"I guess I'll say good-bye for a while," she said at last.
"Wish me luck."

He shook her hand firmly and held onto it, as he had
done the evening before. "Be careful, Joyce. Even after
what I said to you, you came to my house tonight without

a second thought. What made you so sure I was what I seemed to be? For a student of man, you have too much faith in men. Don't you see what could have happened?"

"I had a few misgivings," she admitted. "But I was right about you after all."

"This time. But you go around trusting everyone. It isn't safe."

Glancing around for reassurance, she said, "It's either trust or rampant paranoia. I don't expect the worst of people."

"Well, get in touch with me if you need me. You have my card." Then he put his hands lightly on her arms to hold her away from him before bending down to let his lips brush hers. His intention was not serious until he actually kissed her, and then both of them seemed to feel it at once—it was an electric moment. Joyce put her arms over Antonio's shoulders, and they held the kiss for a long time. When he finally released her, Joyce had been properly kissed, and she wondered if, after all, she had done the right thing. She did not want to become involved, either.

Antonio returned quickly to the driver's seat of his car, and said, "Keep in touch, and remember, if you need any help, call me."

Chapter Four

Joyce did not call anyone when she opened the door of her room and found the contents of her duffel bag dumped out on the floor and all the empty bureau drawers standing open. She just stood in the doorway for a moment, paralyzed, afraid the intruder was still there. Then, leaving the door open for quick escape, she cautiously checked the bathroom and the balcony, but found both empty. Frantically, she closed and locked the door and windows with shaking hands and sat down on the bed. In a way she felt almost relieved to have proof at last that someone was taking an unusual interest in her activities: it was not just imagination. The room had been ransacked when she was at Antonio's. They had followed her there and then had picked up her trail again afterward. But what on earth were they looking for?

Nothing was missing from her belongings: it was not a simple burglary. Repacking her duffel bag carefully, Joyce considered the possibilities. A clever thief would not have left a mess like this. Either her pursuer was incredibly stupid, or he was just trying to frighten her. But *why?* Later, as she began to gather her notes to pack them, the question was partly answered. The notebook containing the description and drawings she had made of the statue the night before was gone; she even looked under the bed and into the wastebasket for it. So . . . the search still had something to do with the statue. Perhaps the collector, realizing that she had been trying to determine its origin, had sent someone to get a history of the statue for himself if she succeeded.

She went over the past two days carefully in her mind, putting herself in the place of her pursuer. There was nothing to make him suspect the possibility of the Pompeii Scroll. Unfortunately, he knew about the Casales, but their discussion tonight had taken place in the dining room, an inside room: no one could have been watching through a window. There was no reason for her watcher to waste any more of his time on the Casales; that, at least, was reassuring. He was only concerned about the statue. *Only*, she thought, realizing how much her statue had receded in her mind. The loss of the notebook meant nothing to her, except that she was grateful she had not put anything about the scroll in it. The important thing, at this point, was to protect the Casales and to keep their secret. And in order to find the urn, she must rid herself of whoever was following her.

While her companions on the London flight relaxed with drinks and newspapers in the pressurized silence, Joyce studied every face in an attempt to find one with a Greek cast to his features.

She saw several likely possibilities on her frequent trips to the plane's washroom, but two of them were soon eliminated when she heard their flawless Italian. The other one, a dark man sleeping soundly, as though he had been up late the night before, bore watching, though. She had not heard him speak to anyone.

After they landed at Heathrow, Joyce lingered in the terminal until the man got through customs, but when his wife and two children met him, she shrugged, picked up her duffel bag, and got on the local bus for Hounslow West that went to the Underground station. Her pursuer could have taken another plane, she thought, as she sped through the tube beneath the city: but if he did that, how would he find me later? Or he could have been someone else on the plane: someone who did not look Greek at all.

Shifting her duffel bag for easier carrying, Joyce got off at Russell Square and walked around the park until she came to a row of attached Georgian houses that designated themselves "hotels." There was no sign above the door where she stopped to ring the bell. Mrs. Amboy's house was a home away from home for many foreign, as well as British, scholars doing research at the British Museum. Word of its unadvertised presence on the square was passed along from professor to student. Mrs. Amboy gave her guests special treatment, clean rooms, and meals at a minimal fee. She had a weakness for archaeologists, and though she had never lifted a spade in her life, had done enough reading on the subject to qualify for a degree.

Mrs. Amboy was getting old. She seemed smaller, frailer than she had a few months ago, and her white apron nearly went around her twice. But her eyes brightened when she saw Joyce on her doorstep.

"Dr. Lacey . . . we've been waiting for you! You just missed the Gardner boy. He stayed for a fortnight, hoping you'd show up."

Her students had already passed through here on their way home, then. It was just as well: it saved a lot of explanations. Joyce hugged the woman affectionately and dragged her duffel bag into the old-fashioned hallway.

Once, Mrs. Amboy had called her by her first name, but that changed abruptly when Joyce got her doctorate. Mrs. Amboy's sense of propriety was rigid, and she would never consider her simply "Joyce," the student, again. Joyce was grateful for the familiar warmth of the old woman's greeting, in any case. Supper was in preparation; the odor from the kitchen penetrated the lower floor. Steak-and-kidney pie, Joyce thought appreciatively, one of her favorites, and a mild relief after all that southern Italian food.

"Are any of my students still here?"

"No. Michael was here a month ago. And that quiet one . . . John Gardner . . . left on Monday. He wanted to talk to you."

"How did they seem?"

"Indignant!" Mrs. Amboy's voice reflected their emotion. "It was a shocking thing. You'd think the Greeks would have better things to do than put people like you in jail. Oh . . . John left a note for you." She disappeared into her private apartment off the hall and returned with a sealed envelope. "He'd been in Switzerland. He was so proud of you! They both were."

Joyce smiled ruefully and looked at her watch: the reading room at the museum was still open. She might be up to discussing Greece, later, but she did not feel like it now. "I'll take my things up later," she said. "I'm going to the museum. Who else is here?"

"Sir James Willis-Parks, the old emeritus. He's getting more senile all the time." The old woman shook her head regretfully. "He's at the reading room now, I think. And another one of the Greeks, a Dr. Arapkilos. Looking at the marbles," she twinkled, "trying to figure out how to take them home!"

Joyce was immediately on guard. "How long has he been here?"

"He came a few days after John. They became great

friends. You'll like him. He seems a nice man, but he doesn't speak much English. . . ."

Everyone was a "nice man" to Mrs. Amboy, Joyce thought dryly as she walked to the museum. Well, at least she and the old woman were alike in that respect. Joyce could not be suspicious of anyone either. There were always Greek scholars staying at Mrs. Amboy's: there was no reason to avoid this one. He had been there for almost two weeks, so he could not be following her. And he and John had probably discussed the whole story of what had happened in Greece, so she had nothing to hide.

Most of the Greeks Joyce had met at Mrs. Amboy's were there for the same reason, and Joyce was sick of arguing about the Elgin Marbles. Lord Elgin had probably saved the precious statues, metopes, and slabs of frieze from total destruction when he transported them, at his own expense, to England. Left in Athens, they would have perished in the civil wars. His intentions had been honorable, and most Englishmen, including Keats, had been inspired by the sight of them. But Lord Byron, Hellenophile and martyr to Greek independence, had called the transport of the marbles theft. And the Greeks still looked at it that way. Until now, Joyce had only half-agreed with them; today, she wondered if they were not right. The preservation of anything is chancy at best. Perhaps everything should be left where it belongs . . . even at Pompeii— if, she smiled to herself, someone like Antonio could come up with a way to cut through red tape and "muzzle" Vesuvius.

When Joyce entered the hollow vastness of the museum, she was tempted to go into the gallery where the marbles were so beautifully displayed, but she went directly to the director's office to present her foreign scholar's pass. The reading room would be closing soon, and she was anxious to start her search.

Dr. Willis-Parks . . . *Sir* James Willis-Parks—he had

been knighted for his Anglo-Saxon discoveries—was ensconced at a table beneath the gold-girdered dome, poring over a volume with a reading glass, as red-eyed as an aging basset hound. Joyce respectfully avoided his table when she put in her book request. She had met him several times as a student, and she would probably be dining with him tonight, but in this solemn room she felt more comfortable at another table. As the *Book of Peers* was laid noiselessly beside her, she turned carefully to *W* and moved her finger down the columns until it halted at *Willoughby*. It was a prolific family, with several branches, so she turned to the most recent entry first:

> Willoughby, Lord Stanton. Seventh Baron of Carrington. b. 1899 d.　　　　Father: James, Sixth Baron Willoughby. Mother: Margaret St. John. Educ.: Eton; Camb., 1920. President, United Sports Cars, Ltd. Res.: Willoughby Hall, Carrington, Wilts.

She suppressed a smile. Seventy-four years old, and he manufactured sports cars. Apparently, he had never married: no heirs were mentioned. She followed the entries backward until she found the eighteenth century:

"Willoughby, Lord Robert. Fourth Baron of Carrington. b. 1770. d. 1843." She scanned his biography: "King's Courier, court of Naples, 1797–1804; Attaché, Moscow, 1806–1812 ..."

She had to suppress an exclamation of delight. Lord Robert Willoughby had been courier to the court of Naples when the urn was stolen! There was no doubt about it: he was her man. She would wire Antonio immediately; no, she was the only one who had needed confirmation of the story. The Casales had believed it all along. Copying the information on both Willoughbys, she noted that Lord Robert had acquired a young Italian wife during his sojourn in Naples, one Contessa Viola Falcone, upon whom he had fathered two sons to continue the line. Joyce was not impressed by the title. Though they were no longer valid in Italy, everyone whose family ever commanded a hilltop fortress seemed to claim one, and the hills of Italy were studded with fortified castles. But the Contessa's name, Falcone, meant something to her, though she couldn't remember what it was. She would think about it later. Chairs were being quietly pushed back from the tables. The reading room was closing.

When she took her duffel bag to her room, she remembered John Gardner's note. Poor John. He had discovered the statue to begin with, and he was more upset than anyone by its loss. A bright, dedicated young man, studious and retentive, he masked his sensitivity with all the outward symbols of rebellion. His beard and long hair had brought the police down on him hardest of all. She scolded herself for not reading the note sooner, but it would have to wait a little longer now. She had a telephone call to make before there was anyone in the parlor. The pay phone was inconveniently located in the downstairs hallway.

As Joyce dialed information, the front door opened slowly and Dr. Willis-Parks placed his umbrella in the stand. He nodded at her nearsightedly before he entered the parlor. Damn, she thought, glancing around the portiere to see if anyone else was settled there. Except for the old professor, the room was empty, and he was already nodding in his chair.

Joyce lowered her voice. "Operator, I'd like the number of Stanton Willoughby, Willoughby Hall, Carrington, Wiltshire, please," she said. "Yes . . . Carrington." She waited breathlessly, listening to the clicks and hums on the line, certain that the voice would return to tell her that the number was unlisted. But when the operator spoke again, she said crisply, "That number is. . . ."

Joyce searched for the pencil beside the phone pad in the dim hall and wrote the number down, but she still did not believe her luck. "Are you sure that's the number of *Stanton* Willoughby at Willoughby Hall. . . ?"

"Carrington, Wiltshire," the operator's professional voice repeated. "That is the number that is listed."

Joyce replaced the receiver weakly and lined up the coins she had brought downstairs with her. She should give herself some time to decide what to say: she had never spoken to a baron before. She suspected it would not be good form to telephone and blurt out, "See here, an ancestor of yours bought a stolen vase about a hundred seventy-five years ago. . . ." But the other guests would be in the parlor later, and she could not use the phone in privacy. Steeling herself for the ordeal, she placed the call.

The voice that answered by repeating the phone number was too upper class to belong to the nobility. Joyce was certain it was that of a butler. Explaining who she was, she asked to speak to Lord Willoughby; no, she could not leave a message . . . it was a personal matter. There was a pause on the other end of the line. As she waited, Joyce worried: What on earth will I say? Maybe he'll refuse to speak to me, and I can write a letter: I should have done that to begin with. The idea filled her with relief, just before a clear voice switched in briskly.

"Willoughby, here. I don't know how an American got into the act, but my answer's final. *I won't have my roses excavated!*"

Shocked into momentary silence, Joyce was surprised at her own poise when she finally spoke. "It isn't about your roses. It's about your ancestor, Lord Robert Willoughby, and a vase he purchased in Naples in 1798. I'd very much like to see it."

"In 1798!" his lordship's voice exploded. "My dear lady, do you know how much junk has accumulated in this house since then? All of my ancestors collected some damned thing, and the place is one bloody big attic. I could never locate a single vase."

He pronounced it *vaus*, and Joyce considered herself corrected. "It's an urn, really," she explained, so she would not have to repeat the word again. "Black . . . with only one handle. Probably Etruscan . . ."

"Etruscan? They lived on the coast of Turkey or someplace, didn't they? I don't think 'Rambling Bob' ever made it there."

Joyce winced. Well, he probably knew a lot about sports cars. "Italy, sir. Northern Italy. But he acquired the urn in Naples . . . and it never should have left the country."

There was a short, thoughtful pause. "Italy, huh? Are you telling me in a polite way that he stole the damned thing?"

He had said it, she had not. "Technically, no," she demurred. "The laws were different then. But I know Italy would like to have it back again."

"Hm," he considered. "I don't want any difficulty there. Not with the Monza coming up. Where are you?"

"In London."

"This is a toll call? What a waste of money! Give me your number, please. I'll call you back in a day or two on my business line. Some of my ancestors' morals may have been questionable, but we've tried to improve on them. I'll look around. To be truthful, any bit of junk you could remove from this place would be a tremendous service to me . . . especially if it makes the Italians happy before their Grand Prix. . . ."

He rang off, obviously a very busy man. Sitting down weakly on the hall bench, Joyce hoped he was not so busy that he'd forget to call.

As she dressed for supper, Joyce suddenly remembered John's note again. She put her hairbrush down and tore the envelope open with her finger:

Dear Doc,

I thought you'd show up eventually and waited as long as I could. I'm almost out of bread, though, so I'm flying home tomorrow before I have to swim. Mrs. Amboy will destroy this if you don't show up within a month.

When you split in Athens, I caught the vibes and knew what you were up to, and I decided to do the same thing on my own. Nosed around Greece for a few days, but there was too much fuzz around . . . I was afraid they'd come after me with a tank. Then I remembered that the sale of the Euphronios krater to the Metropolitan Museum took place in Switzerland, where everything's so nice and neutral, including numbered accounts. I thumbed my way there and picked up some work retouching in a gallery. Some pretty wild things passed beneath my hands, and I don't think the Swiss even know what's going on.

I've turned up a couple of interesting collectors, and one of them is Greek. A fat cat named Priapos Karavitas. Some name, huh? I touched up a red-figured oenochoë for him that had no business outside a museum. Address only P.O. Box 4152, Athens Central.

There's a guy in Rome you wouldn't believe. I packed a couple of figures hacked off the Black Pagoda at Konorak for him. God knows when they were stolen, but Krishnamsetty Das has them now. Address: Villa Regale, outside of Rome.

I've encountered a little problem I should warn you about. Someone's been tailing me, I think, since I left Switzerland. I can't seem to draw him out in the open to get a whack at him. I must have slipped up somewhere. Since this guy hasn't knocked me off yet, I think he's just seeing me safely out of Europe. I'm only too willing to oblige. But be careful. Whoever these people are, they're trying to protect what they have. Take it easy . . . don't try anything alone.

If I don't take your course this fall, it's nothing personal. I think you're one hell of a chick. But, everything considered, I've decided to concentrate on the Indus Valley. I'll never go back to Greece, and those temple figures turned me on.

Come home quickly . . . don't get yourself killed, Doc. It isn't worth it.

Best always,
John

Joyce had not left Athens to search for collectors, but to find a historical context for the statue. But John, misinterpreting her determination, had gone off hunting collectors on his own. Somewhere along the line, John had made someone uneasy enough with his activities that they located Joyce and began watching her, too. Everything fell into place, now. About the time John had left Switzerland, she had begun being followed. So far, everything had been surveillance and scare tactics. Her nerves began to tingle, for whoever had followed John knew about Mrs. Amboy's place.

With singular devotion her student had made the search for the scroll extremely hazardous for her.

Chapter Five

Joyce ate in troubled silence, with only an occasional glance at her table companions. Dr. Willis-Parks was either deaf or did not listen, because Dr. Stephen Hill, a young American professor who had arrived during the afternoon, was having a difficult time carrying on a conversation with him. But the American continued to concentrate his full attention on the revered old man, oblivious to the fact that he was only being answered in grunts and snorts. If Dr. Hill wanted to go home saying he knew Dr. Willis-Parks personally, he would have a difficult time quoting him unless he read his books.

Isolated by language, Dr. Arapkilos, the balding Greek archaeologist, was being left out of the conversation. In spite of everything that had happened to her, Joyce still liked Greeks. The man had been a friend of John's: the least she could do was make him feel comfortable.

"Are you enjoying your stay in London?" she asked in

Greek, and Dr. Arapkilos' swarthy face brightened perceptibly. The timidity left his eyes, as he answered her question with animation.

"Oh, yes! I've spent most of my time at the museum."

She smiled. "You've seen the Elgin Marbles, then?"

"As a matter of fact, my interest is the Romans. I've just returned from a tour of Roman Britain . . . including the new Northumberland excavation. . . ."

Joyce nodded wistfully as he went on about Rome, "the stone rose that seeded the world," left edifices from Palestine to the Antonine Wall. She had always felt that the Greeks had been the most civilizing influence on the Western world, but the Greek had other views. She listened with more attention than she would have done a few weeks ago, though she did not mention she had just come from Pompeii.

Inevitably, the conversation turned to the theft at her excavation. Dr. Arapkilos had read about it before he met John, and his sympathy seemed sincere. "Your student had hopes of recovering the statue, though I pointed out the difficulties to him. It was small . . . only three feet high, I understand . . . easily concealed. The people who do such things are not amateurs, Dr. Lacey. They might hide it indefinitely. The recovery rate on stolen art objects is very low."

Joyce did not believe in statistics any more than she accepted a law of averages. Besides, she had every intention of altering all probabilities, but she did not communicate this to the professor.

"Look on the good side," Dr. Arapkilos said, squeezing her arm. "It's a distinction to spend some time in a Greek jail right now. Some of the best people in the country are there! I'm sorry such a thing had to happen to you in my country, though."

His warmth and good humor were almost too much for her. All her enthusiasm for the Greeks returned in a staggering rush; in another moment she would have asked him about Priapos Karavitas. But Dr. Willis-Parks, who had finished his dinner and was picking his teeth with the social immunity of the very old, made his first pronouncement of the whole meal.

"Stupid ass," he muttered, to everyone's surprise. Joyce, who thought he was talking about Dr. Hill, flushed warmly, thinking that senility had motivated the incredible gaffe. "The whole family's a little balmy, you know. . . ."

Dr. Hill, amused by the old man's outburst, touched his napkin to his lips to hide a smile. "Who is that?" he inquired helplessly.

"The Willoughbys, of course," the old man replied, proving that there was nothing wrong with his hearing: he had obviously picked up part of Joyce's telephone conversation from the parlor. Then he revealed that not only could he hear, but that he understood Greek, as well. "Talk about illegal collectors! If some of the others were alive, I'll wager you'd find what you're looking for. But all old Stanton cares about is his bloody mound of roses! Take my word for it, young lady . . . you're wasting your time."

His drooping eyes stared moodily into space, and Joyce prayed that they would remain that way. All she needed now was for him to say something about the urn. She did not know whether to leave the table, at the risk of the men's continuing the discussion, or stay there to monitor what was said. The young American professor cleaned his horn-rimmed glasses with his handkerchief and yawned. And though the muscles at Dr. Arapkilos' thinning hairline had jerked slightly when the old man spoke, his face was under complete control now. It made her wonder if Dr. Arapkilos spoke more English than he was pretending.

Finally, with a nod to the three men, Joyce excused herself, and went to her room and bolted the door. Once inside, she did not want to come out again. Anyone at Mrs. Amboy's, she realized, might be her pursuer . . . or John's.

Willoughby Hall was not visible from the taxi as it turned onto the drive through the gates. But the mansion began to loom, large and square, as they drove through the extensive grounds, which began with a stand of woods and leveled off into a green lawn, interspersed with gardens. It had not been easy to get an invitation. Only her daily calls to Stanton Willoughby finally wore him down. He had looked for the urn, he said, and could not find anything like it. She asked him to look again . . . and then again.

"Dammit!" he finally exploded over the telephone. "You come down here and have a go at it yourself! I want to return it to Italy as much as you do, but I can't get through all this trash alone."

In spite of his unpleasantness, Joyce was exuberant. She took almost paranoiac care to ensure she would not be followed. Leaving Mrs. Amboy's well before dawn, she dropped into the Underground like an ant. The first train to Salisbury was too early for excursions, so she was alone in the car. When her connection with the Bristol train was delayed, she spent the time waiting in the ladies' lounge. Her only difficulty had been in finding a taxi in the small village of Carrington.

As the taxi driver stopped his ancient vehicle in the rounded drive designed for carriages, he cleared his throat self-consciously. "If I may make a suggestion, love . . . and it has nothing to do with my business. When you want to leave here, please call me. Don't let his lordship drive you back to the village."

"Why not?"

He indicated a low sports car parked ahead of them, silver-gray, almost flat, shaped like the mantle of a jetting squid. "That's his Ray . . . the latest one," he said.

"He manufactures them, doesn't he?"

"Yes. And that's not bad enough . . . he drives them, too. He's smashed two in the past year. Into hedges, lucky for everyone. He likes to see how much speed he can get out of the things."

"Isn't he too old to drive?"

The taxi driver squinted his eyes from the smoke of the cigarette hanging on his lip. "There's that, too. His license has been lifted. But I still see that thing swatting about the countryside at night."

"Thank you." She paid the fare, adding a promise to return via the safe, plodding old Ford. "I'll call you Sunday evening. Maybe sooner. My business here shouldn't take long."

She experienced her first trepidation when she entered the Hall. There was not an empty space against any of the walls in the entranceway; the surfaces were covered by antique furnishings and a remarkable collection of old clocks, none of which was running. Lord Willoughby had not exaggerated the extent of the collections. A glance up the massive staircase confirmed the worst. The Hall was crammed to overflowing with the acquisitions of his ancestors. Joyce wondered how a man interested in roses and the clean line of sports cars could live in such a clutter.

"Do you have to clean all this?" she asked the house-keeper, who had admitted her.

"No," the weary woman said, pushing back a strand of gray hair. "I supervise the staff that does it. His lordship's in his study . . . right there. There'll be tea shortly. Please go right in . . . he doesn't stand much on formality."

The study was as bare as the rest of the house was disordered: Joyce was not sure it was an improvement, though. She had felt more comfortable in the entrance hall than in this futuristic domain of glass and metal, with its blacks, whites, and brilliant oranges. The sofa looked like a segmented caterpillar that might crawl away if one sat down on it. His lordship stood, straight as a spire, behind a smoked-glass desk that floated above the velvety white carpet. Though his bearing was dignified, he struck Joyce as just a gray-haired old man in a casual gray cardigan, a little weary, perhaps quite lonely. But his first words dispelled that impression.

"You're a most persistent young lady," he said coolly. "Please be seated. I'd like more details about this thing."

She glanced at the carpet to see if she had left footprints on its snowy surface. "You certainly didn't exaggerate the collections," she said, sitting gingerly on the edge of the sofa, "Lord Willoughby."

"Call me Stanton . . . unless you're one of those types who want to dig up my garden. They insist there's a filthy burial mound beneath my roses. I must say, you're better-looking than the ones I've encountered before, though. Younger, too."

"Would you like to see my credentials?" she asked, but he waved the suggestion aside.

"They've all been checked out. You're legitimate enough . . . except for some nasty business in Greece recently. In which, I must say, you handled yourself pretty well. So now you've started a crusade to return all stolen antiquities to their proper countries? It's one way to get back at the sort who stole your statue."

"Yes," she said candidly, "I guess that's it."

He observed her closely with puzzled gray eyes. "Like to dig, huh? 'Just because the earth's there,' or something like that?"

"We're digging up history . . . not just making holes in the ground, sir."

"Stanton. Well, as long as you don't have the sandbox mentality of those chaps at Cambridge and Oxford."

A maid brought in a silver tea service and set it carefully on the glass desk. Joyce was struck by the anachronism of the elaborate service in the ultramodern room. His lordship . . . Stanton . . . began to pour for both of them.

"I occupy two rooms in this place," he said. "My bed-

room and this study. I hope you won't mind taking your
meals with me here. There's no place else to go. Now, how
did you hear about this vase Rambling Bob's supposed to
have made off with?"

"From a family in Italy."

"Good family?"

"A very good family . . . still troubled because their
ancestor sold the urn to yours. It . . . wasn't his to sell."

"A thief, huh? I take it we aren't mentioning names."

Joyce hesitated, took a sip of tea. "As in your family,
they've tried to improve the line."

He looked up in surprise. "Good. Jolly good! I think I'm
going to like you, Dr. Lacey."

"Joyce."

"Well, Joyce . . . I've been over some of this blasted
house since we talked . . . and I couldn't find anything like
the urn you described . . . black, blue, or mauve. You're
welcome to have a go at it, but. . . ."

"The collections aren't in order," she said with resignation. She had suspected it: it would not make her job
easy.

"Oh, the ones that fit into little cases are . . . butterflies,
saltcellars, things like that. But everything else's been
shuffled around over the years. It's absolute chaos. Do you
happen to know the family motto?"

She tried to remember what she had read in the *Book of
Peers*. " 'Everything Is Mine,' or something like that, isn't
it?"

"Yes. The words of the first baron, spoken in gratitude,
when he received the title and land for losing a leg in
battle. Everyone since has interpreted the words literally,
though. No one has let anything get out of the family.
They've even stipulated in their wills that the collections
are 'to be maintained on the premises.' Maintained, hell!
It's all got out of hand. . . ."

"Pack-rat mentality," she could not resist saying, though

she was grateful for the clauses in the wills. If everything was still there, she would find the urn.

"Exactly! I can't break the cycle until I die, but after speaking to you the other day on the telephone, I started thinking. If you find Lord Robert Willoughby's collection, I'll have it shipped back to Italy straightaway. . . ."

"Wouldn't that be breaking *his* clause? Besides, some of the articles might be valuable."

"If they were stolen, they should go back to where they belong. As for their monetary worth, I don't care about that. I consider it all dreary junk, and I have enough money. Most of the collections are probably valuable . . . but this is an opportunity to get rid of one of them!" He paused thoughtfully. "I'm an honest man, I think. Or as near as anyone can come to it in business. I'll make a deal with you. If you can find that collection in this mess, you can dispose of the urn as you please."

Joyce, letting out a gratified sigh, explained, "The family only wants what you want . . . to see that the urn is returned to a proper display in Italy. I would like to study it first, though. . . ."

"Then the whole thing's settled. I suppose you're anxious to get on with it?"

Her preliminary survey of the ground floor took the rest of the afternoon. She was only able to identify one item that might have been part of Lord Robert Willoughby's collection: a Scythian metalwork horse of beautiful design, which she found mixed up with some trinkets in the china cabinet in the dining room. Though it was not of Italian origin, she found it encouraging: Robert Willoughby had spent his final years in the foreign service in Moscow. It was evidence that the rest of his collection was still somewhere in the vast Hall. Later, at dinner with Stanton Willoughby in his study, she asked for a plan of the building.

"It's been lost for years," he told her, but he drew a sketch of where he thought the upper rooms were, indicating that he had not visited those areas for some time.

"May I borrow your housekeeper tomorrow?" Joyce asked. "She's responsible for the upkeep of the house. Maybe she knows where things are."

"Mrs. Craig? Certainly. Mind she doesn't keep you away from the parts that aren't maintained, though. She thinks I'm a fool, but I know they can't do it all. Now, tell me more about the Scythians. Do you think I should send this handsome little thing back to *Russia*? It'd be rather embarrassing all around. . . ."

Mrs. Craig was extremely nervous the next morning as she showed Joyce around the clean and polished rooms of the second floor. Finally, she admitted to Joyce that she had seen a man prowling about the grounds the night before.

"I saw him when I was checking the windows before I went to bed. He moved across the lawn and then stood under that old oak tree, just watching. It put a proper scare into me, I'm telling you . . . like one of those horror things on the telly! And his lordship wouldn't call the police, said it was my imagination. But I really saw someone, Dr. Lacey! I'm not the fanciful sort. . . ."

Joyce assured Mrs. Craig that she believed her, without adding just how well she knew that the lurking figure was not imaginary. Promising to speak to Lord Willoughby about better security for a house filled with valuables, Joyce was able to persuade Mrs. Craig to let her go on exploring on her own. So now her shadow had found her even here. Well, she didn't want to think about that for the moment—he couldn't know what she was here for, and her own search was more important for the moment.

On the next floor an encouraging layer of dust covered everything, and since the area had not been converted to electricity, she turned on her flashlight and began to search in earnest.

Opening and closing doors quickly, flashing her light into those rooms with no windows, Joyce worked her way toward the front of the house. Massive collections of junk, which must have meant something to someone at one time, filled every room. No wonder Lord Willoughby was anxious to get rid of what he legitimately could.

After a while, Joyce noticed that her flashlight was giving out. Impatiently, she twisted the grooved cap and shook it, but the batteries were dying, and she did not want to stay up there in the dark.

Before going downstairs to replace the batteries, Joyce glanced into one more room. The feeble light hardly penetrated the darkness, but it caught one object on the mantel, milky-green and vitreous, shining under its layer of dust. Joyce drew in her breath—it could be only one thing . . . an early experiment in glass. A small Roman jar like those she had seen reproduced in abundance in Pompeii. A pulse jumped in her throat as she panned the room with her dying light. Dim figures loomed under drapery, with broken slabs of marble at their bases. She ripped off one of the sheets in a billow of dust and focused her light on a portrait statue, unmistakably Roman, of a matron as stern as Antonio's mother. Joyce stumbled over something on the floor and stopped to examine it, a clay hut with figures on its sides: an Etruscan funerary casket! Not what she was really looking for, but she was getting warmer.

Then her flashlight went dead, and she was left in total darkness. For a moment her elation dispelled every other feeling. She had found Lord Robert Willoughby's collection!

A sudden sound made her turn quickly, just as the Roman matron fell toward Joyce, grazing her shoulder. Joyce made a small noise and held her shoulder as the matron thudded down against a footstool and rolled away

noisily, but apparently unharmed. Joyce was actually unharmed too, but she was sure her shoulder would have a
healthy bruise. As she recovered her wits, she wondered
shakily if the matron had suddenly taken it into her head
to protect the collection, or if the man Mrs. Craig had seen
on the lawn last night had made his way into the house.
Damn! She would really have to tell everything to Stanton
Willoughby so that he could be on guard—but meanwhile,
oh, marvelous meanwhile—she had found Lord Robert's
loot!

Lord Willoughby was in the midst of an open three-way
phone conversation, but he switched it off with composure
when Joyce rushed into the study without knocking.

"I've found it!" she gasped. "I've found it!"

"The vase?"

"Not yet . . . but I found Lord Robert's collection! It's
on the third floor. I need light, though . . . lots of light!"

He pressed a button on his intercom. "Mrs. Craig, please
bring some oil lamps at once," he said, as though this
strange request was most reasonable. He turned his attention back to Joyce, busy putting new batteries from her
purse into the flashlight. "Good God, what's happened to
you? Your face is dirty. And"—he looked at the footprints
on his carpet—"you've acquired a bit of dust on your
shoes, too."

Too excited to apologize, she reached out to lead him to
the treasure, but he fastidiously avoided contact with her
hand. Mrs. Craig appeared at the doorway with her arms
full of candles. Her lower lip was trembling. "Your lordship, I'd like to explain. . . ."

"Forget it. I know it hasn't been cleaned up there for
years. Do you have some matches for those? You'd better
come along . . . and bring a pad and pencil."

In the blaze of candlelight, several articles were tagged
for foreign travel: a flat Greek drinking cup with scenes of
revelry on its sides and the inscription 'Dion is a beautiful

boy' in its interior; not one, but *three*, hut-shaped funerary urns; a head of Minerva with the nose broken off; and all of the statues that Joyce could be sure were authentic. Over her objections, Stanton Willoughby insisted that even the Roman glass be sent back to Italy. But there was no sign of the black Etruscan urn.

Joyce sank down on the dusty counterpane of the creaking bed. "I don't understand it," she said with disappointment. "Everything in the collection points right to it . . . but it isn't here."

Lord Willoughby was so gratified by the number of departing objects that he had forgotten about the urn. "Are you sure that statue of the Roman woman can't go, too? It's so damned big!"

"It's a fake . . . a good fake, but there's no sense in sending it. The Italians are good at that sort of thing. They did a whopping business during the age of the Grand Tour. Stanton . . . are there catalogs anywhere of any of the collections?"

"I really couldn't say. You might look in the library . . . but nothing's in order there, either. Some of the family collected books. I don't think they read them: a lot of the pages are still uncut. I know a dealer in London who's anxious to buy up the entire lot, but I can't sell them, of course. You can have a go at them if you like . . . after you've showered and had some lunch."

Joyce spent the rest of the afternoon in the huge library with its musty odor of old paper, looking for diaries or indices of the collections. Her tea and later her dinner were served to her on trays. She ate without tasting the food. Some of the euphoria she had felt at finding Robert Willoughby's collection still lingered; but she knew that if she stopped to think, she would come down with an emotional thud. Only the activity of climbing the movable ladder and riffling through leather-bound volumes kept her from facing defeat.

On the bottom shelf, their tops covered with dust, Joyce finally found what she was looking for. In a set of thin volumes with false covers, appeared the words *Index of My Collection*. She looked hastily for Robert's list and when she found it she moved it onto the table under the lamp.

Lord Robert Willoughby had entered his acquisitions meticulously, in a neat hand, according to the dates of acquisition, neglecting only to mention the circumstances surrounding their purchase. He had acquired a number of antiquities on his trips to Italy, including all of the objects now safely in Stanton's study. She finally found what she wanted:

"6 May, 1798. Cin. urn, Pomp., black ceramic, still sealed, Circa ?100 B.C."

Circa 100 B.C.! He had no conception of the urn's actual age, but he had known it was a cinerary urn . . . and he had left it sealed! But the entry was followed by a small asterisk, which matched another at the bottom of the page:

"Stolen, with other starred objects, 9 July, 1814."

Stolen . . . and stolen again? She cursed softly under her breath. Stanton Willoughby had not mentioned a theft in the Hall. Of course, his ignorance about the collections was so abysmal he probably did not know about it himself. The urn had not been here from the beginning. Well, she consoled herself, her time had not been altogether wasted. She copied the descriptions of all the stolen objects: there were only four of them, and one might lead to another.

The library door creaked quietly open. She was almost afraid to turn and look. For the past few minutes, despite her concentration, she had been conscious of something else. Her shoulder was beginning to ache painfully from the bruise and the day's tensions.

She was relieved to see that it was only Stanton Willoughby, returned from his drive, nosing considerably into the library, but this did not still the beating of her heart. He moved with abstraction to the darkened windows without speaking to her. "Did you hear anything outside just now?" he asked at last. "I could have sworn I saw someone outlined against the light at this window when I drove up. . . ."

The hair rose on her arms. She had been too occupied since she found the collection to think to draw the drapes. "No. I didn't hear anything. I didn't even hear your car return," she confessed.

"That isn't surprising. The engine doesn't make much noise. The Ray . . ." He seemed about to launch into a description of his favorite car's mechanics, but Joyce cut him short. She remembered her promise to Mrs. Craig and the curious accident upstairs. She was aware, also, of the objects in the study, waiting to be packed.

"You should have better security here," she said. "Some of the things in this house are priceless, Stanton. You should at least have dogs. . . ."

He drew the drapes thoughtfully. "There's supposed to be a watchman," he said. "Maybe it was him I saw . . . come to have a look at a pretty girl through the window. . . ."

She drew in her breath, braced herself for what she had to say, certain that he would not like it, but there was no alternative. She did not want to see anyone in the house harmed later because of her.

"It's possible that I was followed here," she said in a rush. "Someone's been following me for some time. I took every precaution I could think of before I left London, but. . . ."

His reaction surprised her. "My dear girl!" he said, approaching the table. "Why didn't you tell me sooner? Who's following you . . . and why?"

"I don't know," she said, relieved to speak of it to someone at last. "It has something to do with the statue in Greece . . . you know about that." She told him what her student had done. "John didn't mean any harm. He was only trying to find out something about our statue. What he didn't know was that I'd start looking for the scroll. The family in Italy doesn't know about this . . . and they don't want the police involved. It's understandable . . . they're proud people. But unless I get rid of whoever's watching me, I'm going to have a hard time on this project. . . ."

"Scroll?" he picked out of her confession. "What scroll? Are you looking for incunabula in the library now?"

She did not realize she had said it: the slip left her momentarily tongue-tied. Then she decided she must be completely honest with him and added, slowly, "The urn I'm looking for is supposed to contain a scroll. If it does, it would have enormous historic value. Only, with these people sniffing around, thinking I'm still looking for the statue, my hands are almost tied . . . and I may even be in danger."

She spoke softly, still conscious of the heavily draped windows, which were too far away for anyone to hear, anyway.

"It isn't likely that the seal's still unbroken, after all this time," she qualified her statement. "I may not find the urn at all. Your stupid ancestor let it get stolen again." She tapped the pages of the index with her fingers; then she realized what she had said. "Oh . . . I'm sorry. . . ."

"It's quite all right. It was damned stupid of him to buy it in the first place." He began to pace the room. "I don't like this, Joyce. I don't like it at all. If the police can't be told, you're at the mercy of these buggers. A little girl like you . . ."

"Don't worry about me," she said quickly. "I only told you so you could take precautions. Since they've followed me, they might decide to steal everything you have. And someone might get hurt in the process."

He did not seem to hear her. "I have a nephew in Army intelligence," he said. "He's in hospital with a bullet in his back right now, poor lad. But he once told me that the

only way to rid oneself of a pursuer is to reverse the roles
. . . draw the fellow out and pursue him in turn. The whole
trick's in confrontation. Of course, Ian's a big fellow,
trained in the martial arts and all that. . . ."

The bullet lodged presently in Ian's back did not reassure Joyce, but the advice was sensible. She considered her
course of action in silence.

"I wish there were something I could do to help you,"
Stanton Willoughby said suddenly. For a moment she was
touched by his concern; but then he continued, "You've
done a lot for me. You have no idea the publicity my
company will get when I return that collection to Italy!"

"You're going to tell the newspapers?" she asked, appalled. "You won't say anything about the urn . . . the
scroll? You won't mention me?"

"Of course not, my dear. I can understand your friends'
reluctance to have news of the urn spread about at this
time. And I'm very grateful to you. Wouldn't it have been
marvelous, though, if I could have returned that urn as
well! Is there anything I can do to help you find it?"

Joyce tried to gather her thoughts. "Perhaps there is,"
she said at last. "Do you know any reliable dealers in
London I can contact? Someone who's been in business a
long time?"

"There are the big ones, of course, but I'm only familiar
with one. The family's dealt with the firm for years. It's
absolutely reliable. But Churchman and Sons doesn't handle . . . contraband art."

"Churchman and Sons," she repeated, writing it down
in her notes. "They may not deal in it, but they'll probably
know more than I do about how it's handled."

"Jermyn Street, St. James. The youngest son, Lyman, is
in charge now. I'll ring him and tell him you're coming."
He hesitated. "But what about this other thing? Should I
hire a private detective to keep an eye on you?"

"No," she said. "There are too many eyes on me already. I'll take care of it myself."

Joyce left the next morning after thanking Stanton Willoughby for his cooperation and assuring him that he would hear from her if she ever managed to locate the urn. He promised to take all necessary security precautions to put Mrs. Craig's mind at rest and guard his houseful of valuable antiquarian refuse.

Chapter Six

D r. Willis-Parks was lecturing at the Institute of
Archaeology the next evening, but Drs. Hill and
Arapkilos had left Mrs. Amboy's and had been
replaced by an exuberant group of students of
various nationalities. The students had come to
plunder the scholarship of the museum for their theses and
to check out London nightlife in passing. Dr. Arapkilos
had made a sudden decision to return to his country on
Saturday morning, Mrs. Amboy informed Joyce, and the
American professor had left the same day. The students,
who had drifted in separately over the weekend, had already become friends, listening to loud tapes in one of the
rooms in the evening and walking together, in a solid
serious mass, to the reading room every day. Joyce decided it would be to her advantage to blend in with them;
besides, they were her kind of people.

By the time she got around to going to the museum next
morning, however, it was Dr. Willis-Parks, instead, she

found accompanying her. The students had already left. The usual five-minute walk lengthened to fifteen in his company, and Joyce could not think of anything to say.

The old man himself finally broke the silence: "Your student was bold . . . but indiscreet," he said. "He shouldn't have told that Greek so much, you know. Something odd about the fellow. I didn't take to him at all. After a while, you develop an instinct about such things."

"Dr. Arapkilos?" Joyce inquired. "What did John tell him?"

"All about the statue he was looking for . . . about his job in Switzerland. He was pumping Arapkilos for the names of Greek collectors, I think."

Joyce considered this new information. "Did he," she asked, "mention the names he already knew?"

Dr. Willis-Parks coughed loosely and raised a wadded handkerchief to his mouth. "I don't think so . . . did he have some?"

"A couple," she said carefully. "They're probably nothing. . . ."

"Neither was the Greek," the old man said flatly. "He wasn't an archaeologist anyway, I'll wager. That story about visiting the Northumberland digs. No excavation going on right now, you know. He didn't even seem to know that much about the Romans."

"Didn't you warn John, sir?" Joyce asked.

"Too late. When I realized what was going on, it was too late for that. I was happy to see him leave when he did. I trust he's arrived home safely?"

"I just wrote a letter to find out. You've known about . . . everything . . . all the time!"

"There are some things I feel rather strongly about," he said. "And when people think you aren't listening, you hear things. I'm sorry about that Willoughby remark the other evening . . . but you were about to do something foolish. It was the only way I could think of to stop you.

To remind you that even the walls have ears." They
stopped to present their passes. "Dr. Lacey, I'd be honored
if you'd attend my lecture tomorrow evening. I'm going to
twist a knife in an old wound, so to speak."

They parted in the reading room, as Joyce went off to
request all issues of the London *Times* for the two weeks
following July 9, 1814. The newspapers did not appear for
over an hour, and she thought about Dr. Willis-Parks the
whole time, measuring his doubts about Dr. Arapkilos
against her own. Mrs. Amboy had said that the Greek
arrived shortly *after* John did, but he had continued to stay
on even after John's departure. Why? Was he waiting for
her? If she had lost her own pursuer in Italy it was not
impossible that John's had been waiting for her, right here,
when she arrived. And Dr. Arapkilos had decided to "return to Greece" on the very morning she had left for
Wiltshire. Where was he now?

According to the faded newspaper account, Lord Robert
Willoughby had entertained a party of friends over the
weekend preceding the theft of the objects from his collection. One of his guests, his brother-in-law, Count Luigi
Falcone, was quite vociferous to the press about the theft.
It was a scandal, he said: something should be done about
it at once. Valuable pieces of Roman and Etruscan art had
been stolen, a loss to all of Western civilization. An art
connoisseur himself, he was appalled by the ease with
which the Hall had been entered, the way the items had
been "spirited away." The newspaper said the count was
from Rome, instead of Naples, where Lord Robert Willoughby had met and married his sister, the contessa. Joyce
compared the newspaper report with her list from Robert's
index: a small bust of Pluto (or Hades), identifiable by the
crown of foliage around the head; a vase inscribed by
someone called Lucius; a broken stele depicting a beloved
wife being laid to rest; and a black pottery urn. All rela-

tively small objects, but not easily portable. She wondered why the head of Minerva had been left behind.

A sudden feeling, deep inside of her, prompted by something Antonio had said, made her pay close attention to Count Luigi Falcone as she read through the remaining articles. If he had been an "art connoisseur," he probably had been a collector, too. Furthermore, in a later edition the count had described the urn, which Robert Willoughby had merely cataloged "Cinerary urn, Pompeii," as "an Etruscan cinerary urn, at least five thousand years old." Even in the early 1800s the count had known Etruscan from Roman and had come closer to the correct date than Robert Willoughby. Luigi Falcone had been a rare *cogniscente* for his time. There was no mention of what subsequently became of him. As a nobleman, and a relative, no suspicion had fallen on him. In all probability he had simply returned home to Italy. To Rome. But his sister had been married in Naples, so the family was probably Neapolitan. Joyce remembered Antonio's evaluation of the breed. Clever devil, the count, she thought with grudging admiration. Except for one thing . . . he protested too much. And in protesting, he revealed how much he really knew. In a way, what he had done was just: he had returned the objects to the country where they belonged. Though she could not be sure that he had not resold them.

A request for more newspapers finally closed the case. The objects had not been recovered, but they were heavily insured. Joyce decided to look into the financial situations of both families at the time. Stanton would probably provide her with the information here, but she felt a more urgent need to follow the 158-year-old trail of Count Luigi Falcone. She looked at her watch. Antonio would still be at the excavation now: she could not reach him until evening.

With a feeling of accomplishment at having reduced the

last sighting of the urn by sixteen years, Joyce hurried back
to Mrs. Amboy's to change into her one respectable dress,
so she would not be turned away from the door of the
Churchman gallery.

The almost perpendicular ride up the escalator from the
Underground made Joyce feel giddy, so, as she ascended,
she concentrated on the advertisements posted on the wall.
Once out into busy Piccadilly, she observed the foot traffic
behind her by glancing at reflections in the windows of the
stores. Everyone seemed to be hurrying about his own
business, paying no attention to her at all. Though she had
not felt anyone following her since she left Lord Willoughby's, she had a distinct feeling of being watched now.

She passed a church, tucked in between modern department stores, and took the first turning toward St. James.
She had walked only half a block when a swift glance over
her shoulder confirmed that someone had turned the corner after her. She had only a glimpse of the man because,
when she turned, he put his hand to his face to adjust his
dark glasses. She could not dismiss the man from her
mind: something about him was familiar, though she felt
she had seen him under much different circumstances, at-
tired in entirely different clothes. A single glance, a feeling,
a suspicion in her nerves were not enough to turn and
confront someone who might be a perfectly harmless
stranger. If he was following her, he would still be waiting
when she came out of the gallery. Until then she must
maintain her composure in order to get the information she
wanted.

Churchman and Sons Gallery was housed in an impressive old stone building with a doorman out front. The
carpeted foyer was as quiet as a club, and only one gentleman was in attendance on the ground floor. He let her
roam about at will into the side galleries without accosting
her like a salesman. There was not an antiquity in sight,

though a placard revealed that the Oriental galleries were on the third floor. The paintings and sculptures displayed in the first room she entered were modern, strategically placed to get the best effect from the light. An examination of the opposite room only revealed that the paintings were older. She wondered what was on the second floor, and she asked the salesperson.

"Books," he informed her. "If you'd be interested in seeing them . . ."

Of course, she thought: books. Churchman was the dealer in London interested in the Willoughby library. Joyce presented the salesman with her card.

"I'd like to see Mr. Churchman, please. I believe Lord Willoughby has called him."

As she waited, Joyce wondered where the customers were, or if they came by appointment. Except for the dark-suited salesman the building appeared to be empty. It was certainly nothing like Gump's in San Francisco: one hardly felt at home here.

"Mr. Churchman's been expecting your call," the gentleman said when he returned, indicating that she should have telephoned first. But at least Mr. Churchman knew about her. Old Stanton had prepared him, true to his word.

Lyman Churchman was younger than she had imagined he would be, in his late thirties, attractive, with hazel eyes and sideburned hair. He shook her hand warmly and showed her into his wood-paneled office. Though his finely tailored suit made him look like a banker, she suspected his leisure clothing was much more trendy, because of his fashionable hair. There was an immediate rapport between them, generated by him, which Joyce attributed to the fact that Mr. Churchman was extremely fond of women. At least the approving glance he gave her seemed to indicate fondness.

"You made a great impression on Stanton . . . from what I could make of his rather disconnected conversation," he said, holding a chair for her. He moved his own to the side of his desk, so the fine cherry-wood surface would not stand between them. "He told me about your project, and I must say that I'm fascinated by it. I'd be delighted to assist you in any way I can."

"Thank you," she smiled, completely at ease in his presence. "I want to know all about art theft, and I'd like the names of a few illegal collectors."

At first, her request overwhelmed him; then he laughed aloud. "Good God!" he said. "Is that all? Do you realize what you're asking, Dr. Lacey? Surely you aren't going after the collectors yourself?"

"I don't know yet. As an archaeologist I've heard things, of course . . . but I'm a complete novice about the way these things are handled."

He stretched around his desk and reached into a drawer. "Our gallery's old, but not as old as the theft at Willoughby Hall that Stanton told me about. Of course, we have *no* dealings in contraband art. Every article in this building has full credentials and export papers. The bulletins we get from Interpol"—he laid a handful of flyers on her knee— "are our only source for checking what's been stolen, unless we read it in the papers like everyone else. These are the most recent."

Joyce glanced through the bulletins, conscious of his eyes upon her, but her statue was not listed. Most of the descriptions were of paintings taken from museums. "My statue isn't here," she said, disappointed.

"There could be several reasons for that," he said kindly. "It takes time to get these things circulated, and. . . ."

"And?" she asked, looking into his handsome face.

"Well . . . an article has to be reported missing. Some of these collectors are influential men. Influential and wealthy. In spite of the small flurry of publicity the theft of your statue received, political or monetary pressure might have been exerted. . . . I'm not saying it has been," he reassured her quickly. "It's probably just a time-lag sort of thing. I simply haven't had the bulletin yet."

She nodded, "I've heard the recovery rate of stolen artworks is pretty low."

"Unfortunately, a canvas can be rolled up and stored for years, if it hasn't found its way into a collection. Something like your statue . . . well, if the thief can afford to wait, a buyer could be found easily after a short lapse of time. You don't seem to realize how big this traffic is . . . or how little the law's enforced."

"But the Greek antiquities law of 1932 . . ."

"How can it be enforced if the article's already out of the country? I'm not saying they don't try. But it's a hassle all the way around. Look what happened with the Euphronios krater. The claim is that it had been kept, broken, in a box somewhere, since before the law was passed. The museum says it was bought in London before the law was passed. The Metropolitan is in trouble only if it was excavated in Italy as the Italians claim, and not in Greece as the museum claims." He sighed, "For that matter, Turkey's regulation of 1907 absolutely prohibits the export of cultural property, except as occasional awards to directors of field research, but things leave the country every day! You can buy them right in the bazaars, I understand . . . and have them shipped as cheap replicas! Which, incidentally, is the way it's most often done . . . with small objects, anyway."

"You seem to know a lot about all this. . . ."

"I have to, my dear! I'm very careful about what I buy. My father used to deal in antiquities a little . . . cautiously, you understand. Our firm's always had a good name. I've given that up altogether, though . . . gone mostly modern, as you may have noticed. It's just too much trouble to get things verified." He smiled suddenly, boyishly. "But please don't let me run on so. I want to hear about your little cloak-and-dagger quest for an urn that was allegedly stolen from Willoughby Hall over a hundred fifty years ago. . . ."

"No longer 'allegedly,' " she smiled. "I have proof of that now! And the urn was one of the objects stolen."

"No wonder Stanton thinks you're a remarkable young woman!" he said with admiration. "You know, it was sheer luck that you called on him. He has no interest in the collections at the Hall, except to rid himself of the burden, and you gave him a good excuse . . . and a chance to get a little publicity into the bargain. What do you think your chances are of ever finding that urn?"

"I *must* find it. And right now I'm feeling more hopeful. I think it was taken back to Italy, if it wasn't sold here. . . ."

"An Etruscan urn," he considered. "It could have been assimilated into any collection . . . even a museum one . . . or been lost completely, in that length of time."

"I've considered all that. If it still exists," she said, "do you think it might have passed from collector to collector?"

"It's possible, I suppose. Probable, if it isn't in a museum," he smiled. "Now, let me think . . . what sort of a collector might have it now?" He thought about it for a moment and began to frown. "A *bucchero* urn isn't the loveliest thing in the world. It would have to be someone like Lord Robert Willoughby . . . who simply has a passion for antiquities. And if he has, he doesn't care how he gets them. . . ."

"Do you know any collectors like that?"

"No. Oh, I've heard things . . . every dealer has." He put his fingers together thoughtfully. "Once, in Paris, I heard something about a man named Denis . . . Jean-Paul Denis. He'd got himself into a bit of trouble over the purchase of a holograph manuscript . . . it proved to be a fake later, so he wasn't charged. But a French dealer remarked to me that the police would be interested in the things in his house on the Île St. Louis . . . some of them date back to Babylon!"

"Jean-Paul Denis," Joyce repeated. "You didn't report what you'd heard to the police?"

"Good Lord, no! It was only hearsay, and it's better to keep one's name out of such things. Take Mynheer Zee, for example: he lives in Amsterdam . . . or used to. There isn't a dealer in Europe who doesn't know about his collection. It's legend, by now. He collects *everything*. But I, personally, wouldn't buy anything from him if he showed me verification papers ten feet long."

Joyce recorded the name. "Doesn't Interpol know about these people?"

"I daresay . . . some of them, anyway. But what can anyone do without proof? And these collectors are clever. Interpol, you know, is an overworked and undermanned agency, and it can't do anything without the help of the national police involved. Now, if one of the paintings listed here"—he touched his hand to the stack of bulletins—"appeared anywhere in my line of vision, I assure you I'd report it at once. So would most dealers. But after the information got to Interpol the police of the country involved would have to take the necessary action."

"Cooperating with the law would protect your reputation," Joyce suggested. "But reporting hearsay evidence might link you to contraband art."

"Exactly. Now, let me see. . . . There's an Arab, Ibrahim Moab. . . . Oh, my dear, I'm afraid he lives in Libya! Rumor has it that his collection of antiquities is priceless, but that's hardly a place to go stomping around with a warrant right now."

"No," Joyce frowned. "Can you think of anyone else?"

"Your own country isn't free of the scourge, either, I regret to say. In fact, the collectors are quite open there. I suspect they're wealthy enough to be unapproachable. Or maybe America just doesn't respect antiquities laws." He gave her several names. "And there's Alberto Grossman in New York. He divides his time between Central America and New York, transporting pre-Colombian art. He's a dealer, but he collects, too . . . which isn't unusual, if one can afford it."

Joyce was familiar with the name. "I think he's in jail," she said. "A couple of years ago he made the mistake of bringing in some solid-gold objects from Peru . . . more gold than a United States citizen's supposed to own. No one was concerned that the gold was crafted by the Incas. I was a student then, and we were really upset about that. He's probably out of jail by now, though," she said, putting down his name.

She waited, but no other names were forthcoming.

"I'm sorry," he said. "Given a little time, a chance to ask a few questions, I might come up with more, but. . . ."

"You've been wonderful," she assured him. "Tell me, though . . . have you ever heard of a man named Priapos Karavitas?"

He shook his head, smiling at the name. "It does seem to ring a dim bell, you know, but. . . . No, I'm sorry."

"Krishnamsetty Das in Rome?"

"Nothing," he admitted. He studied her with amusement. "May I ask an insane question? What on earth do you plan to *do* with these names?"

"I'm not sure . . . yet," she sighed. "These people are so spread around, aren't they? Ever since Greece, I've been trying to figure out what kind of collector would do such a thing. The middleman . . . the dealer, if you'll forgive me . . . I can understand. But a collector like this . . . someone who hides things away for himself alone. . . ." She shrugged.

He smiled, "The people I deal with, the normal art collectors, fall into two basic types, I think: those who love art, and those who are investors. Often, they're both. But an illegal collector . . . well, he has no intention of either displaying what he buys, or investing, really, does he? The nature of his acquisitions makes them worthless to anyone but himself. It seems to me that anyone who'd go to all that trouble and expense so he alone could view his collection, must have some sort of kink. I'd be very careful if I were you."

"I've been given that advice before," she smiled, rising to leave, "but thanks anyway. You've been very kind . . . and helpful, too."

He escorted her to the door. "Art collecting's big business right now. Even the rich Japanese have got into the market. The value of a work of art doesn't go down with the market: it's safer than gold. Um . . . I say, are you free for dinner this evening? I'd like to tell you about an organization some of us are trying to put together. We want to put a tax on our sales . . . the proceeds would go toward cataloging and protecting the world's great art. . . ."

"I'd like to hear about it," she said, "but I've a call to make . . . and I'll be leaving shortly. Maybe another time . . ."

"You're leaving right away? What a pity. . . . Where are you going?"

She shrugged. "I'm not sure yet. But I've done all I can do here."

He took her arm companionably and accompanied her down on the elevator. "You're quite a woman, do you know that? Do give me a ring when you're in London again. And if I think of anything that might help you, I'll let you know. Keep in touch with Stanton Willoughby."

They shook hands at the heavy glass doors, with the uniformed man standing beyond them.

"Good luck," he said. "I must admit, yours looks like an impossible quest. Incidentally, if you're in Rome you might contact a colleague of mine, Harold O'Keefe. He's a wholesaler with offices on the Via Babuino and an excellent eye for modern Italian art. He's a countryman of yours, who's been in Italy since the war. He may be able to give you some insight into the situation there."

"Thank you. I'll look him up."

"See here," he said, detaining her with a frown, "you won't do anything rash, will you? The collectors you're after are some kind of monomaniacs, I think. I can't explain them, but . . . approach them with caution."

A careful glance outside the gallery and up and down the street did not reveal her suspected pursuer, and Joyce walked slowly back to Piccadilly Circus. She did not know where to begin, and her finances were getting low. If she intended to spend the rest of the summer in Europe, she would have to get a draft on her savings from home. It was too late for a trip to the bank today, and tomorrow she had to follow up the vicissitudes of the Willoughby fortune.

She bought a ticket at the machines in the Underground and approached the steep escalator, wondering where she should have the draft sent. As she stepped onto the escalator she caught sight of the tall man in dark glasses rapidly approaching it, and panic tore through her like an icicle plunged into her heart. He was a few steps above her, but he was *walking* quickly down the moving steps. His hands touched her back just as she shied to one side. Clutching the moving rail with both hands, she clung to it for life. The impetus of his shove, which glanced off her shoulders, sent him hurling down the escalator through the space left by her move. He tumbled several times on the empty stairs before his fall was stopped by a frightened passenger below, who turned in horror, unable to release the rail himself. Joyce watched with dry-mouthed alarm from above, while the imprint of those hands burned into her back like a brand. The crumpled body of her assailant was hauled off onto the platform by concerned and helping hands.

When she reached the landing, a station guard had appeared, and still feeling numb, she joined the curious group around the sprawled figure. She had seen him before, this man with the broken glasses askew on his nose: Dr. Hill, the American professor who had stayed at Mrs. Amboy's!

He was still breathing, but his leg was bent at an impossible angle, and blood oozed through his trousers. A man with an attaché case ran to a telephone while the guard and another man crouched beside the injured Dr. Hill, afraid to move him further. Joyce remained at the edge of the small, sympathetic crowd that was gathering. She was beginning to tremble.

"Nasty tumble," someone said. "Poor chap . . ."

The guard went discreetly through the victim's pockets and extracted a passport folder. "American. Tourist, I suppose. Damn shame. What's this?" he muttered, looking puzzled. "*Two* passports? American . . . and Swiss. Well . . . whatever . . . the police can look into this. He must have come over dizzy. . . ."

As Joyce drifted away, she paused, in complete confusion, before the directional signs to the trains. Swiss. And she had been taken completely unaware, in spite of her intention to draw out her pursuer. If her body had not obeyed an instinctual command of its own, she would be lying there right now instead of her assailant. Since she was half his size, she would have been hurt worse. She might even be dead.

"Antonio!" she cried, when she heard the deep, assured voice on the other end of the line. "Is . . . everything all right there?"

She had waited, allowing for the hour's time difference, until she was sure he was home from work, before using Mrs. Amboy's private phone to call him. The male operator in Naples was singing while he rang the number; she waited in agony until she had her party.

"Of course," he said. "Why shouldn't it be? Nothing ever happens here. Joyce, what's wrong with you? You sound. . . ."

"I'm all right, but someone tried to. . . ." No, she would not tell him over the telephone. "I'll tell you about it when

I see you. Can you get away to look something up for me?"

"Yes. What is it?"

"Try to find out everything you can about Count Luigi Falcone. Go into his finances in 1814 if you can. I'm sure it's a Neapolitan family. . . ."

"Falcone? That's the name of the street where my great-grandfather delivered . . . that package!"

The Via Falcone. That is where she had heard the name: it was in the Casale papers. "Yes! I remember now. Do you think you can do it?"

There was a pause on the line. "I can do it," he said at last. "But when are you coming back? You've been gone almost a week."

"I have to attend a lecture tomorrow evening. . . . And I have some other things to do. . . ." She thought about the names Lyman Churchman had given her. Then she made her decision. "I'll be on the express train to Rome on Wednesday evening. I'll see you in Pompeii on Thursday. It doesn't give you much time. . . ."

"I'll see what I can find out. It's good to hear your voice again. You didn't write."

"I've been *busy*. I must hang up now . . . long distance. I'll tell you everything on Thursday. And, Antonio . . . be careful."

"Yes," he said thoughtfully. "I wish you were coming back sooner."

"So do I! Thursday, though. *Ciao,* Antonio."

"Ciao, amica . . ."

Despite the spur-of-the-moment decision, she felt she had made the right choice. She was in no condition to confront collectors in Amsterdam and Paris right now. The accident in the Underground had happened too late to get into the evening papers, but she had been thinking while she waited to call Antonio. "Professor Hill," the man who had bored her at dinner and then tried to kill her, was probably the person she imagined she had lost at the airport. Yet he had known where to come, so there was communication here with someone else. If Hill was her pursuer, Arapkilos must have been John's, especially after what Dr. Willis-Parks had said about him. She could not complacently assume that Arapkilos had gone back to Greece. If he were still in London, either he knew about his coconspirator's accident by now, or he would read about it shortly in the morning newspaper. And this time he would be on her trail.

She knew she had to cover herself while she was here and somehow escape him to take that long trip by train. The possibilities on a night express made her shudder. She wished she had not promised Dr. Willis-Parks that she would attend his lecture: she wanted to leave right away. Then she remembered that the students had said they were attending the lecture, too. For the next two days perhaps she could lose herself in the smokescreen of those young people. She would not be alone for a minute.

A rumble of amusement went through the Archaeological Institute auditorium at Sir James Willis-Parks's opening joke that he thought the Piltdown Man fraud was perpetrated by archaeology students and that he had never trusted clever students since. Some of the students Joyce was sitting with clapped briefly at the old man's unexpected humor. If the audience had expected the old professor to inch out onto the platform and mumble about his Anglo-Saxons, it was in for a surprise. He walked slowly, but not feebly, and he spoke in the clear accents of a veteran lecturer. But his subject, when he got into it, engendered both shock and dismay: Dr. Willis-Parks was urging archaeologists to forget their individual disputes and band together to prevent art theft.

Dressed in blue jeans and a sheer, wrinkled, embroidered-cotton Pakistani shirt she had bought from a grad student

from Columbia, Joyce listened with interest, but her gaze
hardly left the audience. She had not seen Arapkilos yet,
and if he was here, she wondered if he would recognize her
amidst the students, with her long blond hair hanging
straight over her shoulders and her reading glasses, thin-
rimmed and "mod," pushed down on her nose, so she
could watch while she listened to the lecture. To herself,
and to the delight of the students staying at Mrs. Amboy's,
she looked just like one of them. None of them questioned
her whim to blend with the crowd: they had all known
some pretty "hip" professors at their own schools, and they
knew what had happened in Greece. To them, Joyce was
"with it," despite her degree and her allergy to cannabis,
which had sent them into fits of laughter when it was
discussed.

Joyce did not feel like laughing now, though: she was
still on edge, and the old man's lecture did little to reassure
her. He was listing the number of losses from excavations
in the past fifty years, not excluding the now legendary,
still mysterious, and gingerly referred to "treasure of
Dorak," which had gotten a British archaeologist into considerable trouble in the late 1950s. The man had seen the
"treasure," sketched it, published a paper, and then the
treasure, the house, and everyone connected with it had
disappeared into the desert without a lead. At first, the
archaeologist had been accused of theft; later, his permit to
dig in Turkey had not been granted. Some archaeologists
still thought he was a liar; others believed that he had
simply been used to verify the authenticity and date of the
"treasure" before clever thieves made off with it.

Joyce listened in fascination to the old professor's stories, unable to believe that the traffic in stolen antiquities
was of such magnitude. By comparison, her statue was a
drop in the ocean: it was nothing at all. But she sat up
straight and drew in her breath in surprise when he mentioned that, too:

"Recently, I've noted a trend in our younger colleagues not to endure this sort of thing," the basset-eyed old man was saying. "At peril to themselves, of which they are innocent, they are trying to retrieve their stolen discoveries. As far as I know, no one has met with disaster so far. But is it right or moral for us to make these young people go it alone? I suggest to you that we solve our internal problem . . . the one that's been constant with us . . . what Sir Mortimer Wheeler called our 'vendetta' for permits to dig, and turn our sights outward . . . to *protect* what we have uncovered. And to assist the young people who will take our places in understanding and coping with the eternal problem of art theft. Archaeology should not be a 'vendetta' . . . it should be a passion for discovery, a beautiful science to pass on to the young. . . ."

Chapter Seven

Joyce was so happy to see Antonio waiting on the platform of the Terminal Station in Rome that she would have rushed to throw her arms around him if she had not been hampered by her duffel bag. She had spent a peaceful night, crowded into a compartment with a group of Eurailpass-carrying students on holiday, blending in nicely thanks to her newly acquired jeans and Pakistani shirt. She had not been frightened on the train either, having covered her departure from London neatly enough to throw anyone off, by reserving a seat on a flight to America on the hall telephone, for everyone to hear, and then not claiming the seat. Instead, disguised as a wandering student, with her hair hanging over her shoulders, she had done her banking and had purchased a rail ticket while on an outing to the National Gallery with the students. She left them, after a raid on some of the bookstores, just in time to board the express at Victoria Station, and quickly found herself amid another flock of lively students. One of the boys had a guitar, which he played as far as Dijon, when they all settled down to sleep. She felt as free as they were, now. If Arakpilos was still in London, he was off the scent.

Antonio's neatness made her feel tacky in comparison as she approached him. Clean and cool in his green jersey, he surveyed the people getting off the train with quick, observant eyes. Obviously, he had not seen her descend to the platform.

"Hi!" she greeted him warmly when she stood before him. He raised his arched brows, nodded politely, smiled, and continued to search the platform. "Antonio! It's me . . . Joyce."

Looking down at her with startled green eyes, his glance swept her "hippie" outfit and her hair. Then he reached for her duffel bag with a laugh and threw his arm around her shoulders. "What in the name of the Holy Virgin are you made up for? I didn't recognize you!" He peered closely at the embroidery down the front of her shirt. "Are you wearing anything under that thing?"

"It's none of your business . . . but of course I am!" she smiled, pleased, both by the contact of his arm and the fact that not even he had recognized her. "I'm in disguise," she said ominously; then she, too, burst out laughing. "You thought I was trying to pick you up!"

He shrugged indifferently, a confession that it had happened before. She wanted to put her arm around him, too, as they walked along, but she decided she better not carry this role too far. Her contact with the students had been rejuvenating; dressing like them could be her undoing. Now that she was with Antonio again, it was necessary to crawl back into her own clothing and identity.

"I didn't expect to see you here," she said, more seriously. "I must say, I'm delighted. I have a lot to tell you. Let's go to the Diurno, so I can shower and dress. . . ."

The Diurno, or day hotel, in the station at Rome was

one of Joyce's favorite conveniences in the city, a wonder of the modern world she had encountered nowhere else. Here one could shower in luxury, sleep if one felt like it, have one's hair set, or have lunch while awaiting a train or after getting off one. While Antonio waited in the coffee shop, she took a long, hot shower in one of the clean, modern booths and put on her white dress in an adjoining dressing room. She pulled her hair up into a dignified twist, checked the smoothness of her panty hose, and rejoined him to find sandwiches and coffee awaiting her.

Antonio took in the costume change, and then his manner, too, changed. His eyes were still friendly, but it was business as usual again. Joyce had a vague feeling of loss: she had liked being a student better. She wondered if Antonio, like Mrs. Amboy, was a snob. He was a proud man: did her degree really make that much difference?

"Well, it's all been confirmed," she told him casually, between bites. "The problem now is that the urn was later stolen from Lord Robert Willoughby." She filled him in on all the details as he watched her face with silent tension. "Did you have any luck at all, tracing the count?"

"I found him," he said simply.

"You . . . what do you mean, you *found* him? Is there still a Count Falcone?" She could not suppress the hope that the urn was still in the family.

"I'll take you to him as soon as you finish your coffee."

How remarkably cool he was about the whole thing, Joyce thought, almost as though he were not involved in it at all. "Never mind my coffee! Take me to him now!" she cried.

Outside the station he guided her through a hot, weary line of people waiting for taxis, brushing aside the hustlers with limousines for hire and hotels to recommend. Finally, she caught sight of his friendly, eroded Fiat. He opened the door for her and locked her duffel bag in the storage space in front. Once he was inside the car, Joyce began to bombard him with questions.

"How did you find him? Is there still a collection? Antonio . . . answer me!"

"Later," he said, without looking at her. "I have to watch out for these crazy Romans. . . ."

His driving was defensive, on the theory of "when in Rome . . ." She closed her eyes as he passed someone in the right-hand lane. "For heaven's sake . . . !"

She did not relax until the Fiat was parked, illegally, front end to the curbing, before a hotel on the Via Veneto. Then she began to worry about the police. "Look . . . we have to be inconspicuous," she warned him. "We don't want any tickets . . . any trouble with anyone. Can't you find another spot?"

"It would take hours. Don't worry so much, Joyce. You act as though you're being followed."

His remark made her consider all that she had withheld from him. She would have to tell him now, she decided, as she accompanied him up some marble steps to a brick building with a crest on the stair landing. He motioned her through a wooden door beneath an arch, and the purpose of their visit came back to her. She blinked her eyes. They were in a dim anteroom, face-to-face with a gentle, bearded monk. What sort of place was this anyway?

"Is he . . . ?" she began, but Antonio, shaking his head, led her into a narrow corridor lit only by small windows in one wall and smaller bulbs in chandeliers hanging from the vaulted ceiling. Several dim little chapels were on their left, and the ceiling was decorated in wonderful rococo, the antique gold as delicate as filigree against the white stucco. Antonio stopped short of the end of the corridor and walked to the rail guarding one of the chapels, indicating its interior to her. Glancing into the dimness she emitted a soft cry of surprise.

The altar was composed of human skulls. The niches on

either side of it, containing the mummified remains of monks, were made of bones, too. She looked at the ceiling more closely: the fine designs were not antique gold, as she had thought; they, too, were a grisly decoupage of small yellow bones. The altar was a primitive sacrificial cairn, flanked by angel wings of human scapulae. When her mind finally absorbed what was before her eyes, her professional eye went to work identifying the bones. The old gold scrolls and curlicues on the baroque ceiling were vertebrae and spidery clavicles. The niches were piles of femurs, stacked as securely as railroad ties. A single white plastic lily stuck into a jar at the feet of one of the brown-robed mummies was the only relief in sight. She was appalled by the place.

"Permit me," Antonio said in a courtly way, "to introduce Count Luigi Falcone. Count Luigi . . . Dr. Joyce Lacey, who is interested in your past." He lowered his voice as though they were in church. "The count's the one in the niche on your left. He even rates a flower. . . ."

She stared at the cowled skull covered with dried muscle tissue, at the skeletal hands folded over the flattened chest. The count was grinning at her with teeth as perfect as Antonio's. Her head felt a little light. "Antonio . . ."

"You told me to find out about him. I did," he said, still speaking softly. "He's in good company here. That's a Barbarini princess on the ceiling in the last chapel . . . the child with the scythe."

"Who *did* this?"

He put a finger to his lips and hitched his head toward the sweet-faced monk who had appeared in the doorway. "Over a hundred years ago, the Cappuccine monks excavated their cemetery in the course of remodeling. I guess they had a lot of time on their hands and didn't know what to do with the bones. Or maybe they were trying to tell us something. '*Humo, polvo, nada*' . . . you know Calderón? When you look at it one way. . . ."

"It's disgusting. How did the count get here?"

"That's the real story," he said, moving toward the door, dropping an offering into the collection box, and nodding to the monk. "I'll tell it to you while you finish your cup of coffee. . . ."

"I need it. I thought you'd found a *living* descendant! You did this as a joke!"

He shrugged faintly. "It would have been a good one," he said as they stepped into the fresh sunlight, "only you're too serious, Joyce. Count Luigi Falcone, collector . . . in a collection, himself!"

She smiled in spite of herself. "How did you find him? And . . . what happened to *his* collection?"

They crossed the street to a sidewalk café, where Antonio ordered two cold coffees. "I found a history of the Falcones in the Naples library. I even went to the old house. The street's changed its name now, and the section's gone bad. The house where my great-grandfather delivered the package is divided into apartments with the wash hanging outside. I went through it, but it was just a ritual: there's nothing there but screaming babies. The count was intimately connected with the court . . . and he didn't change his allegiance when Napoleon made his own brother-in-law king of Naples. He'd just about exhausted his fortune in intrigue before he moved to Rome. . . ."

"When did he enter the monastery?"

"In 1817. It was easy to take a vow of poverty by then, I think. It also gave him a chance to repent his sins. The one thing I haven't been able to find out is where he lived when he was here . . . before he took orders."

"He was in England in 1814. I'm sure he stole the urn and other items from Lord Robert Willoughby's collection now. I thought a conspiracy might have been involved— the objects were insured. I didn't get a chance to check out the Willoughby finances at that time, but now. . . . If Count Luigi stole them, he could have lived for the next three

years on their sale, perhaps. He must have sold them here.
We're right back where we started!"

"Not quite. One thing we have learned about the count
is that he was a patriotic man. If he sold the objects, he
sold them to an Italian. All we have to do now is trace the
urn through its successive ownerships. . . ." He sighed
wearily and lit a cigarette.

But the strong, cold coffee had refreshed Joyce. She
explored her handbag for her notes. "Unless we can find
the person who has it now. I have the list of names I told
you about in the Diurno. Maybe we can add to it by visiting
a dealer here . . . Harold O'Keefe, on the Via Babuino. Is
that very far?"

"Within walking distance . . ."

"Good . . . I think I'd rather walk."

Beyond the flower- and tourist-covered sweep of the
Spanish Steps, past a statue of a baboon standing incon-
gruously on a pillar in the middle of the street, the galleries
on the Via Babuino presented an almost solid masonry and
stone face to the pedestrian. Only a few small windows
displayed choice works of art and valuable antiques.
Lyman Churchman had neglected to give Joyce the name
of the gallery with which Harold O'Keefe was associated,
and she and Antonio entered several of the attached buildings before they found his name on an elevator directory.
He had offices on the third floor.

They rang the buzzer and waited. A glance of silent
agreement not to mention the urn passed between them. If
necessary, Joyce thought, I can always turn to the statue,
but she hoped to avoid that, too. It was the statue, not the
urn, that had given her so much trouble so far. When the
office door finally opened, she tried to reserve judgment of
the man before her, but her dislike for Harold O'Keefe was
instantaneous. He was fat, fair-skinned, well over fifty, and
his styled hair and silk shirt were as modish as those of the

persistent young men on the Via Veneto, though, in his case, the shirt was mercifully buttoned. There were probably no pectoral muscles to reveal, the way the young Romans did. But it was his eyes she disliked most, small and cold, as avaricious as a jackal's.

"Lyman sent you?" he repeated, fingering her card. "Well . . . come in, then. . . ."

"I talked to him in London a few days ago. He thought maybe you could help me," Joyce said, surveying the room as she spoke. A clutter of canvases, in sizes ranging from small to enormous, stacked against the wall, face out, exploded color and design in curious confusion. "We're interested in locating some antiquities collectors. . . ."

He did not let her finish. He moved his fat shoulders in a gesture exaggeratedly Italian. "I don't know anything about antiquities. I'm only interested in modern art . . . modern *Italian* art . . . as you can see."

"There must have been a misunderstanding," Joyce said. "Mr. Churchman gave me the impression you were his colleague, and. . . ."

"Oh, I am!" There was understandable pride in his voice at being connected with Churchman and Sons. "Lyman visits at least once a year looking for good new talent. And when I have something really fine, like that painting right there"—he indicated a canvas spewing red and yellow and black, like Vesuvius in full eruption—"I query him first . . . or send it right along. Most of this stuff goes to New York. Americans will buy anything." He smiled disparagingly, trying to draw Antonio into his joke. Then he began to address him in rapid Italian.

"He says," Antonio interpreted, "that the Italian partisans saved his life during the war. He has not been back to the States since. Italy is his life . . . it's everything to him. He should have been born Italian."

This is ridiculous, Joyce thought angrily. This man was an American, and Antonio was having to translate for her.

O'Keefe himself suddenly seemed to recognize the peculiarity of the situation.

"Forgive me," he said. "I've lived here so long, it's become my native language. I'm terribly fond of these people. There's nothing they can't do really well. Through the centuries they've been first in art, music . . . literature. This country's one vast museum, a tribute to their creative spirit. . . ."

"The government's good, too," Antonio said, and his ironic expression told Joyce she could dislike O'Keefe with a clear conscience. Antonio did not care for him much, either. But she tried to keep the feeling out of her voice.

She took a step toward the stack of canvases and considered them for a moment. "It's a shame to see all these leave the country. As a dealer, you must know all of the big collectors."

But O'Keefe suddenly became modest. "I know a few of them, of course. Most of my business is with other dealers, though . . . and the artists themselves. I do hate to see some of these canvases leave Italy. I'm much happier when one of them goes to the Modern Gallery here. Even when Lyman buys one . . . and he gets the best, I. . . ." He did not finish the statement.

"Our basic interest is the same, then," Antonio said. "You don't like to see the paintings go, though it's your business to sell them. We don't like antiquities to leave their countries . . . in a much less legal way."

"Contraband?" There was a trace of indignation in O'Keefe's voice, and his face flushed. "Is that why Lyman sent you here? Surely he knows. . . ."

"He knows you're honest," Joyce said. "That's why he sent us here. He thought you might have heard rumors over the years. We're only trying to get the names of some of the illegal collectors. People like Krishnamsetty Das, for instance."

"You know about him?" O'Keefe wiped his pudgy hands

on a monogrammed handkerchief and opened a small tin of antacid tablets. He tossed one in his mouth and swallowed before he continued. "K. T. Das isn't interested in anything here. His collection's Oriental. . . ."

"But you do know of him," Antonio said with an appealing smile, which O'Keefe returned almost shyly. Joyce noticed the flirtatious look.

"I've heard of one or two like him," he confided, "but I don't know the nature of their collections." O'Keefe again studied Joyce's card, which had begun to go limp in his perspiring fingers. "The kind of thing you're talking about usually takes place outside of galleries. In a private home . . . or a hotel room. Switzerland's a good place for that . . . have you been to Switzerland?" he asked hopefully. When he received a negative reply, he took another tablet. "Not that it can't happen here. A dealer down the street got into trouble a few years ago. But he was released and back in business within a few days. . . ."

"A payoff?" Antonio asked, and O'Keefe looked pained.

"I didn't say *everything* in Italy was perfect," he admitted. clutching his stomach. "The food, for one thing . . . Look, I don't want to get involved in any of this. If you must ask questions, go to someone else, only don't mention my name."

"What's the name of the dealer who was released so quickly?" Antonio asked him.

"It doesn't matter. He's dead now." The words fell heavily into the turpentine-scented room. "It happened a long time ago."

"Then why are you afraid?"

"Afraid? I'm not afraid . . . my stomach's giving me hell, that's all. Have you ever eaten scallopini alla Marsala? Like an idiot I tried some Sicilian food last night."

Joyce commiserated with him, confessed that she, too, had had to buy some antacid tablets. He responded at once to her concern.

"I have an ulcer," he said, with his hand on his middle. "The food . . . and any unusual tension . . . play hell with it. I'll give you the names of a couple of people who might help you . . . but keep me out of it."

"We aren't trying to make waves," Joyce said. "We're just looking for something."

"Well . . . you might call on Carlo Montebello in Trastevere," O'Keefe said, relieved at having the burden lifted from his stomach.

"Trastevere? What's an art dealer doing there?" Antonio asked.

"You'll see. If you can overlook the nature of his enterprise . . . I told you before, Italians do . . . almost everything . . . well . . . you may learn something. The other person I'd recommend with more caution: Johnnie Aramidian." He gave them the address of his gallery. "He may be all right, but . . . he lives too grandly for the size of his business. And his connections are in the Middle East. I understand he's *persona non grata* in Lebanon, his own country. What I'm trying to say is . . . he may be into something else, too."

Joyce remembered the Baggies of hash in Greece. They would be extremely careful around Johnnie Aramidian. Looking for an antiquity was one thing; getting involved in the drug traffic was something else again.

"*Persona non grata* in Lebanon! Jesus, I thought anything went there," Antonio said.

O'Keefe shrugged dramatically. "It's only a rumor. Now, if you don't mind, I have business to attend to . . . ."

He was obviously anxious to be rid of them, and they did not linger.

Joyce's mind was ticking like a computer as she walked toward the door, but it stopped in midthought and flashed red lights when Antonio carelessly threw back over his shoulder, "By the way, how was that dealer killed?"

"Shot. Someone shot him," O'Keefe said absently; then

his face blanched like a ball of bread dough. "But I didn't say . . . I *didn't* say. . . ."

She waited until they were in the elevator to smile her approval. Harold O'Keefe was right: Italians did things very well. When she tapped her temple in imitation of one of the dealer's exaggerated gestures, Antonio smiled and closed his hand around her arm, looking at her fondly. It recalled the good-night kiss at Pompeii and his amiable camaraderie at the station. They could not see the other dealers today, which meant they would have to spend the night in Rome. She decided there were several things she should explain over dinner.

After a trip to the Villa Giulia, the most elegant of all Etruscan museums, in which they studied the detail on every *bucchero* urn in the spotless glass cases, often crouching on the carpeted floor to get a better look at them, they found a small *trattoria* off the Piazza della Repubblica.

Joyce was tired, and her eyes burned from studying so much fine detail under fluorescent light, but she was relieved, too, that the urn had not found its way, without its clay seal, into the museum. She wished she had known about the urn when she visited the archaeological museum in Florence on her earlier travels, though it would have been nearly impossible to distinguish the patterns on the Etruscan urns there without a flashlight. The difference in the funding of the two museums was almost a national crime: the one in Florence housed a remarkable, if haphazard, collection, without adequate security and poorly lighted; the Villa Giulia was a dream museum, perfectly laid out and modern, with security guards at every turn.

"You're tired," Antonio said, closing his hand over hers on the table. "I should have slowed you down. You did too much in one day, after such a long trip."

His tone of voice, his consideration, wrenched her, and

she answered him with a smile. "I have a lot of energy, usually," she said, "but the past few days have been awful. There's . . . something I have to tell you, Antonio." She took a deep breath. "I should have told you sooner. Someone's been following me for weeks. I don't know why . . . but it has something to do with the statue. I was being followed when I met you. But I wasn't really sure of it until that night before I left Pompeii to go to England."

She watched for some reaction in his face: it was troubled, thoughtful. As briefly as she could, she outlined what had occurred after she left him that night: the ransacked hotel room, the figure on the grounds at Willoughby Hall, the incident in the Underground. "Hill's name was Roerig . . . he was Swiss. It was in the papers the next morning, but there was no mention of the dual passports. His condition was listed as 'satisfactory' . . . a compound fracture of the leg will keep him laid up for a while. I think I've lost them for now: I hope so. But I probably shouldn't have become involved in looking for the scroll under the circumstances. . . ."

His fingers tightened around hers, and she trembled. His face was very serious. "Never mind that," he said softly, perturbed. "You might have been killed. . . . Joyce, I . . ."

"It was all because of that student of mine," she cut in quickly. "John was the one who put them on my trail. I don't even know whether he's all right. I don't know what they're up to . . . or whether they intend to keep me under surveillance. That last night in Pompeii . . . remember, you thought we were being followed? Well, so did I. I didn't want whoever was watching us outside the hotel to tie you in with my activities. I didn't want anyone to stay there watching your family, so. . . . I mean, I let you kiss me then, but. . . ."

He withdrew his hand slowly and lit a cigarette. "I see." His voice was toneless, and she could not read the expression under his lowered lashes. Then, a smile touched the corners of his mouth. "So you fabricated a little romance on the spur of the moment . . . a good-night kiss from the guide. Why are you telling me all this now? You said you'd lost whoever was following you."

"I . . . just thought you should know," she said weakly.

"Yes." The smile did not leave his lips, but it did not reach his narrowed eyes, either. "You thought I should know before we go to the *pensione*." When she protested faintly, he raised his hand and let it drop to his side. "I'll admit I considered . . . momentarily . . . the economy of just one room. But"—he sighed—"when you live beneath a volcano, you don't take anything for granted . . . especially a woman like you. There are *two* rooms waiting at the *pensione*, Joyce."

"Oh . . ." Her voice fell, embarrassed. It was unnerving to have put something so delicately and then have a man see right through it.

"Do you think you've really lost those fellows?" he asked, practically. "Tell me about everyone you met. . . ."

Relieved to change the subject, she told him about the guests at Mrs. Amboy's, and how she had suspected Arapkilos, before "Hill" had attempted to push her. She related what she had done before she left London to throw off the other pursuer, if there was one. She went into detail describing Lord Willoughby, Lyman Churchman, Dr. Willis-Parks. She even told him about the old man's lecture and the students who had accompanied her. They were all nice people.

"I wish I could tell the wolves from the sheep," she said desolately. "Arapkilos seemed like a nice man, too . . . but now I'm not sure."

Antonio picked up the check and reached for his wallet at the same time that she reached for her purse. One glance warned her not to open it, and he put some bills on the plate with the check.

"What'll I do if they show up at Pompeii again?" she asked. "I can't let them find out about the urn!"

He laughed. "If they come there, you'll just have to continue your summer romance with me. You're altogether shameless . . . and Italians are like that. . . ."

She did not like the sarcastic tone of his voice; she flushed with anger. "I suppose you wouldn't mind?" she said, mustering all her dignity.

"I guess I wouldn't object," he said indifferently. "Anything for the scroll. If the end justifies the means . . ."

"Machiavelli again!" she exclaimed with disgust, but he looked surprised.

"No . . . St. Jerome, the Latinist ascetic who translated the New Testament."

"You've lifted him out of context then! You're . . . you're a. . . ."

He leaned back in his chair and laughed softly: then he said seriously, "I'm not . . . really. But of course you don't know that, do you?" he added. "You don't know what I am. You've looked into the past so much, you've grown nearsighted. You don't know what goes on in the mind of a man . . . any man."

She had had quite enough. "I know one thing . . . you're a devil!"

"No," he objected calmly, "but I'm not an angel, either. I'm just a simple Neapolitan."

"If that was meant to reassure me, it fell flat! Look, Antonio, don't fluster me . . . I have a lot on my mind. You're as subtle as a Jesuit . . . you're playing with me!"

"Now, *that's* an interesting idea. . . ."

"Please . . . stop it! You've gotten me to the point where I don't even trust myself. I'm suspicious of everyone."

He gave a sigh of satisfaction. "Good. Maybe someday you'll get the message. Don't trust anyone. Now we can go to the *pensione* . . . to the separate rooms *I* booked."

Chapter Eight

Whether it was Antonio's instruction in distrust or Johnnie Aramidian himself, Joyce was reluctant to ask questions when they visited his small gallery the next morning. Playing the rich American tourist and her interpreter, Joyce and Antonio tried to look properly bored. Joyce browsed among the Eastern imports, touching a teakwood table here, a carved ivory figurine there, but focusing most of her attention on the office area cut off by a beaded curtain in the rear. The dealer had appeared from there promptly when an antique Indian temple bell on the door rang at their entrance. He was a mild man with soft ripe-olive eyes and crinkly black hair rising from his sallow, polished forehead. Though he was dressed in clothing from the Via Condotti, everything about him reflected the unctuous Eastern merchant. Joyce found the wide gold Arab bracelet he wore on his right wrist and the odor of incense that clung to his clothes mildly repellent.

Watching them as though they were going to take something, Aramidian moved forward quickly when Joyce approached one particular glass case displaying flints, polished obsidian mirrors, and a small terra-cotta "Venus" fertility symbol from ancient Turkey.

"You're interested in antiquities?" he asked, holding his hands together and bowing slightly.

"Are they authentic?" she asked matter-of-factly, though there was no doubt in her mind that they were. "I'm not interested in anything that isn't absolutely authentic."

"I assure you," he smiled with a flutter of his hand. "These objects· are from Catal Hüyük . . . verified."

"By whom? The Turkish government?"

His smile became wary. "No, signorina . . . by the man from whom I purchased them. He found them at the site."

"They're very small," Joyce said hesitantly. "Not very attractive. I don't know *where* I'd display them. Do you have anything larger . . . a pot or something like that?"

The Armenian glanced toward his bead-draped office: there must be a safe there. "In a few days it might be . . . arranged," he replied carefully.

In a few days he could have her all checked out. Since he was not going to show her anything else without knowing her credentials, and she was too suspicious of him to ask questions about collectors, Joyce decided to hazard everything just to get a reaction.

"What I'd really like is a gold bracelet," she said. "Something so old it might have been worn by Helen of Troy!"

The muscles at his hairline twitched; he blinked his eyes. His swarthy complexion took on the pale green of pallor. Joyce could almost hear his heartbeat from where she stood.

"I . . . don't have anything like that," he said at last, mustering all of his composure.

She sighed like a disappointed shopper. "Well, in that case . . . Thank you very much. Perhaps another time . . ."

He stood frozen like a statue beside the glass case as Joyce, nodding pleasantly, motioned to Antonio and breezed out of the gallery to the ringing of the temple bell. Neither of them spoke until they had turned the corner and regained the security of the Fiat, which Antonio accelerated at once.

"What the hell did you say to him?" he asked as they merged with the traffic. "You nearly frightened him to death."

"I broke a taboo." She smiled thoughtfully. "I referred to something no one talks about much. A theft Dr. Willis-Parks mentioned in his lecture. I only wanted to judge his reaction, but. . . ."

"Well," Antonio said, "you certainly got one! Was that a safe thing to do?"

"I don't know." She considered his question, then smiled again. "It's only dangerous if he has part of the Dorak treasure stashed away, back there, in his safe. You know, the possibilities of doing this sort of thing are endless. . . ."

"Please . . . don't do it again," Antonio said. "We've enough to think about as it is. I don't think I want you to call on Carlo Montebello in the mood you're in right now."

"Well, O'Keefe warned us about Aramidian. Speaking of Montebello, why did you question an art dealer's being in Trastevere when O'Keefe told us Montebello's address?"

"It's a poorer quarter of the city. There are some good restaurants there, a few shops on the main street. But art dealers? It sounds very strange. Pushcarts, yes. A flea market on Sunday, where you can buy everything from broken combs to antiques. . . ."

"Antiques?" she raised her eyebrows hopefully, and Antonio smiled. "Yes, *antiques* . . . the things people live with until they can be replaced by something modern. I didn't say antiquities, Joyce."

They drove through a maze of narrow streets, some wide enough to accommodate a single car, some dead ends, blocked off for vending stalls. When Antonio finally located the elusive address O'Keefe had given them, they parked and stared at the decrepit square building without leaving the car.

A peeling sign, which read "Montebello, Ceramics and Metals," hung over the door of a small factory.

"Signor O'Keefe's done it again," Antonio laughed. "Was he just trying to get rid of us?"

"I feel as though I'm on a scavenger hunt with the wrong list of clues," Joyce sighed. "Let's have a look, at least. You'd better lock your car. . . ."

"It isn't exactly a Ferrari," he said, but he, too, had observed the young men on the corner showing an unusual interest in the rusted white Fiat. "For once, you're right."

The aproned potters at creaking wheels were too occupied to notice them when they entered the single long room on the ground level of the factory. Behind the austere, lazy front of the building, a lot of activity was taking place within. There were at least fifteen men, ranging in age from young to elderly, turning out ceramics alone. Wheels were turning, painters were glazing, and the kilns in the rear wall let off a tremendous amount of heat. Outside the work area, along the wall, a long table displayed samples of what all the activity was about; it was a showroom of ancient reproductions.

Joyce picked up one of the plates. "They're like the ones in your grandfather's shop," Joyce smiled. "It's only a fake factory, all open and aboveboard. . . ."

Antonio held up a terra-cotta pitcher of lovely proportions, with the black figure of a Greek warrior on its side. "These are much better than the ones Nonno buys. I'll have to tell him about this place."

Joyce wandered along the display table until she came to something that absorbed her attention: a pile of large green

Roman coins and a sticklike Etruscan charioteer. As she motioned to Antonio, her eye was caught by a young man in the working area deftly smashing a completed vase with the tap of a hammer. The youth then glued it back together again with fingers so nimble that she envied him. She could not have assembled the shards of an ancient pot so quickly herself. But he left one broken fragment inside with a small hole gaping in the mended artifact, and she stared in disbelief. To an inexperienced eye, the vase might have been excavated in Etruria a few nights before. As O'Keefe had said, the Italians did things very well. When Antonio rejoined her, she indicated the phenomenon to him.

"It's almost funny," she whispered. "Who'd be taken in by something like that? And look at these." She touched the small charioteer and the verdigris came off in flakes on her fingers. "What are they using to produce the effect of oxidation . . . Paris green?"

Antonio scooped up a handful of the coins and smiled. "They're only museum reproductions. They sell these in the shop at Pompeii. . . ."

"What about the vase? I've never seen a broken vase on sale in any shop. Only an idiot would buy such a thing!"

"That's right, signorina," an unfamiliar voice said. "Idiots and tourists. Permit me to introduce myself. I am Carlo Montebello. May I show you around?"

A fat man with a mustache, who had been tending the kiln, had come forward with an amiable smile. Removing his apron, he paused to pick up the freshly glued vase. Joyce was embarrassed. He had overheard everything, even her remarks about the broken "antiquity." Noting her discomfort, Antonio broke the silence.

"The work in your factory is very good, signore," he said. "The signorina pays you a compliment by suggesting it could be used in such a way."

Signor Montebello was amused. He proffered Joyce the vase with a challenge. "What's wrong with it, huh? If you saw it in the flea market next Sunday, would you just pass it by?"

"No," she said. "I'd look at it, out of curiosity. But one glance would tell me it wasn't newly excavated. The clay's not discolored . . . it's never been used." She pointed to the interior. "You can still see the grooves from the potter's fingers in here. The work's nice, the repair job was stupefying . . . but it wouldn't pass for ancient."

Instead of diminishing Signor Montebello's smile, her remarks broadened it. "A knowledgeable young lady. And you're absolutely right. I wouldn't dare put it up for sale as a genuine antiquity: the police wouldn't like that. It's the same with the charioteer. Only an idiot would buy 'bronze' shedding green like this; therefore, it's deliberate. I'm doing nothing wrong. I don't even charge much for them. I'll ask"—he appraised the vase—"maybe twelve thousand lire for this. All the tourists know they should give only fifty percent of the initial price at the flea market. They'll go away happy, thinking they've cheated the vendor. Who's being robbed? And everyone's happy: The tourist, the vendor . . . and me!"

If he was an old rogue, he was a charming one, and Joyce smiled at him. "Is it fair to capitalize on the night digging in the Etruscan tombs?" she asked. "Just because the whole world knows it's taking place and no one's doing much about it . . . is it right to profit from the publicity?"

"It's such a *small* profit," he said, raising parallel fingers to indicate the extent of his operation. "And . . . it's fun! I don't get anything like the *tombaroli* . . . that's real money. But, you know, they do it mostly for fun, too."

"The *tombaroli*?" she asked.

"The night diggers . . . up there." He indicated a vague, northerly direction, which included all of Etruria. "My profit comes from the sale of ordinary souvenirs. It gets a little dull. This adds some spice to my life, signorina. You should hear some of the stories that vendors tell me! The recent scandal over the krater that was sold to the Metropolitan Museum in your country gave me the idea."

"That scandal isn't funny at all," she said, shaking her head. "It's tragic for everyone concerned. The Euphronios krater, wherever it came from, is the most magnificent thing I've ever seen . . . and its history's been lost."

"Ah . . . you're concerned about such things," Montebello said sympathetically. "So am I. . . ."

"Dr. Lacey's an archaeologist," Antonio said. "Naturally, these things bother her."

"An archaeologist," the old man mused. "Yes . . . I think I sensed something."

"Come, Antonio," Joyce said a little wearily. "It was just a wild-goose chase. Thank you for letting us see your factory, signore. I'm sure Signor Casale's grandfather will be placing an order with you."

Antonio had already opened the door for her when Signor Montebello came running after them. "Please . . . *Dottoressa!* May I ask you what wild goose you are chasing?"

Without hesitation, Joyce smiled, "It isn't important."

"Then . . . may I ask you to come with me, please. Just for a moment." His eyes were almost shy, but they were pleading, and a frown crossed Antonio's forehead. "You, too, signore. I'd like the *dottoressa's* opinion on something."

Joyce nodded. She liked the old potter. She and Antonio followed his round form to a wooden staircase beyond the display table, and he motioned them up the stairs like an eager child. Leading them through a paper-cluttered office that did not speak well for Nonno's ever getting his order filled, he inserted a key in the lock of the door beyond. The room into which he led them was darkly shuttered, and Joyce gripped Antonio's hand in apprehension.

Groping in the dimness, Signor Montebello threw the wooden shutters wide and turned to study her reaction, which was one of overpowering disbelief. Before them on a highly polished table were five of the most perfect Greek vases she had ever seen outside a museum, but it was the large krater in the middle that attracted her. She stepped forward warily, drawn by curiosity. Very carefully, she examined it from all sides, studied the painting depicting the death of Serpedon, with Thanatos and Hypnos supporting his body. She was so overwhelmed that she dared not touch it, except to inspect the black rim and an area near the shoulder of one of the athletes. She drew her hand back as though it had been burned.

"Where did you get it?" she breathed. She groped for Antonio's hand and drew him to the table. "It's the duplicate of the Euphronios krater," she told him. "They've been searching all over Italy for this!"

"Please," Signor Montebello said, wringing his stubby fingers, "examine the others."

She moved from one vase to another, exploring them with care. They were remarkable, perfect, except for one of them, which had an ancient mend, a staple inserted to hold a crack together. When she completed her examination, she sank down on a chair. "Signor Montebello," she said, "I've no right to ask . . . but, since you showed me these treasures . . . where did you get them?"

He kneaded his pudgy hands. "They're genuine, then?"

"Yes . . . I'm sure of it. I'd have to examine them more closely, under better light, but . . . the staple in that one . . . the clay." She pulled her gaze from the krater to the smile of satisfaction on Signor Montebello's cherubic face. "They belong in a museum . . . you know that," she said, and he giggled. Then he looked worried.

"But you're very young. You can't have much experience," he said. "The curator of a great museum, he could tell. . . ."

"Tell what?"

"That . . . I made them. A real authority could tell, couldn't he?"

Joyce jumped to her feet. "You *made* them! I don't believe it. . . ."

Her incredulity gratified him even more. "But it's true, Dr. Lacey. They're my own work. I'm an artist!"

She inspected the vases again and shook her head. "The clay, the glaze," she pondered. "That glaze hasn't been used since ancient times. It was clear when it was applied, difficult to work with . . . it had to be fired almost at once, and then it turned black. . . . I'd swear this krater is the matching one they've been searching for! Only . . . it isn't signed."

"The clay came from Greece," Signor Montebello said, with tears in his eyes. "I've experimented with pigments and glazes for years. I tell you, they would even pass the carbon-dating test. Oh, I've never been so happy in my life!" He kissed Joyce's hand impulsively. "Thank you! Thank you, Dr. Lacey!"

"What are you up to, Montebello?" Antonio asked suspiciously. "Why have you asked Joyce . . . Dr. Lacey . . . to verify these things?"

"For no illegal purpose, I assure you! I'll never sell them. Have you ever heard of Dossena?"

"He was a . . . forger," Joyce said.

"A most magnificent forger! The best! His works are still in museums everywhere. They are almost as important as originals. He was a master. A good man . . . he didn't know his copies were being sold to the museums." Observing the expression of displeasure on Joyce's face, he added hastily, "I have no intention of doing the same thing. I just wanted to see if I could do it, that's all. And you've confirmed that I can. It is enough."

"I wouldn't get too ambitious, if I were you," Antonio said, plunging his hands into his pockets and staring out the half-shuttered window onto the street. "Dr. Lacey's opinion's given you satisfaction. Now perhaps you can do something for her. . . ."

"Anything . . . if it's possible, of course."

"Your 'ancient vases' are a complete secret?"

"Only a few people know about them. My family, some close friends . . ."

"Any collectors? Dealers?"

A shadow crossed Signor Montebello's face; he lowered his eyes. "Once . . . only once . . . did someone like that come here. I don't know how he heard about it. It was a few years ago . . . he was an American. He wanted me to make something for his own collection, he said. But I thought, 'Why does this rich collector *want* a forgery in his collection?' It sounded fishy, you know . . . even though he said I'd only be making a copy of something he already owned. I thought maybe he was going to have the copy 'stolen,' for insurance or something . . . while he kept the original. When I told him it would take me a whole year to duplicate the object, he went away."

"Did he give his name?"

"No."

Realizing that they could learn nothing more from Signor Montebello, Joyce said, "Thank you for showing us these pieces. Your work is very interesting."

"Thank *you*," Signor Montebello smiled. "I called upon your expertise in an underhanded fashion, Dr. Lacey. I reproach myself. Vanity . . . that's what it was. But you've made me feel very good!"

"Don't get into trouble," Antonio said heavily, as they descended the stairs. "You're good . . . but you may not be *that* good. Instead of becoming another Dossena, you could end up in jail. . . ."

"*Ciao*," Signor Montebello said happily as they departed. "I hope we meet again! If we can't keep antiquities in our own country, we should at least have copies of them, huh?"

They were on their way back to Pompeii when Joyce thought over that last statement.

"Antonio? What do you suppose he meant?" she asked.

The next day Joyce waited, full of excitement, beneath the vines of the outdoor restaurant at Pompeii. She had something to tell Antonio, and she was impatiently studying each patron who entered.

After a good night's sleep and a lazy morning, her mind had turned in earnest to the list of names in her purse. They were complete with addresses now. The number of collectors had decreased in Rome, when she had crossed Alberto Grossman off the list; but then, Antonio found an address for him in the New York directory. He was out of jail, apparently, and had opened his gallery again. She put his name back on the list. She had enough names to start with, and if the art world had the grapevine she now suspected, her interest in the urn would leak to other people. It was like throwing out a net: one might catch some strange species in the haul. She was excited, but she was nervous, too.

Then Antonio strolled beneath the arbor. "You look happy," he said, as though it were a rare phenomenon. "What does it mean?"

"I've written a letter. I want you to read it." She handed the carefully composed draft across to him and scrutinized his expression closely while he read it. He sipped his beer slowly as he read, and every shift of feeling exposed itself in his face, from a cocked eyebrow, to a frown, to the faint smile that touched the edges of his mouth when he put the letter down on the checkered cloth.

"Dr. Lacey," he said with mock formality, "I don't think you're aware of it, but . . . what you're contemplating is almost blackmail."

"No!" she protested. "It's a plain, straightforward statement of the facts. An Etruscan cinerary urn is the object I want to buy: the complete description of the urn is enclosed. I'm interested in studying the urn for my work, and I'm willing to pay three hundred dollars for it. The catalog price on an urn like that is a little less. Of course, the museum letters will be different: I won't ask to buy it. I just want to see if any of them have it."

"You didn't mention that the urn's sealed."

"It may not be . . . now. That's something I have to find out, too."

Antonio slouched down in his chair. "The *dottoressa* has *furbo* and doesn't know it. What makes you think that a rich, illegal collector is going to come out in the open to sell the urn for three hundred dollars? His dedication to science?"

"The fact that I know his name!" Though it had not entered her mind when she was composing the letter, Antonio's smile made her realize, now, that she was using her knowledge of the collectors' names as a lever to make them move. "It isn't really . . . *blackmail*," she said slowly. "I haven't said anything threatening. . . ."

Pointing to his eye in the gesture for *furbo*, he explained, "No. You've just appealed to a man who doesn't want his activities known to sell you a *bucchero* urn, if it happens to be in his possession. You don't really give an adequate reason *why* he should do so . . . and therein lies the threat."

Joyce scanned the letter again. It was simple, direct, but what Antonio saw in it was there: a hidden hook to catch the collectors' interest. "If it fell into the wrong hands, it couldn't possibly be construed as blackmail," she said. "It's just a business letter."

"The wrong hands?"

"The police," she said, and his face grew stern. An obvious conflict of scruples had arisen between them. "Well, can you think of a better way to get the urn? We can't contact all these people in person!"

"I don't know," he confessed. "I was hoping we could locate the urn through our research, I guess. Then if one of these collectors had it, we could steal it." Her expression made him quickly justify the statement, "Well, everyone else has! I've been thinking . . . I wish we could find out who Count Luigi Falcone knew in Rome before he entered the monastery. . . ."

"You still want to follow the urn through all its ownerships? Antonio, it will take years!"

"I suppose so, but. . . ."

"What about the letter? Shall I tear it up?"

"No," he said reluctantly. "It's the only way, I guess. How many languages will we need?"

"I think four will do it. I'll write the English and Greek, if you'll take care of the Italian. And your French is better than mine. We'll use French for the Arab in Libya . . . and . . . for Zee in Amsterdam . . . English, I suppose. The Greek one to Karavitas will have to be handwritten. I can use the hotel typewriter for the rest."

They wrote with concentration for half an hour, sipping their drinks. There were two variations of the letter: one for collectors and dealers, another for museums. Antonio finished his two drafts first, while Joyce was still checking the Greek syntax in her mind.

"Be careful of the accents on the typewriter," he said. "The French are particular about that . . . so are Italians."

She looked over his letters while he puzzled over the Greek.

"Do you think we should send a letter to Johnnie Aramidian?" she asked suddenly. "He's the only one we've left out."

Antonio hesitated; then he said recklessly, "Why not?

The person we leave out might be the one who can help us." He grew quiet again, squinting thoughtfully. He had not finished his beer.

"What's the matter?" she asked.

"I have an odd feeling. I don't know what it is. Do you think we're still alone here?"

"Yes. I haven't noticed anything out of the ordinary. I keep watching everyone, though. . . ."

"We'll have to be careful of that, now. You're doing exactly what they don't want you to do. Before, it was only the statue . . . but once the letters are in the mail. . . ."

"Once they're in the mail, they'll know I'm not interested in the statue anymore," she said hopefully. "Maybe they'll give up entirely."

"Mm. And maybe they'll get interested in the urn." He put his hand on hers as he rose to leave. "Be careful. If anything happens, you have my phone number." He paused indecisively and took a deep breath. "Keep in touch, huh? And . . . watch out for the accents on the typewriter."

The rest of the evening was spent typing letters on hotel stationery in the manager's office. When Joyce stamped them and walked across the parking area to the postal box, it was past ten. She could hear a watchdog barking within the dark excavation. Watchdogs were nothing new to Pompeii, she thought: a mosaic entrance hall depicted one in ancient times, with the inscription "Beware of the Dog" beneath it. Even when the city was alive, the houses were not safe from pilfering. Now, along with the dogs, guards patrolled the excavation nightly, to protect the art still in place.

Only after the last letter was irretrievably deposited in the box of the square little postal station did she begin to feel the discordant jangle in her nerves again. She looked around her quickly and knew she was not alone on the dim, deserted street. From one of the many deep shadows,

a dark figure moved slowly toward her. In a sudden burst
of panic she ran back across the street to her hotel and
dialed Antonio's number from her locked room.

"*Pronto,*" he answered wearily, though she knew he had
not been asleep. The telephone was in the parlor, where he
worked at his drafting table.

"They're back," she said tightly. "I was mailing the letters. . . ."

"I'll be right over."

"No . . . it's all right. I'm locked in my room. I just
wanted to tell you, so we can try to spot him."

"You shouldn't be alone. . . ."

She laughed nervously. "I don't think anyone can get in.
I'll put a chair beneath the doorknob to warn me. I'll bolt
all the windows and the shutters."

"Do that. I'll come by on my way to Scavi tomorrow. I'll
check the hotel registers on the way. I can do that . . . an
interpreter looking for work can do anything. The clerk
there is on the premises. He'll probably be asleep, but call
him if you need him. . . ."

"Yes," she said. "I'll see you in the morning, then. Good
night . . . and thank you, Antonio."

With his voice no longer in her ear, she sat on the edge
of the bed, trying to steady her knees with her hands. Then
she rose quickly, checked the balcony, and bolted the triple
windows. She pulled a chair across the room, secured it
firmly beneath the doorknob, and rechecked the lock.

She thought she would be relatively safe until the letters
were delivered; in the meantime, maybe she and Antonio
could identify this new pursuer, find out what this was all
about. For the first time, she wished she had recourse to
the police.

When she finally went to bed, she did not sleep well.

Chapter Nine

Joyce spent the next day with Antonio at the excavation. They walked together, hand in hand, between his tours, and lunched on the food he had brought from home, in the middle of the Amphitheater. When she was not with him, she concentrated her attention on the area excavated before 1826, which was the earliest diagram she could find. Only the portion directly adjacent to the city wall and the Porta Marina had been excavated then, along with the Amphitheater in the southeastern corner and a tiny preliminary investigation at the end of the Via di Nola, near another city gate. Though she was studying the areas closely, trying to match them with the cross-section drawing in the Casale papers, she tried to do it in an offhand, almost cursory, way. To any observer, she hoped to appear just a vacationing archaeologist on the prowl, waiting, between tours, for her handsome lover. As soon as they were together again, they behaved in a light-hearted, affectionate way. But by three o'clock she was totally exhausted from lack of sleep the night before. She kissed Antonio on the cheek, bought some books and other materials at the excavation shop, and returned to her hotel.

An hour's nap in the tightly closed, locked room restored her somewhat. Showered and dressed, she went to the arbor restaurant to meet Antonio again, with her thoughts very much on the Via di Nola and the still unexcavated region beyond it. She thought Nonno Casale was right. The urn must have been found during that preliminary dig, which had been filled in again later.

Antonio arrived, rubbed his cheek against hers, and found her lips in a kiss that was more than endearing.

"That was a bit much, wasn't it?" she smiled fondly, for anyone to see, though she spoke in a whisper.

"Not nearly enough," he said, kissing her hand, his eyes melting into hers. "You don't know how these things work . . . *carina*. I checked the hotel registers again: nobody's stayed on."

"Do you think I was mistaken?"

"No. The timing's too right. He could be staying somewhere else and just coming here at night. Or he could be moving from one hotel to another. I'll watch for that tomorrow. He'd need a passport to check in."

"The man in London had *two* passports," she said with some trepidation. "Good God . . . he might be in my hotel!"

"It isn't the most popular one here," he considered. "What did you do, choose it for economy? But it's certainly worth considering. . . ."

"I hardly slept a wink last night," she admitted. "I have a feeling tonight isn't going to be much better. . . ."

She was reading in bed when the light tapping on the door nearly made her heart stop. The door was locked, and the chair was in place, but suddenly she felt terribly vulnerable. She put her book aside and pulled her robe on to cover her short nightgown. Then, hoisting her heavy handbag by the strap, she walked softly, barefoot, to the barricaded door.

"Who's there?" she asked steadily, wondering what she would do if the person outside identified himself as part of the hotel staff.

"It's me . . . Antonio," his familiar, resonant voice whispered back. "Let me in, Joyce."

She put her bag aside and removed the barrier of the chair; but when she opened the door, it was only by a foot, until she assured herself that it really was Antonio standing in the hall. He walked quickly across the room and looked onto the balcony through the shutters, scanning the vines below.

"What is it?" she asked.

"Close the door. You're right about someone following you here. A hired limousine's been parked across from Nonno's shop for more than an hour. Whoever it is . . . he's watching me, too."

"Did you see *him*?"

"Yes. He's young . . . a flashy dresser. A proper Roman dandy type. He followed my car in the limousine when I left. . . ."

"If he was watching you, why did you come *here*? I don't want him around, either."

For the first time since he had entered the room, he turned to look at her. She drew the tie on her robe more tightly and secured it with a double knot. Her self-conscious action made him smile.

"If he's trying to find out what's between us, I don't want to disappoint him. I want him to think I'm here with you at night. You could sleep, then . . . because he'd never be sure if you were alone."

It sounded reasonable enough, though awkward to carry on for over a week. And in another way, it sounded slightly more hazardous than being locked in here alone. There *was* something between herself and Antonio: she was not sure what, yet, but she knew she did not want a casual affair with him.

"How long will you have to stay?"

He turned away, but she saw the amusement in his face before he could hide it. "That depends."

"On *what*?" she asked suspiciously.

But his answer was simple and honest. "On what kind of woman you're supposed to be. On the . . . intensity? . . . of our 'relationship.' " His green eyes stared directly, impersonally, into hers. "Are you just a career woman on holiday . . . or are we very fond of one another?" Antonio smiled, but Joyce refused to find the situation amusing.

"How long will you have to stay every night?"

He sighed; then he approached the problem as though it were a mathematical formula. "In the first instance, only an hour or so. But if we're really supposed to be fond of one another . . . I'd be here all night, sleeping beside you."

"Isn't there something in between?" she asked. "I don't want to look like a . . . but I don't want you here all night, either."

He laughed outright at the statement. "I'll only stay a couple of hours, then. And I'll come at different times on different nights. That'll keep them away from you, I think."

Silence fell between them. There was an unusual tension in the room. Finally, Antonio lit a cigarette and studied her with curiosity, as though she were a mineral with a streak of some rare element in it.

"Joyce, are you . . . ?" he began, but he decided to reword the question. He considered it for a moment, and when it finally came out, it was more like an accusation than a question. "You aren't very liberated, are you?"

"I'm my own person," she said carefully. "I haven't had

much to do with 'causes.' There's no discrimination in my field. For years, some of the best archaeologists have been women. I've worked hard, and my life's been reasoned out according to my own standards. There are many changes taking place in society, but I'm not involved in Women's Lib."

"You sound just like a professor!" he marveled, as though he had just seen another side of her. "It's always been my impression that professors know more about facts . . . than life."

"I was engaged once . . . but it didn't work out. When it came to a choice I chose my profession."

"You're young . . . as you say, you've worked hard to do the thing that interests you," he reflected, snuffing out his cigarette. "And . . . of course . . . you didn't love the man enough."

She did not want to talk about it; perhaps she had already said too much. But her remarks seemed to have served a purpose.

"Tomorrow night," he said gently, "I'll bring a deck of cards."

"I don't play cards, either," she had to confess. "I've never taken time to. . . ."

"All right. I'll bring a book, then." He rose and looked at his watch. "I have a lot of studying to do before I enter the institute. Well . . . it's almost time now. Our desire has been satisfied, we've dallied a little, affectionately and tenderly. But . . . you're discreet and rather proper . . . you don't want anyone to see me here in the morning." He looked down at her seriously. "You are neither predatory . . . nor passionately in love, either. You're 'something in between.' "

Antonio varied the hours of his visits on the following nights, with the time set beforehand, so his light knock on the door would not frighten her to death. While she studied the material on Pompeii at the writing table, or washed out her things in the bathroom, he lay on the bed with his head propped on the pillows and a textbook on his chest. Sometimes they talked, and she was able to draw out of him how difficult it had been to pursue his studies in a country that almost disdained adult education. He had even had a hard time finding a way to finish college at night, and the scholarship to the institute meant a lot to him. She, in turn, confessed that all her undergraduate work had been done while holding two outside jobs, and scholarships had taken care of the rest of her studies. He seemed relieved that she was not the privileged American he had imagined her and was interested to learn that a large proportion of students in America had to do things the same way. And though no one was observing them in the room, he kissed her gently before leaving every night, as though hesitant to abandon her to the chance of their unknown pursuer's intrusions.

Their pursuer, bewildered or bored by their amorous activities, seemed to have left them to their diversions. For several nights there was no sign of him. Joyce hardly had time to breathe a sigh of relief, however, before Antonio appeared at the table one day and blurted out as he was sitting down, "The letters have been received. O'Keefe was at the Scavi today: I gave him a two-hour tour."

"We didn't send *him* a letter. He said he wasn't interested in antiquities. . . ."

"He is now . . . and he's particularly interested in vases. He didn't come right out and ask questions, but you should have seen the way he sniffed around the *bucchero* urns in the museum . . . and appraised the stacks of wine bottles in the old taverns."

Joyce whistled through her teeth. "The word's out, then. He hasn't had a description of the urn, but he knows what we're looking for. I thought something like this might happen . . . that word of the letters would get around. I wonder how he knew we were here, though?"

"I wonder how many other people know it, besides the ones you wrote. Before, we had only one person at a time to contend with, but now. . . ."

He compressed his lips and glanced across the parking area toward the entrance to the excavation, with the tangled overgrowth on the ancient wall behind it, and her eyes followed his. She saw nothing unusual, only the cars and buses and the permanent stalls vending brochures and souvenirs.

"Is there something you aren't telling me? O'Keefe left, didn't he?"

"See that fellow over there, lounging next to the entrance? He's the one who followed me in the limousine that night . . . and O'Keefe stopped to talk to him before he left. . . ."

"The good-looking one in the embroidered shirt?" she asked, picking out the pretty young man, and he nodded. "Well, he looks like O'Keefe's sort, all right. But he came before O'Keefe did! Before the letters could possibly have been received! Why would O'Keefe send someone to spy on us beforehand?"

Antonio sighed with exasperation. "I'm tired of this!" he said angrily, rising. "I'm going to have it out with him. At least he's out in the open now. . . ."

But she restrained him by putting her hand on his arm. "No. We can't have any trouble with the police . . . remember? Now that I've seen him I'm not afraid of him. Actually, I'm curious to find out what they're up to. . . ."

"And what if there are others . . . whom we can't see? Joyce, I'm worried about you. I know what it was about those letters that bothered me, now: I shouldn't have been so stupid! The whole illegal art world might come down on you because of them . . . like seagulls fighting over a beached and very tasty fish. You're in more danger than you were before. . . ."

"It may be worth it," she smiled, with another glance at

O'Keefe's flunky. "In a way, I was bargaining on it. We didn't have many names, you know. . . ."

"You knew what might happen?" he exploded. "I thought you were only trying to blackmail the collectors to get the urn! Holy Jesus!" He ran his hand through his hair.

"I'm sorry, Antonio . . . I really am. Maybe I used bad judgment," she said.

"Judgment!" He laughed harshly. "I could strangle you myself. If we've convinced that one"—he indicated the young Roman across the street—"how do you think it's affected my mother? She hasn't shut her mouth, except to pray, for nearly a week!"

Joyce was beginning to enjoy Antonio's company in her room at night too much, and not just because he was someone to talk to. She looked forward to that good-night kiss, but she knew Antonio did not want to get seriously involved. She had a feeling, deep within herself, that anything less than a really serious involvement would not satisfy what she was trying to control in her emotions about Antonio. Unless they were to be much more than friends, it was time to put an end to this, and she told him so when he kissed her that night.

"This is . . . really too much trouble for you," she said. "I'll be all right. The hotel staff alone is scandalized enough to pass the word. . . ."

"Who ever scandalized a hotel staff?" he asked, but no smile accompanied the remark, and he did not remove his hands from her shoulders. "It hasn't been easy, you know . . . I'm not the paragon you seem to imagine."

In proof of this, his lips stroked her cheek, caressed her face, and touched her own lips, gently at first, then forced them open with a kiss so sweet that she surrendered to it for a moment. It would be easy, too easy, to give in right now. But if they made love, she knew her commitment

would be total: she would never be her own person again
. . . and even Antonio was not interested in that. She
dragged her lips from his with an effort and disengaged
herself from his arms.

"I'm sorry," she said, knowing the words were inadequate. "I'm not ready for this . . . love has to come first."

"But Joyce, I . . ." he began, but checked himself with a
frown. He bit his lip, and his lashes concealed his eyes.
"Yes," he said, as though he really understood.

Joyce explained, "You're an exciting man, Antonio. But
we don't really know each other, do we? You have your
plans and I . . . well. . . ."

His eyes, deep with emotion a moment before, grew
calmer. "Someday you may beg me to take you. And . . .
someday . . . I may not want you at all. Shouldn't we 'seize
the moment'?"

She was glad he had said it, if only to protect his mascu-
line ego. "I've been avoiding that philosophy for a long
time," she smiled. "I don't want any perfect moments . . . I
want something permanent. We're in a tight corner right
now . . . we could say that one of us might be dead
tomorrow. It would be easy to rationalize, wouldn't it? I've
never done anything just because it was easy." She realized
she was talking too fast, too much, saying too little, and
only taking her own point of view into account. "I know
you feel differently about these things," she added. "You're
a man."

He paused only long enough to tousle her hair. "Well,
thank you for that, anyway!" he smiled, with the old teasing expression in his eyes.

If Antonio had not come across from the excavation
early to see whether there were any answers to the letters,
he would have missed the arrival of their next visitor: it
might have been better that way. Anticipating his daily
mail check, Joyce—drinking a lemon soda, which she had

learned by now to order with ice—had two letters on the
cloth before her. The young Roman, invisible until that
moment, made his appearance as suddenly as Antonio and
leaned against the wall across the street. Joyce had almost
forgotten about him, and she wondered about the prudence
of passing the letters in public. If O'Keefe were waiting for
the answers, too, his flunky would report it.

Antonio hugged her, but he did not give her a kiss. "You
received something?" he said at once, when he saw the
letters. "Who are they from?"

"Museums," she said rather flatly. The senders had disappointed her, too. "One of them's interesting, though, I
think. I couldn't read much of it: it's in Italian. From a
curator who seems to be an Etruscan scholar. . . ."

He picked up the envelope with Italian stamps and read
over the thin sheet of paper inside. "But . . . this is *very*
interesting," he said, beginning to translate, "There are the
usual salutations and . . . the urn isn't in his museum, but.
. . . 'The pattern you describe on the *bucchero* urn is most
unusual. Though the variations of design are almost infinite, governed by the taste of the artisan, there are re-
gional differences. From your description, the urn you are
seeking did not originate in northern Italy . . . or at a date
as early as you place it. I cannot be certain, of course. But
from the description I would place it in the pre-Samnite
period in Campania, in the area of the Sarno River, dominated by the Etruscans until 474 B.C. Of course, the urn,
being Villanovan, before Etruscan contact with the Greeks,
probably dates somewhat earlier: it would be impossible to
give an opinion without observing it.' "

"It didn't come all the way from Tuscany, then," Joyce
smiled. "Someone uncovered it around here . . . and kept it
in his house."

"Yes. There aren't many Iron Age artifacts in this area.
But at least we don't have to worry about how it got so far
south!" He looked at the frown on her face and became

more subdued. "What is it, Joyce? Doesn't this make you happy? It should."

"I was just wondering whether that scholar will ever be able to see it." She sighed and, indicating the youth across the street with a toss of her head, said, "Besides, I'm getting claustrophobic."

They both looked up at once when the desk clerk, in his formal black suit, appeared beside the table. "A Signor *Sinjun* inquires after you, *Dottoressa*. . . ."

Joyce was so dumbfounded that she could not speak. She exchanged a cautious glance with Antonio, who gave instructions to the clerk in Italian.

"I told him to send him out here," he said doubtfully, staring at the entrance to the indoor restaurant.

"The name sounds Indian," she said. "Do you suppose K. T. Das has sent someone?"

"Or Johnnie Aramidian?" he answered grimly, taking her hand in his. She tried to extricate her fingers, but he clung to them with an expression of warning.

They pretended a casualness they did not feel and did not look up until the clerk had brought the visitor to their table.

"Dr. Lacey? I'm Ian St. John. You know my uncle, Stanton Willoughby, I believe."

The man who stood beside them was extremely tall and well proportioned, with searching blue eyes and fair, disheveled hair, which he smoothed back unconsciously as he addressed Joyce. Ruggedly handsome, with an almost dashing air about him, he was modishly but properly dressed, in a light suit with slightly flared cuffs. Disregarding the southern Italian heat, he wore a striped tie, a symbol of whatever school he had attended, Joyce thought: it was neither Oxford nor Cambridge, because she knew those stripes. Having expected a small, dark-complexioned Indian, both she and Antonio stared at him in dismay.

"I beg your pardon . . . you are Dr. Lacey, aren't you? Or did that fellow make a mistake?"

"Yes. Uh . . . Mr. Sinjun . . ." She knew the way the name was pronounced in England, but she still wanted to say St. John. "Allow me to introduce my friend, Signor Casale. Antonio . . . Mr. St. John."

Antonio rose to shake the tall Englishman's hand, measuring him with his narrowed eyes like a gladiator about to face another in the ring. "I suppose," he said amiably, "you have proof of your identity?"

The question surprised Joyce, and Ian St. John was completely astounded. The color rose to his strong cheekbones, and his eyes snapped. He reached into his jacket pocket and tossed a heavy British passport on the table, with a small plastic card stuck inside.

"I have all the bloody identification I need," he said sharply. "Casale, is it? Wasn't it your thieving ancestor who started this bloody mess?"

In the weeks she had known him she had observed a variety of expression in Antonio's fine eyes, but she had never seen them filled with distilled fury before. Fearing an attack on the Englishman, she put her hand on Antonio's arm.

"Please . . . sit down. You, too, Mr. St. John. Antonio, be reasonable about this." She glanced at the passport and Army identification card and passed them on to Antonio. "Forgive us," she said to Ian St. John. "We've been having some trouble here. . . ."

"These say he's a British subject and a major in the Army," Antonio cut in. "They don't prove he's related to Willoughby. The papers could be forged. . . ."

"Lord Willoughby told me he had a nephew in the Army. And I seem to recall the name St. John in the family biography. He's all right, Antonio . . . I think."

"Thanks," the major said drolly. "Now, if I've cleared

immigration"—he shot a glance like a bullet at Antonio—"maybe we can get down to why I'm here."

He was a commanding man in his early thirties, and Joyce studied him carefully. His fair, crisp hair was too long for Army regulations, but he did not wear sideburns. Then she remembered that Stanton Willoughby had told her his nephew was in the hospital with a bullet in his back. He might have let his hair grow while he was there, and the pallor of his lips bore out the story she had been told. He was all right, she decided, aside from the fact that he was still very angry. His vivid eyes flashed blue fire. And with good reason: after such a long trip, their reception of him had hardly been cordial.

"Why did you come?" she asked.

"Not out of choice, believe me. I was on sick leave and enjoying it immensely. Then, Stanton summoned me to the Hall with some cock-and-bull story about a stolen scroll. . . ." She motioned for him to lower his voice, and he obeyed automatically. "He's gone out of his mind. The police have finally grounded him, and he's had to stop those kamikaze missions in his car. With all the publicity he got for returning those other articles to Italy, the . . . urn . . . has become an obsession. He wants it back, so he can return it, too. Since he hasn't heard from you, he sent me along to help find it. He's contributing a thousand pounds to expedite the recovery of the damned thing. From what he told me, it sounds damned near impossible. But," he said carelessly, "I decided . . . why not? I haven't anything against a holiday in Italy when it's offered. So I'm really here on vacation."

"A thousand pounds," Joyce breathed. "We won't need that much money, Major St. John. But it would give us a chance to buy the urn if we found it. I only offered three hundred in my letters. . . ."

"Letters?" he said, immediately alert.

She looked at Antonio for permission to tell St. John about the letters. He had been silent during their discussion, but he still was not subdued. She could tell he did not like St. John, though he was convinced of his authenticity now. When he caught her nervous glance, his hand closed protectively over hers again.

"We sent a lot of letters to collectors," Antonio said. "And to museums, too. So far, only two museums have replied: they don't have it."

St. John's attention fixed briefly on their entwined fingers; there was neither disapproval nor approval in his expression, but he scanned Antonio's face more closely. "What collectors?" he asked.

Joyce explained to him how they had obtained the names, and told him of the trepidation they had felt about sending the letters. "I'm not sure what will happen. Already, we've acquired one watchdog, besides. . . ."

St. John produced a thin IBM printout from an inside pocket. "Were any of these names on your list?"

Many of the names were repeated, but the printout was more complete. "Where did you get this? You didn't go . . . to the police?"

"No . . . it's strictly Army. The Allies tried to locate a lot of objects commandeered by the Germans during World War Two. A lot of things fell into private collections and have never been found. . . ."

"I think you can cross Hermann Göring's name off," Antonio contributed quietly, shoving the list back to St. John.

"Yes . . . it's old. But by your admission some of these people are still around. When did you send the letters?" he asked with resignation.

"About a week ago. Why?"

He frowned. "I'd like to see a copy of that letter . . . and I'd like to see your list. We must contact these people personally. I'm surprised someone hasn't appeared here. . . ."

"But someone *has*! That's what I've been trying to tell you," Joyce said, indicating the pretty Roman at the entrance to the excavation. "He arrived yesterday."

St. John's quick eyes settled immediately on the culprit, and a smile twitched his lips. "The gay fellow? I can see I came just in time . . . you're positively under siege. Even in my condition I can get rid of him."

Another memory broke in Joyce's mind, and she dragged her hand free of Antonio's to lean forward eagerly toward St. John. "You're in Army intelligence!" she cried. "Oh, God . . . you're just what we need! Major St. John, you're . . . a *deus ex machina*!"

He looked at her uncertainly. "A what? Am I being insulted again . . . or flattered?"

Antonio leaned back in his chair with a smile while Joyce explained about the mechanical device used in ancient plays for extricating the characters from otherwise impossible situations. But his smile faded when St. John replied, "Oh, yes . . . like the chariot in the last act of *Medea*. I'd forgotten. I studied the humanities for a couple of years at Cambridge, before my father, who was career Army, became alarmed about the whole thing. I shouldn't have told him I wanted to write, I guess. Anyhow . . ." He shrugged his broad shoulders.

"And the tie?" Joyce asked.

"Regimental. It's a rag, but I didn't bring any others. See here, we're going to have to make some plans in a hurry. I don't like those letters bouncing around. But first"—he pushed back his chair—"I'll take care of this other thing."

Without announcing his intention he strode across the parking area and confronted the young Roman, who looked frightened and confused with the major's tall figure hovering over him. He shook his head in violent denial when the restaurant was pointed out to him. But he moved quickly enough when St. John's large hand closed on his arm and pulled him, not gently, toward the low-slung, silver-gray sports car parked in front of the hotel. St. John forced the youth into the passenger seat, and the Ray took off like a laser, without even a warmup.

"Lord Willoughby's car," she said, smiling at Antonio. "He's even brought the chariot!"

"A man of action," Antonio responded, glancing at his watch. "If we don't watch out, he'll get us all killed."

"Don't *be* like that! You do believe he is what he says, now, don't you?"

"Yes. And we need the money his uncle's putting up. It's the only way to find the scroll."

They discussed various methods of action until the car returned, shrieking to a stop, twenty minutes later. St. John untangled his long legs and maneuvered himself out of the almost-ground-level seat with a look of satisfaction on his face.

"You've seen the last of him," he said efficiently. "I bought him a one-way ticket to Rome and put him on the first train. His English was pretty good, really. Insisted he was just an art student on holiday, and all that. Whatever . . . he won't be back, I presume."

Joyce felt an overpowering sense of relief, but Antonio put his knuckles to his lips to keep from laughing. "There isn't a direct train to Rome from here. If you bought a ticket, it was with a change in Naples. However . . . you didn't send him there, either."

St. John was appalled. "Where the hell did I send him?"

Antonio looked at his watch again. "Salerno . . . or any of the stops in between. He can be back within"—his eyes sparkled—"one hour."

Instead of being humiliated, St. John seemed to share Antonio's amusement. "I didn't say I was James Bond," he protested with a smile. "It was Dr. Lacey who wanted to think that. I told you . . . I'm just here on holiday. One hour, huh? Well, we needn't worry about him. We should make plans for tomorrow, though."

When Joyce heard his plans, she began to wonder whether his head was completely on holiday, too.

Chapter Ten

They were to leave first thing in the morning for Rome, Paris, and Amsterdam to confront the collectors face-to-face, but Ian St. John would not say why. Furthermore, the three of them were to travel in the fast sports car, which was designed for only two people; Joyce, who was the smallest, was assigned a small shelf behind the seats. If she lay on her side all the way, she would be quite comfortable—only, for God's sake, she was not to bring a lot of luggage. Antonio was not asked if he could get away from his work at all: it was just assumed that he was coming, and he raised no objections. He even volunteered that he had a passport, and it was still good: he had worked in Switzerland a couple of years before.

"Switzerland?" Joyce asked, with pictures of her pursuers and the illegal sale of antiquities in her mind, but he shrugged by way of reassurance.

"At a ski resort, in the winter. I was a waiter. But it was too cold there . . . I didn't go back again."

St. John informed them, further, that though he was providing the transportation and his uncle the money for the endeavor, he was not involved in it at all. He was "just along for the ride," and he would like to see the affair wound up as quickly as possible, so he could spend a few leisurely days on the coast of France before returning home.

"There isn't a snowball's chance in hell of finding that urn," he concluded, "but I promised Stanton I'd try. And that's what we're going to do . . . try! When the money's gone, and I return empty-handed, my uncle will know, at least, I've done the best I can. I have my own life to live. This cloak-and-dagger stuff no longer amuses me; I was cut out for other things. I was about to resign my commission when the old boy packed me off here. All I want to do is think."

Joyce tried to find a delicate way to word the question. "Where did you get shot?" she finally blurted out.

"In Northern Ireland," he replied, his blue eyes candid. "Sniper, from a rooftop. Oh, it wasn't in the line of duty! I was set up for it . . . by a girl with the loveliest Roman Catholic complexion. For a while I thought I was dead."

"No . . . I mean, where did the bullet hit you? Your uncle said in the back."

"That's right. It's still there, too. Too close to an artery or something to get it out. There's a possibility of an operation, though. . . . But I'm perfectly all right now," he said quickly, observing the shadow in her eyes. "As long as it stays where it is. It won't begin to travel for a while, you know, and when it does. . . . Well, that's what I have to think about . . . what to do with my life. My plans are rather limited right now. Choosing a new career might be premature, you see. I may decide on some vice instead, only I haven't made up my mind which one yet. . . ."

Antonio left them together a little cautiously; with a warning signal of the eyes to watch out for the man, he went home to face the explosion of his mother and to pack.

"You aren't interested in the scroll at all," Joyce said, with obvious disappointment, when Antonio had gone.

"Oh, I might be, if there were any chance in the world of finding it. But I'm more interested in humanity right now . . . aren't you?"

"What do you mean?"

"The Italian. It's a pity we didn't meet under different circumstances. You have wonderful eyes. But I'm afraid Casale would kill me if he caught me looking at them." There was an attractive crease in his cheek when he smiled. "Tell me, would you have been quite so interested in the urn if he hadn't been involved with it? I think people should be honest."

"Certainly," she said calmly. "If that scroll's still in existence, it's an important document. . . ."

"To whom?"

"Why . . . to science . . . to the world! Nothing like it has been found in Pompeii before: it's unique!"

"Worth a lot of money, too, I suppose."

"You couldn't put a price on it."

He winced and his white teeth dug into his lower lip.

"Are you all right?" she asked with concern. "It . . . doesn't give you any pain, does it?"

For a moment he did not know what she was talking about. Then he patted her arm reassuringly. "No. We'd better get some sleep, Joyce. The sooner we get going in the morning, the better." He watched her out of the corner of his eye. "I say, you wouldn't . . . ? No. Better not. No sense in hastening the end. You know, I think I'm getting my health back!" he announced, as they ascended the stairs. "It came over me all at once, just this afternoon. . . ."

K. T. Das's residence, the Villa Regale, was the first stop on St. John's mad itinerary; it was located in a wooded area on the outskirts of Rome. When Joyce opened her eyes from her sleep on the shelf, the men had changed places and Antonio was driving. The first thing she saw was the whitening of St. John's knuckles on his seat-belt halter. They were moving at considerable speed, and a car coming from the opposite direction had to swerve to miss them.

"I'll be all right on the Autostrada," Antonio said. "It's this damned steering wheel. It's on the wrong side."

"You might ease your foot on the petrol," St. John suggested coolly. "Just because I told you how fast it would go doesn't mean you have to do it."

Joyce tried to sit up. Her neck cracked, and she wished she had brought along a pillow. With an effort she managed to turn completely on her side, facing the men's shoulders. She had not noticed before the rather special way the hair curled on the back of Antonio's neck, or that St. John's had a little gray mixed in with the blondness. She wondered if that had been quite recent. Though she did not believe that anyone's hair turned white "in a single night," she had observed that under extreme mental pressure grayness did appear. And small wonder, she thought: the man might have only a few years to live.

Joyce tried to remember what she could about foreign bodies imbedded in tissue, but all that came to mind were the old wives' tales communicated by her mother. If you broke a needle off in your foot, the fragment would advance itself, inch by inch, until it got into your bloodstream . . . and then, *poof!* It hit either your heart or your brain: she could not recall which. A bullet, however, might move a millimeter at a time, over many years, until it. . . . She wondered whether it would nose itself gently into the wall of the artery, or make one grand, heroic plunge. The thought was depressing. She liked Ian St. John, in spite of his temporary determination to live in a hurry. If she were in his position, perhaps she would try to seize the moment, too. With a deep sigh she looked away from the men. Perhaps she was in an even more precarious position than St. John. I'm living now, she thought: the problem is for how long, and what am I to do with the time? Essentially, their predicaments were the same.

They passed the Villa Regale and had to back up to stop in front of the sagging gate, from which one of the wrought-iron letters was missing like a tooth from a neglected mouth. The gate was rusted, the grounds overgrown, the house surrounded by a high wall of lichened stone. Joyce, who had expected a rich villa, complete with Indian servants, was mystified by what she saw. She wondered if K. T. Das, like Count Luigi Falcone, had been reduced to selling off his collection in order to live.

"Maybe we should have telephoned," she said uncertainly.

"Good manners, bad judgment," St. John replied, surveying the ruined grounds with interest. "These people can't ring off on a caller on their doorstep."

But when a man is "not at home" he cannot be reached, anyway. Though a highly polished old Rolls stood in the driveway, the Italian servant insisted that her master was not there. From the commotion behind the half-open door, either Das had a huge family or in his absence his servants had taken over the house.

"Ask her about the car," St. John said, and Antonio translated quickly.

"She says the signore took a plane. He only uses the automobile for short trips. When he flies he leaves it behind. . . ."

"Where did he go? When will he be back?"

The heavy woman either could not, or would not, answer: her attention was conveniently distracted by the noise inside the house. Joyce detected the shrill voices of children.

"What about Mrs. Das?" Joyce asked. "Antonio, ask her whether the lady's at home."

The servant sniffed and replied that the signora had not lived here for a long time: there was contempt in her voice. The lady was French and spent most of her time on Capri. Without further amenities the woman began to close the door.

Joyce put her hand to her stomach and reeled weakly against Antonio, who supported her with concern in his face. "Are you all right?"

"I . . . don't know. I'd like a glass of water, please."

The woman hesitated briefly when Antonio spoke to her, but her maternal instinct prevailed over her doubts about admitting them to the house. She assisted Joyce to the parlor with a flood of questions, calling over her shoulder to a little girl observing through the rungs of the staircase. The child ran to get the water. Antonio's arm closed around Joyce on the brocaded sofa. He brushed back her hair.

"We should have stopped for breakfast," he said accusingly to St. John.

The interior of the house showed none of the ravage of the outside. The terra-cotta entrance was clean and shining; the parlor, lavishly furnished in the French style, was immaculate. The scolding voices in the rear of the house ceased abruptly, probably with the appearance of the little girl in the kitchen. Antonio remained beside Joyce as she accepted the glass of water with a shaking hand and began to drink in little sips. He was concerned and unusually solicitous. Antonio's protectiveness had been evoked with intensity.

There was no sign of the collection in the large room,

only the French antiques and a darkening oil painting of an Italian cavalier over the marble hearth.

"I need air," Joyce said, disengaging herself from Antonio. With the water glass still in her hand, she moved slowly to the open French windows. St. John, who had been completely helpless during the emergency, folded his arms across his chest and watched her. After a few deep breaths she rested the drinking glass against her lower lip.

The windows let out onto another unkempt garden, this one so overgrown that only the marble tops of the short benches could be seen in the weeds. A pretty girl in her teens was washing her feet in a rain barrel close to the drain under the ivy of another wing that extended parallel to the parlor. St. John moved to the window to relish the small tableau. Joyce indicated the other wing with her eyes; he scanned it, but he looked baffled.

"I'm better now," she said to the matronly servant, returning the glass. *"Grazie infinite, signora. . . ."*

Antonio, leaning against the mantel, beneath the portrait of the smiling cavalier, was watching Joyce. His face was serious. Either he was embarrassed at her behavior or he was worried and unwilling to show it. As they turned to leave, he said a few polite words to the woman who had offered her aid.

"Well?" St. John asked, when they reached the car outside the gate. "Did you see anything?"

"The collection's in the far wing, the one I indicated to you," Joyce said. "It's so overgrown with ivy you can hardly see the windows . . . but I caught a flash of gold, two arms of a gilded Siva, on the upper floor. What I can't fathom is why the place is so poorly kept. At first, I thought Das was in financial trouble. This house interests me. What do you think, Antonio?"

"I think the *cavaliere* over the mantel was a nice touch," he said quietly. Joyce did not like the look of his narrowed eyes, his compressed lips; he was angry again, but she did not know why. "They used to call some of them *cavaliere servente* . . . ladies' men, who followed everywhere, carried their gloves . . . and their smelling salts. Get back on your shelf, Joyce."

Hearing the tone of his voice, she did not question the order: she climbed into the car with alacrity, wondering what was bothering him. He backed the car up, made a U-turn in the middle of the road, and headed in the direction from which they had come. Joyce tried to determine what she had done to infuriate him so. She had only seen him like this once before, when he had first met Ian St. John yesterday afternoon. She finally decided that Antonio was embarrassed for having been so concerned about her when she was only pretending to be ill.

"I had to get into that house, Antonio," she said from behind him. "I didn't mean to take advantage of that woman. . . ."

He did not answer, and she watched his expressionless green eyes in the rearview mirror. "It's all right. I explained things to her. She understood. She's a mother herself."

Joyce was shocked. If he was joking, there was no lightness in the remark: it was a well-thought-out put-down. In a few words he had reduced her to a mere biological entity, confirmed what St. John suspected, and taken complete possession of her. Unable to think of a reply, she blew her hair away from her face in anger.

"Good God," St. John said easily, turning to inspect her. "You aren't . . . pregnant, are you?"

"Of course not!" she snapped. If Antonio had not been driving, she would have hit him with her handbag. "That's his idea of humor! He's just being hateful. I don't know what makes him think of things like that."

St. John looked from her to Antonio, who was intent upon his driving. If he thought that one of them was lying, St. John kept his own council. He put his arm on the window and watched the cypress-shafted countryside. It was clear that their intimate spats had nothing to do with him, especially when they were so irrational that they could not even agree on something that important.

When they turned onto the Autostrada, heading north, St. John leaned his head back and went to sleep, and Joyce followed his example by turning her back to Antonio and using her handbag as a pillow. The traffic was fast, but if she was going to die it might as well be while she was sleeping. They had breakfasted in absolute silence at the last stop before the turnoff, and she was emotionally exhausted. There would be no more scenes in front of Major St. John, she decided: she would wait until she and Antonio were alone to tell him what she thought of his idiotic implication.

She dreamed she was on a jet liner during takeoff; she even told herself, in the dream, to relax so the pressure would lessen. She awoke in alarm. It was hot. The bit of sky she could see through the rear window was blue and unrelenting; the perspiration on her face made her stick to her handbag.

St. John awoke at the same time. "For Christ's sake, Casale!" he yelled. "If you smash this thing, we'll have to pay for it! On both our salaries combined, it should take about twenty years!"

Joyce propped herself up on her elbow. The green blur of countryside edging the freeway gradually took on the forms of trees and hedges. She was finally able to distinguish a fortification on a hilltop, though the other cars were still falling behind them. Antonio should not drive when he is angry, she thought, wondering how fast they had been going.

"Someone was following us," he said, with his eyes still on the rearview mirror.

"You're damned right they were!" St. John said. "Every

car in northern Italy was following us, except the ones you'd already passed. I thought I heard a siren. Old Stanton'll be gratified to know his car outran the Italian police. . . ."

"Someone *was* following us," Antonio insisted evenly, and Joyce believed him.

"Was it the limousine?" she asked, forgetting they were not speaking.

"No. A Ferrari picked us up shortly after we left Rome."

"You mean, this sort of thing's happened before?" St. John asked, regaining his calm.

"Someone's been following me all along," Joyce said. "In Pompeii, in London . . . didn't your uncle tell you about the man at Willoughby Hall?"

St. John was thoughtful for a moment. "No. With his usual candor he neglected to mention it. . . ."

Joyce told him about the incident in the Underground. "The paper said the man was still in serious condition. For one thing, he had a compound fracture of the leg. I thought maybe I'd lost them, until after I'd mailed the letters in Pompeii. Someone in a hired limousine . . . we thought he'd gone away. . . ."

"Well, I suspect few people rent Ferraris. If there'd been one behind us, we'd have noticed it earlier."

"It was dark until we reached Naples," Antonio said. "Or maybe we picked it up after Das's villa."

"The only thing I saw there was that ancient Rolls. Of course, there was some distraction when we were leaving." St. John rubbed his face wearily and muttered into his palms. "How do I get into things like this, anyway?"

"It isn't over the urn," Joyce said quickly, "or at least it wasn't. It had something to do with the statue that was stolen from my site in Greece."

"It doesn't really matter, now, does it? The point is, we have a tail. Why didn't you tell me before?"

"You didn't give us a chance."

Ignoring her remark, he directed all his attention on Antonio. "How fast were you going? I did hear a siren, didn't I?" He tapped the glass over the speedometer with his fist. "It's stuck at a hundred fifty. You outran a Ferrari . . . and dammit, I did hear a siren!"

Antonio's response was carefully worded. "That was only after I lost the car that was following us," he said. "When the police started chasing me, I didn't want to get your car in trouble."

"Turn off the Autostrada directly," St. John instructed him. "There may be a roadblock up ahead by now. We'll let Joyce drive for a while."

They took turns driving after that, stopping only to eat and fuel up the car. St. John hardly gave them a chance to stretch their aching limbs before he had them on their way again: he seemed motivated by more than just the desire to complete his mission, now. After his brief remarks about being followed, Antonio did not say another word. Their passports were checked at the border, and after that, St. John stopped once during the night to ask them whether they wanted coffee, but he received only negative grunts in reply. Asleep in the front seat, Joyce was dimly aware that he was gone for a while, but she went into a deeper sleep as soon as the car began moving again. Antonio, sleeping soundly in an impossible position on the shelf, had not stirred.

When she heard the swish of tires on wet pavement, she opened her eyes: St. John was shaking her by the shoulder. It was raining, and they were in a city: his face was weary under the street lights.

"Joyce!" he whispered, trying not to arouse Antonio. "We're here . . . in Paris. I have to speak to you."

She sat up straight and watched the reflections of colored lights flicker on the wet asphalt. "Yes?" she said sleepily.

"I know a nice little hotel near the Place des Invalides. What sort of accommodations shall I ask for?"

She looked at him without expression.

"Are you quite awake?"

"Yes," she said, imitating his whisper.

"Good. Look, I don't give a damn one way or the other, you know that. But do you want a single or a double room?"

St. John indicated Antonio, sleeping like a modern Endymion behind them, with one arm over his face, the other falling loosely over the seat.

"A single room for me," she said shortly. "You two can do as you please."

He turned the wheel sharply, and the tires made a crescent whisper on the wet pavement. "You needn't be so touchy," he complained. "It just had to be sorted out, that's all."

When she reluctantly inquired about her companions the next morning, she was informed that the major was breakfasting in the dining room and Monsieur Casale had asked for directions to Napoleon's tomb an hour before. Not surprisingly, the hotel was called the Angleterre, and most of the staff spoke English. After acquiring a map of the city, Joyce sought out St. John at his table. Though he was working his way through a large English breakfast, he still looked unusually tired. Without greeting him she ordered café au lait and croissants and spread the map beside her plate to see how far the Île St. Louis was from where they were.

"Good morning to you, too," St. John said. "I hope you slept well."

"Yes, thank you . . . and the weather's fine, too," she said glumly, without taking her finger off the Seine.

"Obviously you haven't looked outside: it's still raining.

Joyce, what the hell's the matter with that friend of yours?"

"I'm sure I don't know."

He slammed his teacup down on the saucer, and she looked up with concern, realizing that Ian St. John was just as out of sorts as she was.

"I've bunked with all kinds of men," he brought out slowly, "but I've never had a night like that. I wouldn't mind if he snored: I can sleep through that. If he sang in the shower, it'd be natural . . . he's Italian. But Jesus Christ, who can sleep with someone padding about the room like a panther? I couldn't even hear him . . . all I could do was lie there with one eye open, watching the light of his cigarette. . . ."

"He slept in the car. He was probably just restless."

"He reminded me of Cesare Borgia plotting his next assassination. It was downright eerie. My nerves aren't what they should be, and I didn't close my eyes until close to morning."

She laughed incredulously. "You weren't *afraid* of Antonio? Why would he want to hurt you?"

"I don't know," St. John said, considering the reasonableness of the question. "Unless he knew that I was thinking about you."

Joyce lost patience with him completely. "I don't know Antonio's habits. All I want to do is find a certain street on the Île St. Louis, and this map isn't detailed enough . . ."

Her denial did not satisfy St. John, though. "What kind of relationship do you two have, anyway?"

"None," she said. "He's a friend, that's all."

"Nothing?"

She hesitated. "No . . . nothing. I don't know what's wrong with him. Something happened at the villa that made him mad. He's usually very pleasant. How well do you know Paris? I've only seen it as a tourist."

"I've been here a lot. The Île St. Louis is a charming

place," he said in a friendlier tone of voice. "Most of the houses are divided into expensive flats. Where does Jean-Paul Denis live?"

She told him the address, and they bent their heads over the map. Joyce liked the scent of his aftershave. His smile, his candor, his predictability made her feel comfortable. Their cultures were similar enough that she knew what to expect of him most of the time. She knew he liked her, too, and she was relieved that they had straightened out the misunderstanding about her friendship with Antonio in a straightforward way. After two weeks of emotional sparring with Antonio, it was nice to know exactly where she was and what she was doing. Maybe Ian St. John was right when he presented himself at Pompeii with the remark that he had arrived just in time.

But when Antonio joined them for coffee a few minutes later, she was thrown into upheaval again. His long walk to Napoleon's tomb had brought him back to normal. He did not greet her with a kiss or attempt to hold her hand, but he was no longer angry, either. The shoulders of his suede jacket were spotted with rain, and the light drizzle had curled his hair around his ears like Michelangelo's *David*, a condition he unconsciously tried to correct by smoothing it with his hand. He seemed to have contracted St. John's eagerness to reach the collectors.

"I've been thinking," he announced without preliminaries, "any collector we contact might know what's in the collections of some of the others. Joyce has started at the bottom with the dealers, but if we ask the right questions, there might be a pyramid effect, narrowing things down until . . . *presto!* . . . we find the man on top. Anyone might tell us something to protect himself, providing he doesn't have the urn. And if he does have it, he might just let us buy it to keep himself in the clear. They've all had Joyce's letter by now, and"—he smiled—"it had a very faint perfume of blackmail in it."

St. John listened with growing respect. "The letter had something else about it, too," he said, without elucidating. "What did you do, jog all the way to the Place des Invalides? You made it in record time."

"I walk fast . . . from being a guide," Antonio smiled again. "Actually, I was looking for anything out of the ordinary while I did it. We shouldn't have left the Ray on the street last night. It's a conspicuous car."

"You didn't see any hired limousines, did you?" St. John asked with amusement. "Or Ferrari's?"

"No, of course not. They'd have changed cars by now, though; whoever they are, they aren't fools, you know."

"You're right. See here, it's past ten . . . we'd best get cracking."

Though Jean-Paul Denis wore a mourning band on his sleeve, he invited them into his flat with curious elation. He was a short, hunched man with heavy features that bordered on the grotesque. At first glance, Joyce imagined that one of the gargoyles had flown over from Notre Dame for the specific purpose of opening his door. Denis was the ugliest man she had ever seen. Antonio had to act as interpreter: his French was more fluent than either hers or St. John's. Monsieur Denis explained that he was a recluse and that his own language served him well on his infrequent travels. He was an "islander," he pointed out, as he led them through the elegant rooms of his apartment to his study; many who lived on the Île St. Louis never ventured across the bridges to greater Paris. The island was a village in itself.

Wondering why such a recluse was being so pleasant to them under the present circumstances, Joyce felt a little frightened. Ever since they had crossed the bridge from the Left Bank, the sensation of stepping back into history had been steadily increasing. The almost medieval atmosphere of the island was intensified by the spires of Notre Dame on the adjacent island. The narrow streets were damp from the morning rain, and moss grew in clumps at the bases of some of the older, gray-stone houses that once had been regal but now showed the deterioration of age. Though St. John explained that the oldest dwelling was probably no older than three hundred years, Joyce felt that she was back in the Middle Ages when they had to abandon the car in a narrow alley to proceed on foot, with the high, shuttered houses on either side of them. Located as it was in the center of modern Paris, the island was an anachronistic impossibility on which she felt extremely uncomfortable.

Denis's section did not get much sun, though it was trying to come out now. The streets were not only wet, they smelled dank as well, and Antonio only increased her apprehension by remarking that the island, he understood, "had an unpleasant history." A picture flashed through her mind of bodies being silently dumped into the Seine at night.

Denis's extreme cordiality increased her apprehension instead of lessening it. If he was the illegal collector she had been led to believe, why was he being so polite to them? She had not expected to gain entrance, but there they were in his paneled study, sitting on brocade with crystal glasses in their hands, and their strange-looking host was acknowledging receipt of her letter. She sniffed the contents of the glass and put it discreetly aside.

"I suppose I should have answered," Monsieur Denis was saying, "but I seldom respond to any correspondence. And in this case it was a waste of time: I don't have an Etruscan urn. The Etruscans do not please me with their silly dancing and feasting and pretty, smiling people. They must have been a giddy, beauty-oriented society at best. So unlike that of . . . say . . . the Babylonians, who thought of more serious things. Not that I collect ancient art, you understand: I don't, with one or two exceptions that wouldn't interest you much. Old art, yes . . . but ancient?

The only pieces I'd like to have are mostly unavailable . . ."

Joyce studied the books in the glass-fronted case behind him: *Là Bas* by Huysmans; Rimbaud; Baudelaire; and shelf after shelf on diabolism and witchcraft. She recalled Lyman Churchman's mentioning a scandal about a book, but this did not look like a total collection, only a reference library. "In strictest confidence," she asked, "what do you collect, monsieur?"

She did not expect an answer, but the misshapen face broke into a leering smile. "I was afraid you weren't going to ask. I consider it rude to show my things unless someone expresses an interest . . . and that," he sighed, "is seldom. I'm glad now I didn't answer your letter. By not doing so, I brought you to my door! As I told you, I keep to myself."

He dangled a small key on an old-fashioned watch chain. "The only time my situation becomes uncomfortable is when something so extraordinary happens that I *need* someone to share it. I've just returned from a most joyful trip." He unlocked a cabinet below the bookcase and removed a dark piece of stone, which he cradled gently in his hands. "This," he announced, "is from the church of St. Pierre in Louvain. I've been after it for years. . . ."

"Louvain?" Joyce asked, looking helplessly at her companions: the name meant nothing to her. The broken stone head that Monsieur Denis laid lovingly on the table for their appreciation had the grinning face of a demon.

St. John studied it for a second, and a light of recollection flooded his eyes. "Wasn't that the Belgian city the Germans destroyed completely in World War One . . . because a single shot of resistance was fired?"

Monsieur Denis nodded enthusiastically. "It was the only perfect gem of Gothic architecture in Europe," he said. " 'A tapestry in stone.' And this is all that's left of it . . . all that's authenticated!"

Antonio stared with distaste at the charred, diabolic head. "It's appropriate it should be the face of the devil," he said.

Denis's thick lips twisted into a grin. "And so apt that it should fall into my hands at last!"

This man not only looks like a monster, Joyce thought, he *is* one. His only feeling about the devastated city was that it had yielded up this trophy for him. She did not have to inquire further into the nature of his collection; his remark about Babylon tied in with what she saw before her, with the books behind him. Jean-Paul Denis, so ugly himself, collected only what was ugly and diabolical. Small wonder he scorned the beauty and gaiety of the Etruscans.

"I suppose it's useless to ask where you acquired it?" she said.

"As a matter of fact, I can tell you, because of the circumstances involved. I bought it at a closed auction in Amsterdam."

"A *closed* auction?" St. John asked.

Denis rubbed his hands together and leered. "*Mon Dieu*, you really are innocents, aren't you? A closed auction is one to which one is summoned by invitation . . . because of the 'delicacy' of the articles on sale. This piece"—he put his hand upon it—"is *not* illegal . . . the limitation of the law has run out on it. An old acquaintance of mine died, and his collection was sold."

Antonio asked a quick question of his own, to which the well-weighed reply was, "Mynheer Zee."

"Zee's dead," Antonio told them. "His collection's gone. . . ."

St. John cursed softly, and Joyce was thoughtful for a moment. "The object we're looking for . . . did you see it at the auction?"

Denis's attention was on the precious relic on the table in front of him, but he shook his head.

"I'm sorry to hear about your friend," St. John said politely. "May I ask how it happened?"

"A misfortune. A misadventure. A dizzy spell, perhaps. He drowned in a canal when he was taking his evening walk." He could not keep his white fingers away from the stone. "What do you think of my little devil? He's beautiful . . . yes?"

They agreed that it was well crafted, and that seemed to satisfy him. Joyce wondered what inner spring of greed made it the most beautiful object in the world to him. She suspected that its brutal, bloody history was not the least of its value. Antonio turned imploring, disgusted eyes on his companions, almost begging them to leave.

"We have to run along," St. John said, rising to place his glass upon the table. His glass, too, was still full. In fact, when all three glasses were lined up, it was embarrassingly evident that none of them had touched a drop of the pale green liquor. Bracing himself, St. John shook Denis's maggot-white hand. "It's been a pleasure. May I ask one more question, though? Was there any reaction to Dr. Lacey's letters at the auction? You weren't the only one to receive one."

"I don't recall its being mentioned," Denis replied. "But I do keep to myself, even on such occasions. . . ."

They started to leave, but St. John turned back again in spite of himself. "I know you're excited about your new acquisition," he said, "but may I suggest you keep it to yourself for a while? You shouldn't admit anyone the way you did us today. Don't even show it to friends."

"What a peculiar request! But it hardly applies to me, Major St. John. I have no friends," Jean-Paul Denis said.

Once outside, Antonio moved to a patch of sunlight and stood there with his eyes closed, drinking the clean rays into his pores, and Joyce massaged her hands together to restore their warmth.

"What a sad, sick little man," she said to St. John.

"You didn't touch your drink," he smiled.

"I don't like anisette. I don't like any liqueur at this time of day. . . ."

"Anisette, hell. That was absinthe, my dear . . . the stuff that used to be accused of addling one's brain."

"What was all that talk about not showing off his devil?" she asked.

"Something struck me, that's all. Something that's been on my mind from the beginning. Look, there's someone I have to see this afternoon. Can I drop you somewhere? I'll meet you later at the hotel. . . ."

"Antonio, where do you want to go?" she asked, and in spite of the sun he suppressed a shiver.

"To church," he said.

Chapter Eleven

S he did not know whether he was praying in Notre Dame or not: Antonio did not kneel. He stood beneath a stained-glass window and let the color flood him, as he had the sunlight on the island, and she did not intrude upon his thoughts. Something had disturbed him very much in Denis's apartment, but it might not be the same thing that had bothered her: their frames of reference were different. Joyce tried to avoid looking at the reverential stream of cathedral blue and ruby red and medieval yellow on his clear-cut features: the sight was unnervingly like seeing the aura around an archangel under Kirlian lights.

When he had finished meditating, Antonio took her arm and silently escorted her from the church. As they crossed the Petit Pont he paused to look into the river, dull gray even in the sunlight. He was quiet for so long that the familiar depth of his voice startled her.

"This city is younger than Rome," he said. "It seems

older . . . as though all the evil of the past is trapped here."

"Your introduction was a bad one," she sympathized, and pointed back to the Île de la Cité. "There was a pagan shrine on that island before Caesar. It does go back a long time. . . ."

"Pagans are innocent," he said paradoxically, beginning to walk on. "Joyce . . . do you think that unfortunate man killed Zee to get that ghastly head?"

"If he'd wanted to do that, he'd have done it years ago." Then, with curiosity, "What makes you think Zee was killed? Denis said it was an accident."

"When a lot of people profit from an accident, it makes one wonder. And Denis's complete lack of concern over the man's death, in spite of the mourning band . . ."

"Maybe he wears mourning all the time. He's an odd man. And he was preoccupied with showing us that head. Maybe all collectors are like that. Anyhow, if we can take his word for it, the urn didn't exchange hands in Amsterdam. That's our real concern."

"You're right. We're in Paris! Wine, laughter, and song, and all that. But we mustn't forget our *idée fixe*."

"Well," she said, unable to ignore the irony in his smile, "I don't think we should forget it. Isn't that what it's all about?"

She shifted her jacket to her other arm and tried to keep pace with him as they walked along the embankment, dodging students, tourists, and motorcycles to cross the street. She hated Antonio's silences, distrusted that grim, inward smile: somehow, she had lost contact with him since St. John appeared in Pompeii. Or was it after her bit of playacting at the Villa Regale? She still did not understand why that had made him angry: After all, it had gotten them into the house. They had been so close, but now he would not share his thoughts with her. He was dispirited: something had really brought him down. She wanted to coax him out of it, but she did not know how to begin. She wished he would start teasing her again: anything but silence.

After the long walk back to the hotel Joyce did not see either of her companions again until dinner. When Antonio appeared in the dining room with a folded newspaper under his arm, he was still pale. Even St. John, upon whom she was depending for stability, was agitated, but he came right out and said what was on his mind.

"I called on a friend at Interpol today. Don't get excited, Joyce . . . it wasn't about the urn! It was about Mynheer Zee's sudden demise. That's the thing that's been troubling me all along about those letters you sent. I know it was the only way you could think of handling things at the time, but . . . what neither of you seemed to consider was the impact of those letters on the whole world of contraband art. You didn't send inquiries, my dear: you sent letter-bombs. You have no idea how dangerous some of these people are—though Denis may have given you some indication this morning—and now they are really at one another's throats."

Joyce went numb. "What did your friend say about Zee?"

"Just what I expected, really. His death's being investigated as a homicide. A man who walks along the same canal every evening for fifteen years doesn't just suddenly tumble into it, even with a dizzy spell . . . there was a barrier. There was a hairline fracture of the vertebrae just below the skull, and there wasn't any water in his lungs. . . ."

Joyce put her fork down; Antonio had not lifted his at all. He had sat immobile, waiting for both of them to finish eating.

"You don't really think my letter had anything to do with it?" Joyce implored. "Couldn't it have been done over something like . . . that devil's head?"

St. John comforted her by touching her shoulder. "What prompted the murder was greed, in any case. You didn't commit it."

"Something about those letters worried me when I sent them," she confessed. "Only . . . why would anyone get so greedy over a simple Etruscan urn? The urn itself isn't valuable. . . ."

"I don't know," St. John said. "Look, I'm sorry . . . you've hardly eaten a bite. And . . . Antonio, what's the matter with you? You look like the wrath of God. . . ."

Almost apologetically, Antonio put the evening paper on the table. A small picture of Jean-Paul Denis leaped up from the front page, and Joyce and St. John looked worried.

"What on earth . . . ?" St. John began, turning the folded pages to have a better look at the picture.

"He's dead, too," Antonio said, with troubled eyes. "It happened this afternoon. He fell from that little balcony over the courtyard. They're calling it suicide. . . ."

"But that's nonsense!" St. John exclaimed. "He wasn't suicidal when we left him. He was as gleeful as a demon over that damned head!"

None of them spoke for some time. They stared into their coffee cups as though they were crystal balls, their expressions portraying disbelief, calculation, and outright depression. Finally, Antonio began to drink his coffee and nibble on some bread.

"I think we'd better leave here," he said. "Not in the morning . . . tonight. Someone may have seen us at his apartment today. The sooner we're out of Paris, the better."

St. John agreed, with an almost imperceptible nod. "Zee died a week ago: the auction took place quickly. I suppose they'll auction Denis's stuff, too. Whoever's doing this is working his way down through Europe. We must get in touch with Das in Rome and warn him. . . ."

"Providing he isn't the one who's doing it," Antonio said "He was out of town when we called."

"If he's still away, it'll look bad for him," Joyce said, pushing back her chair. "I don't know about you . . . but I'm packing my duffel bag!"

They knew Das was in residence again at his villa the moment the servant opened the door properly dressed for her duties, and from the quiet and order inside the house. None of the children was in evidence now. Krishnamsetty Das agreed to talk with them "for a few minutes only." He was an unctuous Indian scholar with glasses so thick that the convex lenses made his eyes appear unusually small. He received them in the parlor dominated by the painting of the smiling cavalier. Unlike Denis, he was not anxious to show anyone anything, though he was content to spend the "few minutes" talking over small bronze cups of Darjeeling tea: he spoke Oxford English. And he displayed no emotion when St. John immediately informed him of Jean-Paul Denis's death.

"Denis?" he said, reaching for a cashew from the bowl on the table. "Peculiar man. I saw him only recently, as a matter of fact. But I didn't *know* him. What makes you think this information would interest me? I'm currently working on a book: it occupies most of my thoughts. And though your call is welcome, it does somewhat interfere with my work right now. I regret his death . . . is that what I'm supposed to say, according to Western tradition? I have a dual view of such things. According to my own belief death does not exist at all."

"You won't be going to the auction of his collection, then?" Joyce asked, but she was unable to read his expression behind the thick lenses over his eyes.

"Not even if I'm invited," he replied smoothly. "What makes you think there'll be an auction, anyway?"

"An educated guess," St. John said. "That's where you saw him last, isn't it . . . in Amsterdam?"

Das threw back his head to catch another nut, which he chewed slowly, savoring its flavor. "Yes. But Zee's collection was unusual: it had no nucleus . . . no focus. He was an importer, you know. He had objects from all over the world, chosen at random, just because he fancied them. There was something of interest to everyone there. But Denis . . ." He shrugged affably. "His collection has a slant that, frankly, I myself find repulsive. . . ."

"We know your interest is in Eastern art," Joyce said, placing her small metal cup on the table and staring out the French windows into the overgrown garden. The light was not the same this morning: she could not see through the ivied windows of the wing beyond. The Roman sun was directly overhead, shining on the weathered tops of the marble benches.

Das smiled. "You seem to know a lot about me: I suppose I should be complimented. You realize that if it hadn't been for your . . . naive . . . letter, I wouldn't have admitted you today. I wanted to have a look at the author of that masterpiece. I'll tell you quite simply, though, that I have no Etruscan or Roman objects whatsoever"—he paused—"with the exception of those Roman sarcophagi in the garden that you're studying so fondly. They came with the house. Yes, they're quite genuine . . . and of no interest to me at all. They're rather badly weathered, but they were that way when I came. Someday, perhaps, I'll sell them, or"—he smiled again, this time at St. John—"donate them to the government, as your uncle has done."

Joyce was shocked at her stupidity. In her preoccupation with the far wing, in which she had first seen a flash of Das's collection, she had not registered the width and shortness of what she took to be the tops of marble benches. There were three Roman tombs in the wilderness just outside the window, all of them wedded, perhaps irrevocably, to the plants and growth around them. She wondered if the roots had penetrated the stone.

"Why are your grounds in such deplorable condition?" she asked impatiently, turning from the window. Measuring her quietly, Das took no apparent offense at the question.

"Dr. Lacey, the truth is that I'm not a rich man. I'm not impoverished, but I'm not wealthy, either. The grounds were like this when I took the villa seventeen years ago, and in a way, this suits me. It's the only security I have. Oh, I have some of the growth cut back from time to time, but I can't afford a guard. And who'd dream of burgling a decrepit old villa like this? It costs enough just to keep the interior in order." His flattened hand indicated the splendid room.

The man is a slave to his collection, Joyce thought: the bulk of his assets are in the rear wing, hidden from any view but his own.

Perhaps he was writing his book about the objects he owned, though she did not really think so; the places the pieces came from would be more likely. She did not trust Das much, but she did not think he had killed Denis, either, though he might know more than he was pretending.

As though he had reached the same conclusion, Antonio, who had gone back to his study of the painting of the cavalier, shifted his weight in the delicate chair and fastened his green gaze full on Das's glasses. "Two of the people to whom Dr. Lacey sent those 'naive' letters are dead now. We don't think it's a coincidence. We only interrupted your studies to warn you that you may be next. So . . . even if you don't believe in death . . . please consider yourself warned."

Das's hand stopped halfway to the nut dish. "Why would the recipients of that silly letter be marked men? An Etruscan urn . . . the museums are full of them."

"What about private collections?" St. John asked.

"I'm sure they're full of them, too." Das stopped to consider his statement a moment, pursing his narrow lips. "Actually, I can't think of any in private collections off-hand. . . ."

"And you didn't see the urn at the auction in Amsterdam?"

He shook his head. "No. Zee's collection was more exotic. I didn't see any antiquities there. Now, if you don't mind, I must get on with my work." He smiled distantly. "Thank you for your warning. I'll take precautions that no one . . . catapults me onto the next plane . . . prematurely." He assisted Joyce from her chair, but he was addressing the men when he added, "This just illustrates the possibilities when amateurs get involved. An unfortunate intervention, to be sure."

Joyce was too angry to speak until they were outside; then she completely lost her temper. "Amateur!" she cried. "Seven years at the university and two in the field, and he called me an amateur! I'll bet he picked up that accent from listening to the BBC!"

St. John tried to placate her. "He wasn't talking about you, my dear," he smiled. "He was referring to the contraband art world. In which, all things considered, we've struck out pretty badly. But I think we're learning right along."

"I think he meant Joyce." Antonio volunteered this opinion with a touch of his old humor as he slipped into the driving seat. "She missed by a hundred percent on those sarcophagi in the garden. I could tell by the look on her face."

"I suppose you knew they were there?" she flared at him. "With all those weeds they looked like benches to me."

"I'm not an archaeologist," he said modestly. "Besides, I was looking at something else."

"Well, it doesn't matter," St. John mediated amiably.

"Joyce, if you don't want to get into the crawl space again, why don't you sit on my lap as far as the city? I have to stop there to get that letter from Moab translated. It's a damned nuisance, but we'd better find out what he has to say."

He pushed the seat back, and Joyce sat down on his lap. The arrangement was not much more comfortable than lying on the shelf. "This is the damnedest, silliest car," she said with asperity. "I hope I never have to ride in it again!"

St. John pulled her closer and folded his arms around her waist. "You're just out of temper from the long trip," he said. Then, "I was thinking . . . Moab's the only collector we know of whose safety we don't have to worry about. It would be too much trouble to kill him. But Moab's far enough away to give us some information, perhaps." He paused for a moment to consider the possibility. "My word, you're light," he said suddenly. "This is really rather cozy. We should have thought of it sooner."

"Joyce can drive the next shift," Antonio said, leaving a streak of rubber on the pavement that nearly drowned out his voice.

When they separated in Rome, Joyce had formulated her own plan. More upset by the rash of deaths following the route of her letters than she cared to admit, she decided to act rather than sort out her feelings. The only way to check the wave of catastrophe on the trail of the urn was to find the urn itself. She told her companions she was going to do some shopping, and Antonio dropped her off on the Via dei Tritone, pursuing some thought of his own. Joyce went to the nearest pay phone and called Harold O'Keefe.

He had been the first person to develop a sudden interest in ceramics after the letters were sent. If anyone could give her an answer to what was happening, she thought it might be he. She did not like the man, nor the way he had left someone to watch them at Pompeii, and she would not go alone to his third-floor office. Calculating the risk, she decided she would ask to meet him elsewhere, out in the open, where she would be relatively safe. To her surprise, O'Keefe sounded relieved to hear from her.

"I've been trying to reach you," he said quickly. "I've telephoned your hotel twice. It's important, but I can't get away for a while. I'm expecting someone. The foot of the Spanish Steps would be fine . . . in about two hours?"

"I'll be there," Joyce said, estimating the time before the Ray returned for her.

Suddenly his voice sounded pressured, as though someone were buzzing at his door. "Look . . . I'm sorry about the boy I left there. I want you to understand. It was in your best interest, and mine. I'll explain later. Whatever happens, what you're looking for must remain in this country! I have to hang up now. *Arrivederci!*"

Two hours: that gave her two hours to kill, and only a short time with him after they met. As she walked toward the Piazza di Spagna, she began to window-shop; then, to pick up her spirits, she started to buy. She had not had anything new for a long time, and trying on dresses kept her mind momentarily off her problems. She arrived at the boat-shaped fountain at the foot of the Spanish Steps in a new dress with two other boxes under her arm, but she still had an hour to wait. Then she spotted the Elizabeth Arden salon. Her hair needed shampooing after that awful trip. She wondered whether the salon would be able to take her on such short notice.

When she emerged an hour later, every hair was held in place by spray, and her head was full of fragmented information about film stars and fashions from Italian magazines. She looked for O'Keefe in the crowd at the foot of the stairs, but she did not see him at first. Then she saw him, perched on the metal barricade at the edge of the fountain, taking some of his antacid pills. He did not recognize her until she waved and started toward him. Half-rising, he greeted her with a smile, but the expression remained fixed on his face as, to her horror, he clutched at his middle and tumbled into the fountain.

Joyce dropped everything, her boxes, her handbag, and rushed to help him before anyone else had registered the situation. His feet were still hanging over the metal barrier, but his head was under the shallow water, and he looked ghastly. She tried to pull him out, but he was too heavy. Ignoring the stares and sniggers of the crowd, she waded into the fountain, slipped, rose to her knees dripping wet, and hoisted him up by the shoulders. What she was doing suddenly registered on some men standing nearby, and they helped her haul the limp man to the pavement, laying him gently on his back. Respiration first, Joyce remembered, wondering if any water had gotten into his lungs. He had only been under for a short time, though. She pushed his head back and clamped her hand around his jaw to open his mouth for resuscitation. If it was a heart attack, he would need massage, too: she could not accomplish both at once.

She looked up briefly and cried, "Get a doctor! *Un dottore*! The police . . . *polizia*!"

She went back to mouth-to-mouth resuscitation until she heard a broken siren and two men in uniform relieved her. She sat back on her knees, feeling dizzy, her wet clothes clinging to her. O'Keefe's chest did not move; his round blue eyes stared blindly at the matching Italian sky.

"*Morto*," one of the policemen pronounced, finally. His companion rose to move the crowd back so an ambulance could get through; then he went back to their car, while Joyce stared uncomprehendingly at the body. She began to shake.

Within minutes, there were other uniforms around her, light beige and white, and the crowd had been moved back to the flower stalls on the steps. Questions were being asked of the men who had helped her pull the body out of the fountain.

"I don't speak Italian," Joyce said, dazed.

"Please, signorina . . . sit down," the beige-coated officer said in English, assisting her to the low concrete curb. "You're an American? You've done a very good thing. What is your name?"

She told him. He would want to see her passport, she thought, groping for her handbag. "My purse . . ."

At an order, her handbag and her packages were handed through the crowd to a waiting policeman. As she groped through her bag for her wallet, she kept seeing the fixed smile on O'Keefe's face before he tumbled into the water.

"Where are you staying, Signorina Lacey?"

She brought herself back to the present with an effort. "In Pompeii," she said, and gave the name of her hotel.

"One more question only. I can see you are upset. This man also was an American. Did you know him?"

"No," she said at last, weakly. In a way, she was telling the truth. She did not really know Harold O'Keefe, though he had been waiting for her when he dropped dead. Waiting for her, at her suggestion, she thought miserably, turning her eyes away from the officer.

"You are wet and distressed. Is there somewhere we can take you?"

"My friends will be picking me up soon."

When the Ray finally edged through the police-directed traffic, the covered body was already in the ambulance. Leaving the car in the middle of the traffic, St. John and Antonio erupted from both sides of it and approached her at a run. Joyce rose uncertainly and pulled at the officer's sleeve. "May I go now?"

"Yes . . . of course, signorina. We have all the information we need." Then he added gallantly, "We regret this unfortunate incident. You think very fast. It's too bad the man was already dead when you gave the kiss of life to him."

"My God, Joyce, what happened?" St. John exclaimed. "You look like a drowned rat!"

He surveyed the confusion of uniforms and blinking lights and reached for her hand, but Antonio had already claimed it and was leading her to the car with one arm around her for support. The question of who was driving did not arise. Antonio pulled her into the passenger seat onto his lap and held her closely, stroking her wet hair.

"What on earth happened?" St. John persisted as they cleared the traffic. "It looks as though you tried to pull a *Dolce Vita* . . . I've never seen so bloody many uniforms in my life!"

"The police . . . and the carabinieri," Antonio explained to quiet him down. "They were the ones in the fancy uniforms . . . they're part of the Army."

"All because Joyce took a swim in the fountain?"

She could not hold the tears back or control the break in her voice. "It was O'Keefe. I called him . . . he came to meet me, and he dropped dead!"

"You called him?" Antonio asked. "That was pretty dangerous. . . ."

"No I thought so, too, at first. But Antonio, he left that young man at the excavation for our own protection, I think. He knew what we were looking for, I'm sure of it . . . and he didn't want it to leave Italy. He knew something else, too: he'd been trying to reach me. He sounded frightened. He was waiting there to tell me something. He smiled. . . ." She buried her head against Antonio's shoulder. "I am dripping all over you. . . ."

He held her tighter, ignoring the dampness soaking his clothes.

"I want to go home," she said.

"Home?" he asked uncertainly.

"Back to Pompeii."

"If the police weren't in this before, they are now," St. John reflected. "And they jolly well should be! It's time we told them everything."

Cradling Joyce's head against his shoulder, Antonio raised his hand for silence. Her despair began to drain a little in the comfort of his embrace. She turned her mind off, tried to blot out the painful incident. The dampness of their clothing grew warm from the skin beneath the sogginess. Joyce loved the feel of Antonio, the smell of him, his quietness. She felt like a child in his arms. Before they reached the Autostrada she was fast asleep.

Joyce came down too late for breakfast in the hotel dining room, and she was surprised to find Antonio and St. John chatting amiably in the outdoor restaurant. Antonio should have been at work by now. Within a few minutes, however, she realized that a full-blown conspiracy had developed in her absence. She had never seen them get along quite so well, and when she joined them they both rose to greet her as though nothing at all unusual occurred the day before. She was grateful for their consideration; she was not yet ready to think about it herself.

Antonio ordered her coffee and rolls, and St. John held her chair so handsomely that she was bewildered. "Do you have a swimsuit in that awful duffel bag you haul around?" he asked, more in character.

"A thousand lire it's in her handbag," Antonio smiled. "You do have one, don't you?"

"Yes," she admitted uncertainly.

"Good! We're going to the beach. In *my* car, so everyone can sit down. In all the time you've been here, you haven't seen Sorrento. We plan to bask in the sun all day."

What she really wanted to do was go back to bed, but

she did not have the heart to raise an objection. She had planned to spend the day in total regression, curled up in a fetal position, trying not to think. But Antonio had not gone to work, and St. John had ordered the hotel to pack a lunch. The waiter brought it to the table in a basket before she finished breakfast. The mere thought of the bread and cheese and prosciutto it undoubtedly contained turned her stomach, but she attempted a smile.

"I'll get into my suit."

The calm beauty of the sea and the blue sky, with Sorrento perched on the cliffs above the beach, had a healing effect on her spirit. Lying lazily in the hot sun with the feel of warm sand beneath the large white bath towel she had confiscated from the hotel for the day was much more beneficial than taking to her bed. Antonio and St. John took brief swims, one at a time, never leaving her alone for a minute, shaking like dogs and splattering her with salt water when they returned from the sea. She watched them through half-closed eyes, thinking how nice they both were, how fortunate she was to have them for friends. There could not have been two men more different in every way, but she loved them both today: St. John, fair, well proportioned in trunks he must have bought for the occasion, candid, humorous, dependable in every way; Antonio, too dark and beautiful to dwell on, still something of an enigma, with an attraction she did not define, moody, but a warm friend . . . almost more than a friend. . . .

As St. John flopped down next to her on his confiscated towel, Joyce noticed the red scar on the clear skin alarmingly near his spine for the first time.

"You were lucky," she said. "An inch closer, and you wouldn't be doing any swimming."

"Hm? Oh . . ." He touched the wound below his neck. "The bastard shot down at an angle. The bullet was deflected by muscle, the doctors said. I'm probably the only officer in the British Army ever shot by a twenty-two-caliber bullet. Probably some hotheaded kid full of illusions about the IRA . . ."

It had been close, though, she thought: it still was. She had almost forgotten that the bullet was still there, moving a millimeter at a time toward an artery. "A twenty-two?" she asked. "He must have been right on top of you to do that. . . ."

"Very aptly put," he smiled at her. "The street was narrow . . . have you ever been to Belfast? He was on the roof of a garage right across from where that little . . . the young lady . . . lived. I think it might have been her brother. . . ."

When Antonio returned again, he dived immediately into the lunch basket and began to pass the food around. The menu was what Joyce had expected, but it tasted wonderful now, and there was wine and fruit to round it out. In the middle of her sandwich, she asked suddenly, "What did Moab's letter say?"

The men glanced at one another and did not answer at once; they had obviously discussed it beforehand, and the subject of the urn was not supposed to be mentioned today.

"It's all right," she said practically, brushing the sand from her legs. "We're going to have to talk about it sometime. O'Keefe is dead . . . I hope from natural causes. Denis and Zee are dead, too. If we don't find the urn soon, we'll have to warn everyone on my mailing list. What did Moab's letter say?"

"A lot of nothing . . . which cost me twelve thousand lire for translation," St. John said. "I don't think he likes you. In fact, he called you a meddlesome American . . . female. His words, not mine. The rest was a lot of political balderdash. He's glad his country took over *your* oil companies. He didn't even mention his collection. Antonio made out better than I did. . . ."

Antonio's expression became shrewd, and a thoughtful line appeared between his strongly arched brows. "It may be nothing," he cautioned her. "It was the artist's signature on the portrait of the *cavaliere* at Das's place: *Di Angelo*. There's only one Di Angelo I'd ever heard of . . . Giorgio, who did a lot of portraits of the Neapolitan nobility a couple of hundred years ago. Most of them are in museums now, with neat little plaques identifying the subject. Anyhow, I had St. John drop me off at the library, and I looked for a biography of Di Angelo, to see if the *cavaliere* was mentioned. It wasn't . . . not as that. But he did paint a portrait of Count Luigi Falcone . . . and that portrait's been lost. A contemporary description of it matches the *cavaliere* at Das's villa. . . ."

"But what would Das be doing with it?" she asked. "He doesn't collect that sort of thing."

"I don't know . . . unless the painting came with the house, like the Roman tombs in the garden."

"That painting's fascinated you from the beginning," she said. "You kept looking at it both times we were there. . . ."

"Yes," he said, almost reluctantly. He poured her another paper cup of wine. "It was the teeth . . . he was smiling, you know."

"The *teeth*?" she asked, bewildered.

"Well," Antonio began, "they were good teeth, but with one peculiarity . . . the right incisor wasn't even, it overlapped a bit. I'd seen teeth like that before . . . at the Cappuccine cemetery chapel, Joyce."

She remembered the grinning skull of the cowled mummy. Only an artist would have noticed a detail like that, and Antonio was an artist, of sorts, himself.

"We think maybe the villa was Falcone's before he entered the order," St. John said bluntly, and held up his hand to check her enthusiasm. "We couldn't confirm it . . . not at the Cappuccine monastery and not in old records. The villa belonged to someone else at the time, as a matter of fact. Falcone didn't own it."

Joyce considered the facts for a moment; then, suddenly,

she exclaimed, "But that's what we've thought from the beginning! He was almost broke when he came to Rome. He didn't have the money to *buy* a house. He probably leased it. If he lived in the Villa Regale, it was from there that he disposed of his collection, bit by bit, to keep alive. Only," she added with less enthusiasm, "if he did that, why did he leave the sarcophagi in the garden? And why didn't he sell his own portrait?"

"Maybe he made a sudden decision to enter monastic life," Antonio shrugged. "I could understand that. He was on his last leg . . . those objects wouldn't have sustained him long. And selling his portrait would only publicize his ruin. Maybe," he sighed, "the landlord kept the pieces for back rent? We already know that Falcone was both proud and patriotic. Joyce, has anything else struck you about him? Consider the pieces stolen from Robert Willoughby's collection."

"The urn, a broken grave stele, part of what seemed to be a head of Pluto? They were all Roman or Etruscan. None of them was large. Is there something I've missed?"

"Maybe . . . maybe not." Antonio pondered what he was about to say. "Except that all of them were associated with death; a funerary urn, a gravestone, a head of the god of the underworld . . . a rare piece, because he's seldom represented. Count Luigi may have had a morbid mind, along with his other virtues. Look at the order he entered, noted for its bizarre cemeteries in Rome and Palermo. . . ."

"And the sarcophagi would fit, too!" Joyce cried. "We have to get back to that villa! There's no telling what might have been left behind!"

St. John had been listening respectfully, but now he intervened. "I had the distinct impression that Das dismissed us summarily. He won't allow us back there again. And," he added firmly, "there'll be no breaking and entering. I adore you, but I wouldn't put anything past you. As

I said yesterday, it's time to call in the police. They could get a warrant. . . ."

Together, Joyce and Antonio turned on him as though he were a traitor. "No!" Joyce cried, and Antonio's deep voice was final. "We promised my grandfather we wouldn't do that. He'd die of shame if they knew."

Chapter Twelve

The suggestion about going to the police was dropped: St. John seemed to understand, though he was reluctant to accept their reasoning. He might have brought it up again later, but it was unnecessary. When they returned to the hotel late in the afternoon, a sleek blue Alfa-Romeo with CARABINIERI stenciled in white letters on its sides was waiting, unoccupied, in the parking area. Antonio noticed it first.

"*Gesù*! The bloodhounds are after us!" he exclaimed in alarm.

St. John weighed the situation. "It might have nothing to do with us," he said. "There are other people at the hotel. . . ."

"It's from Rome," Antonio said quickly. "A *pronto intervento* . . . a fast-intervention car. There's nothing we can do . . . they're watching us from the lobby. We'll have to keep our heads . . . and *say nothing*."

Joyce hesitated when she saw the two officers in beige uniforms standing at the reception desk: one was tall and one was short, and the smaller one had the insignia of an exploding gold bomb on his hat. He carried an attaché case and approached them leisurely, with correct military bearing, though his small bones seemed to suppress the quickness of a bird. His gray face wore an expression of infinite weariness, but his blue eyes brightened when he addressed Joyce.

"Dr. Lacey? Permit me to introduce myself," he said, his English retaining its Italian syntax. "Captain Giulio Vizzini, at your service." Antonio stiffened as though he had been touched by an electric wire: the name obviously meant something to him. "The incident in the Piazza di Spagna has come to my attention. I'd like to speak about it with you for a moment."

She nodded mutely as the captain indicated the empty dining room. The tables were set with clean white cloths for evening; usually, the room was off limits at this time of day, but the hotel staff seemed to have vanished. Joyce looked at her friends. Antonio was frightened into immobility, but St. John spoke up at once, consciously pulling rank on the other officer.

"I'm Major Ian St. John, British Army," he said, "and this is Signor Casale, our interpreter. We're Dr. Lacey's friends. May we join you?"

Captain Vizzini shook hands all around with the greatest amiability. "Of course! My intention is only to make apologies to the remarkable young lady. If the man had lived, she would have deserved a medal!"

Reassured, Joyce was more relaxed when the captain held a chair for her: it was only a follow-up on what had happened in Rome. A few questions and the whole thing would be over. St. John appeared to share this opinion, because he dropped his formality and lounged back easily, with no evidence of concern. Antonio lit a cigarette with a shaking hand, which he took care to cover, though the captain was not even looking at him. Vizzini's bruised blue eyes were fastened on Joyce's face.

"Your reaction yesterday was instantaneous," he smiled. "We have it from witnesses that while others were laughing you were already trying to pull him out of the water."

"I . . . thought I could help," she said. "I didn't know he was. . . ."

The captain shook his head sadly. "Yes. Since you acted so quickly, I assume you saw him fall."

"I was . . . looking toward the fountain. I'd just come out of the beauty parlor. He got an odd expression on his face and fell backward. I thought he'd had a heart attack."

"An odd expression? Did he clutch at his chest?"

"Well . . . sort of at his middle." She imitated the placement of O'Keefe's hand on her own bare stomach. "It all happened in a few seconds. . . ."

"He smiled at you?"

Her pause was minimal. "You know *Rome*," she said.

The captain raised his shoulders, and his whole face lit up. "And you'd just come out of a beauty salon! I don't blame him, poor devil." His eyes swept the bikini-clad body under her jacket. "But this man was no Italian *pappagallo* . . . he was an American like you. You stated to the lieutenant that you didn't know him." He opened the attaché case and extracted some papers, too many papers for a report on a mere sudden death in the street, while Joyce watched in blank-faced shock. St. John's chair creaked uneasily, and she could not hear Antonio breathing at all. "Papers . . . always papers," Captain Vizzini said with disgust. "You have no idea how many pass over my desk! Ah . . . here it is! The man's name was Harold O'Keefe. He was an art dealer on the Via Babuino, just down the street. . . ."

"We read that in the paper this morning," Antonio put

in to cover any slip Joyce might make. "We were curious to know what had happened to the man."

Joyce tried to control her pounding heart. The captain, she realized, had called her *Dr.* Lacey: she had not given that information to the carabiniere in Rome.

"Poor fellow must have come out for a breath of air," St. John said reasonably. "That affects the breathing, too . . . heart attacks, I mean."

Vizzini's washed-out blue eyes were mournful. He sighed, but it was not Antonio's kind of sigh: it was one of extreme fatigue.

"All kinds of peculiar things are channeled over my desk," he complained. " 'Unusual occurrences,' they call them. Sometimes I'm able to tie a few of them together. The job itself is 'unusual,' you might say."

"It sounds dull," St. John smiled, but Joyce's hands were sweating in her lap. Captain Vizzini reminded her of a psychiatric resident she had known in grad school, a man too sensitive for his job. He had acquired the same pallor, the same smudged look about the eyes, from looking at the darker side of human nature. But there was something else about Vizzini, too: something with which she could identify. She sensed he had more vitality than he was displaying, that when he appeared weary and bored, he was most on the alert.

"Dull?" he smiled in response to St. John's remark. "No . . . never dull. It's like doing Chinese puzzles all day long. It's made a compulsive reader out of me, though. I read everything: police bulletins, newspapers, any little thing that's put on my desk. I even read the labels on wine bottles, tomato cans . . . and menus! While we've been talking, I've read that you're having veal parmigiana for dinner . . . with green beans. *Again,* I suspect." He indicated the menu, half hidden by the oil and vinegar cruets, and Joyce's uneasiness continued to grow: she had not noticed the menu was there. She began to understand Antonio's reaction when he heard this man's name, and she wondered who he really was.

"Interesting," St. John said, "but what good is so much useless information? You must have disoriented dreams to remove all the trivia from your mind at night."

"That's the interesting thing!" Vizzini said, snapping his fingers, displaying some of the vivacity Joyce felt was hidden in him. "It's often in the middle of the night, when I'm sleeping, that everything falls together in my mind. You call these things trivia. But . . . suppose an autopsy report crossed my desk tomorrow . . . it usually takes longer than that. But just suppose," he shuddered, "that one of you met with a misfortune and wound up in the morgue with this menu in your stomach. I'd know where you had dinner!" he smiled. "The menu wouldn't be trivia anymore."

"Unpleasant thought," St. John countered mildly. "I must say, it sounds as though you're in intelligence work, though."

Captain Vizzini denied the very thought. "I'm a *feeling* animal altogether. It has nothing to do with intelligence. A puzzle's never all in place until it feels right to me. It's only then that I begin to gather evidence. There have been quite a few 'unusual occurrences' lately . . . that fit into something else I'd read. But I must be boring you. . . ."

"Not at all," St. John countered. "What I can't understand is why you joined the Army. Detective work would have been more appropriate."

Vizzini raised his shoulders modestly. "I was a young man then," he said, "I liked the uniform. In Sicily, even joining the carabinieri was an odd choice. . . ."

"These occurrences you speak of . . . do they feel right to you now?"

"I'm glad you asked that question," the captain said, to Joyce's dismay: she wished St. John would shut up so this man would leave. "Maybe you can help me . . . since you *are* in intelligence."

St. John's facial muscles did not register his realization that he, too, had been investigated prior to the visit. "That's a misnomer, too," he said. "You know how the Army fouls up classifications."

"Yes," Vizzini admitted frankly. "But let me present to you the pieces of the puzzle, Major, and we'll see what you make of them." He put his fingers on the white cloth as though he were laying out a puzzle, contemplating its dimensions and shapes. "You must understand that they did not come to me all together, in a box, but one by one, with a lot of 'trivia' in between. Here are the pieces:

"First, an Interpol report . . . an art collector found in a canal after taking his evening stroll. The only sign of violence was that his neck was broken by a single blow. Naturally, this doesn't feel right . . . I consider, as the Dutch police do, that he was killed by someone familiar with the martial arts: a karate chop on the back of the neck is suspected. I can't do anything about it, and it was a painless way to die. But I store it in my mind. Then there was an amusing newspaper article . . . which *you'll* appreciate, Major St. John. An English sports-car magnate returns several objects of ancient art to this country. A nice gesture, except that it comes a few months in advance of the Grand Prix at Monza! He was quoted as saying that the objects were discovered in his house by a young American archaeologist, a lady who must remain nameless. I laugh at this article . . . his lordship, I believe, is in his seventies . . . and a woman for the weekend? Forgive me, but the British always amuse me. We Italians are rather smug. We always tend to underestimate the sexual prowess of others . . . and we're always proved wrong. . . ."

St. John did not let his feelings show, but Antonio made a motion, appeared about to say something, then clenched his teeth.

The captain amended the statement: "Not that the visit was necessarily like that. I forgot all about the article shortly . . . or thought I had. It reminded me of something, but it wasn't important at the time. In the meantime, among all the other material I had on my desk, I had something I had never had before: an undelivered traffic citation! This made me tear my hair. But apparently the Autostrada patrolman was so outraged that he had it passed on to me. He didn't even get the license number, because his own engine boiled over chasing this unusual car at such high speed. He thought that it was gray and he thought it was foreign. His virility was threatened: he was traumatized. I'm vaguely amused by this impotent officer, but it makes me think of Lord Willoughby again." He gazed through the lace curtains on the window at the silver-gray Ray in the parking area near his own vehicle. All three of them were silent, holding their breath. If St. John had encouraged the captain to find out how much he knew, he was getting more than he had expected, Joyce thought. She was afraid of what would come next.

But Vizzini's smile was still open and friendly. "Then, there was a newspaper article about an art collector who had met with some difficulty in Paris. He was a recluse who lived in the same house for many years. He fell from his own balcony . . . *plop!* . . . right into the courtyard, though he never opened the shutters and hadn't stepped onto that balcony for as long as the other tenants could remember. Suicide? Perhaps . . . Sûreté is content to think so. Two art collectors in as many weeks does look strange to me, though. Shall I continue? I don't want to depress you. . . ."

"Please do," St. John said curtly.

"Well, I've no sooner digested this information than the autopsy report of an art dealer in Rome comes from the coroner. A good man, Chiara. This was the report on the man Dr. Lacey tried to resuscitate." He nodded respectfully toward her and picked up one of the papers from his case. " 'Final Diagnosis' . . . I hate that phrase! . . . it is so

. . . final," he said with distaste. "This part of the report lists everything that was wrong with the man, summarizes all that's said above. '1. Old gastric ulcer, healed; new ulcer, causing mild inflammation. 2. Perforation of the stomach with massive intestinal bleeding. 3. Perforation of the duodenum and several loops of small intestine. . . .' And the laboratory report attached reads only 'sulfuric acid.' " He glanced at them for a reaction, but all he saw was three faces, shocked expressionless, so he continued, "The stomach was nearly empty . . . he had not eaten lunch yet, a time when, I can assure you from personal experience, an ulcer acts up worse. He had drunk some milk and taken an antacid. An *antacid*!" His eyebrows rose. "Yet another acid besides the gastric ones killed him . . . almost instantly. In powder form, sulfuric acid does not act without water. The liquid normally in his stomach would have activated it. But how, in broad daylight, alone in the Piazza di Spagna, was sulfuric acid administered? Maybe disguised as one of his own tablets? Whatever . . . This rather clever poisoner miscalculated his chemical . . . and when it would be taken. If O'Keefe had taken it in his office, or at home, there may not have been an autopsy, with his medical history. The fact that the acid burned, not just through the stomach, but right through his intestines like a bullet, might never have been known. . . . It goes without saying that his antacid tablets alone would not have stopped it." He paused. "And that's another thing. People don't swallow those tablets whole; they *chew* them. At least I do . . . but there were no burns in the mouth."

Joyce's lips felt pale. Her hand moved upward to her diaphragm as though it hurt. She knew she had to tell Vizzini about the antacid tablets, and she did not know how Antonio would take it.

"I knew Mr. O'Keefe," she said uncertainly. "I met him once. He *did* swallow his tablets whole. And now that you mention it, he was taking some just before he saw me from the fountain. . . ."

"He was waiting for you?"

"Y-yes. I had telephoned him earlier . . . he was expecting someone else then."

"And what did you do in the meantime?" the captain asked more closely. She was surprised that he did not pursue the reason for the meeting.

"I went to a dress shop and . . . had my hair done."

Her account of her activities seemed to please him immensely. He gave a sardonic smile. " 'I went to the dress shop . . . I had my hair done,' " he quoted her. "You know, if I'd had a chance to interrogate Lucrezia Borgia, I bet I'd have gotten the same answer! Not that she did all the things attributed to her. . . ."

"Good God, you're not implying that Joyce killed those people!" St. John cried, losing his calm. "She's the gentlest person alive. She wouldn't harm a fly! Furthermore, she doesn't know karate. . . ."

"No, but you do," Vizzini said. "And your interpreter friend here is a geology student . . . engineering, isn't it? . . . with a knowledge of chemistry. Isn't it sulfuric acid they use to identify minerals?"

"No," Antonio said, "hydrochloric. Look, I can see that you might suspect us, Captain Vizzini, . . . but not Joyce. She's never hurt anyone!"

"No? When I heard it was Dr. Lacey who had tried to resuscitate the corpse, my mind jumped backward again. I told you the 'young American lady archaeologist' at Willoughby Hall suggested something to me. It was an article in *Time* magazine. A small bronze statue was stolen from her excavation, as you probably know. This, too, had an amusing side . . . not that I consider theft amusing. But Dr. Lacey's reaction to the theft was so . . . delightfully unprofessional. It's always funny when someone steps out of character and reverts to a primitive instinct. She was in no danger of going to jail herself . . . until she hit a policeman with her handbag and nearly fractured his skull. . . ."

"She . . . *what*?" St. John asked in disbelief, while Antonio despairingly put his head in his hands.

"I can only guess what was in the handbag," Vizzini shrugged. "Oh, the policeman recovered! She was only in jail for a week. But it appears that the young lady has a low frustration level, to say the least. She may be downright violent. She might not hurt a fly . . . but she certainly did a job on that Greek policeman. Dr. Lacey? . . . are you all right?"

He's going to accuse me of murder now, she thought. He's going to arrest all of us. All she could think to say was "It wasn't over the statue . . . it was because of my students."

The corners of the captain's mouth went down, and he nodded vigorously. "No doubt the policeman had it coming," he agreed. Then he began to shuffle through his papers again. "It was only this morning that reports of this letter began to come in." He pulled out a teletype printout of the letter, in French. "They were both the same, signed by Dr. Lacey . . . and they mention, not the statue, but an *urn*." He leveled his weary eyes at her. "What the hell are you up to, anyway?"

The block type on the yellow paper moved like ants before her eyes. She could not explain the letters without telling him everything, and this, she could not, would not, do. She had promised Nonno Casale.

"I can explain everything," St. John said, with his usual self-assurance, and Joyce had a dreadful premonition. He had wanted to go to the police all along. "The urn in question was stolen from my uncle's estate, Willoughby Hall, a long time ago. Joyce is working for him. He wants to retrieve it so he can get more publicity by returning it to Italy, too. My uncle, as you've pointed out, is mildly eccentric, and he sent me along to help. We're shocked that two of the people who received Joyce's letters later met with foul play. As for the Ray speeding on the Autostrada . . . well, something went wrong with the carburetor: it just opened up. We adjusted it later."

"It did not occur to you to *stop* the car when you heard the siren?"

"I wasn't driving. I was asleep. We had a long trip before us. We were on our way to Paris to talk to Jean-Paul Denis."

His account was quite natural, because it was more fact than fiction, and Joyce marveled at him. He was unruffled, because most of what he was saying was true. And when Antonio spoke up, with the same level of assurance, her heart rose.

"I was driving," he said. "The car was unfamiliar to me, and I panicked. I'm sorry if the officer lost his. . . ."

"And did you see Denis?" Vizzini asked shrewdly, his attention still on St. John.

"Yes." St. John gave an accurate account of all that had transpired in Paris, including their reading about Denis's death in the evening paper. "He wasn't in a suicidal mood when we left him. He was as elated as hell over the purchase of a monstrous stone head. However, we thought it best to return to Italy."

Vizzini's eyes became bluer: he measured St. John. They stared at each other like poker players. The captain finally smiled, the first honest smile he had allowed himself: it made him look younger. Whether it was a smile of relief, or of pleasure at finding a worthy adversary, it was impossible to tell. He fingered two more thin files on thc table and turned suddenly on Antonio.

"How did you get mixed up in all this? From what I have here, you're a hard-working, ambitious young man . . . devoted to your family. Aside from a single report that you're the terror of the countryside, you haven't been in any trouble at all."

"The terror of . . . Who told you that? It isn't true."

"I can't reveal sources. You're still a bachelor. I suspect" —he appraised the handsome face—"you don't suffer much. In a place like this, with so many pretty tourists . . ."

Antonio narrowed his green eyes. "I don't know what my morals have to do with my character," he said.

Even Vizzini was stopped by the remark. He weighed it for a moment, then he laughed. "You have a point there. You're free to do as you please. The only application your love life has in this case is in regards to your relationship with Dr. Lacey."

"Relationship!" Antonio cried with flashing eyes. "You're insulting Joyce. Captain, I insist that you apologize. We're . . . friends, that's all."

"Mm. Friends who greet each other with kisses, hold hands everywhere . . . and spend weekends together in Rome. To say nothing of the hours spent together in her room here. . . ."

"I can explain that," Antonio said. "She thought she was being followed. It was all for her protection. . . ."

Vizzini's eyes narrowed with speculation. "I know a lot about protection rackets, but I've never heard of one like this before. I take it you enjoyed your job?"

Antonio said grimly, "Joyce is . . . not like that."

"I do apologize," the captain said to Joyce. "In my work, it's important to . . . ferret out affiliations. May I see the list of people to whom you sent that letter?"

She gave it to him after a momentary rummage in her handbag, upon which he seemed to be searching for blood-stains. She wished Das's name were not on the list: she did not want the police near that villa. He hardly glanced at the list before returning it to her.

"All this over a stupid Etruscan urn!" he sighed. "Now, if I may see your passports to confirm a few dates. . . ."

He glanced at Antonio's passport and jotted down a few dates of entry into France and Italy, while St. John continued to grope in his pockets for his own. He finally turned them out and put everything on the table.

"What about the glove compartment in the Fiat?" she suggested, and he excused himself to go to Antonio's car, leaving everything on the table before her. His car keys jumped into focus, as though a light were shining on them: she had an idea. When the captain asked for her passport, she slid her hand back across the table and dropped the keys to the Ray into her open purse. St. John reappeared almost at once, waving his bulky passport in his hand. She felt vaguely guilty when he stuffed his belongings back into his jacket without even looking at them, but something had to be done, and quickly: the world was closing in on them.

"American passports are so seldom stamped," Vizzini said, returning hers. "It's as though American tourists are citizens of the world. According to yours, you've only been in Greece and England. You aren't in Italy at all . . . and you've never been to France."

"Is it out of order?"

"No more than any of them." He looked at St. John's and wrote down a few dates. "*Va bene* . . . that's it! Though this is a peculiar place to stay, I must request that you don't leave here. You must understand my position. In case you don't, the local police will be checking. An extreme precaution, perhaps . . . but murder's involved. As an ulcer victim myself, I don't like the way death was administered to Signor O'Keefe. And as a police officer I don't like policemen being hit over the head by loaded handbags. It's rather personal, you see. Oh," he said, returning to the table and handing something to Antonio. "This is for you. I've filled your name in on the traffic citation."

They watched through the window until the blue car was out of sight, and Antonio exhaled until there was no breath left in his lungs.

"We're in trouble," he said.

Joyce did not ask who Vizzini was, now; instead, she

said, "*What* is he? How did he find out so much so fast?"

"He may have more. You can be sure he didn't tell us everything." Antonio reached for his pack of cigarettes. "They call Giulio Vizzini the 'Sicilian Carabiniere' . . . a term at once derogatory and admiring. I saw an article on him a few years ago, after he had put the 'pieces together' and broken up a whole drug ring. No one knows how he does it. He finds missing persons, too . . . he's very good at that, especially if they happen to be dead."

"You mean . . . he's a kind of Croiset or Hurkos?" she asked, realizing at once what she had sensed about the man.

"He's supposed to have the sixth sense. When he was a boy in western Sicily the villagers came to him to locate things before praying to St. Anthony. . . ."

"He's nothing but a bloody computer," St. John said, "and he has a damned dull job. He programs himself and makes a few educated guesses, that's all. If he were what you say, he'd *know* we're all right. He wouldn't put a watch on us."

Though St. John's argument was more sensible than Antonio's information, Joyce had her doubts about it. She, too, had experienced peculiar mental phenomena, which she could not altogether laugh off.

"Do you suppose," she asked, lowering her voice, "he knows about the scroll? No one must learn about that. . . ."

"Of course not," St. John said. "Don't be taken in by this ESP stuff . . . it's a weapon, Joyce. He couldn't know about it unless he's been to Antonio's house. And no one would tell him there."

Antonio leaped to his feet with a troubled face. "I'd better find out if he's been there. Mama will be screaming her head off if he has! I'll see you both tomorrow."

Joyce watched the parking area from the upstairs hall window for over an hour after she said good night to St.

John. During that time the police drove by only once to check on the Ray. In a few days their vigilance might be relaxed, but she had to get to the Villa Regale tonight. She might never have a chance at the keys again: by morning St. John would discover he had lost them. He and Antonio would not like what she was doing, but there was no other way.

Immediately after the police car passed a second time, Joyce descended the stairs, pausing to survey the lobby at the landing. It was empty, the desk unattended. After midnight the clerk usually slept in the office. She walked quickly, silently across the carpeted floor, grateful that there was no bell on the glass doors. Within a minute the engine of the Ray had begun to purr, and she eased it out of the lot, without lights, onto the Naples State Highway. She would keep off the Autostrada tonight: it was the first place they would look when they found the car was missing.

She was too excited to be tired, in spite of the afternoon in the fresh air and sun; and mindful of Antonio's experience she kept well within the speed limit so she would not attract the police. With the long drive before her she would have time to think. Her idea of investigating Das's villa tonight had formulated itself on the spur of the moment: it still had no definite shape. She did not even know how one went about breaking into a house, but she had her usual tools in her handbag, and her navy denim jeans and jacket were dark enough for concealment, though the jacket was warm. The French windows in the parlor seemed a likely point of entry: she had not seen the rest of the house. If she could get into that funereal garden over the wall . . . *Funereal*: she had not thought of the overgrown garden that way before; the word must have suggested itself from Antonio's remarks this afternoon. The word made her pulses jump hopefully. She would have a look at that garden, too, before she attempted to get into the house.

The picture of the dark-eyed, sardonic, smiling cavalier drifted through her mind. Luigi Falcone, she thought with despair, I wonder if you'd be distressed or amused by the mess you caused by your visit to England such a long time ago!

Joyce drove the car beyond the darkened villa and parked it in a little growth of poplars a quarter of a mile away. Checking the light of her flashlight, she switched it off again and retraced the distance on foot in the bright moonlight, staying as close to the trees at the edge of the road as possible. Her heart beat almost painfully. The idea of entering someone's grounds, let alone his house, frightened her more than she had thought it would. She wondered how burglars could accomplish nightly what it was taking her so much determination to do. They must not respect other people's privacy, she decided: they had no respect for any law but their own. She had to remind herself that she was not there to steal anything, only to have a look around. In a way, she rationalized, she was really protecting the occupants of the house: the sooner the scroll was found, the sooner the murders would stop.

Though she knew the front gate was an eroded disaster, through which she could gain easy entrance, she was afraid it would creak. It was after three in the morning, and there was no light on in the house. She followed the broken stone wall on the parlor side of the building, flashing her light only occasionally, when she lost the wall in the shrubbery. When she finally found a place crumbled enough to climb over, she stopped for a moment to steel herself. This was the point of no return: beyond this wall, she was clearly trespassing. But beyond it lay Count Luigi Falcone's garden and access to the parlor windows. She took a deep breath, clutched at the roots of the foliage growing out of the wall, and hoisted herself over, dropping noiselessly into the tall weeds on the other side. She crouched

there for a moment, listening, but there was no sound
beyond the throbbing in her own temples.

She had underestimated the distance only slightly: she
was closer to the parlor than the center of the garden. But
the surfaces of the marble tombs she had mistaken for
benches were picked out boldly by the moon in the jungle
of growth, and she decided to investigate them first. With
her handbag still looped around her body and the unlit
flashlight in her hand, she plowed through the fragrantly
scented weeds as quietly as possible until her sneakers
touched stone and she realized there was a path that ran
between the sarcophagi.

She felt, rather than looked at, the carvings on the base
of the nearest tomb, separating the weeds to do even that.
Her fingers were fairly sensitive, and she could tell that
Das had not lied to her. The frieze of carved men and
animals on the side of the tomb assured her that his claim
was true: the "bench" was indeed a Roman coffin, one of
the few surviving pieces of Count Luigi's collection. A
sudden impulse prompted her to have a look inside, but
years of moss and lichen had sealed the heavy lid tightly to
the base. Applying all her strength, she could not move the
lid.

After several attempts she paused to catch her breath,
wondering whether it was really worth it. She had seen the
insides of Roman coffins before; there would be nothing
there but a man-shaped groove for depositing the body.
Once in Bath, she had observed skeletons *in situ*, and she
was not interested in finding one here. Kneeling beside the
sarcophagus, she surveyed the moonlit garden uneasily: it
was as quiet as a cemetery after dark. Nothing moved.
There was no reason for the jangling in her nerves except
her feeling of guilt at being there.

The urge to open the sarcophagus was strong: it presented an archaeological problem, and curiosity was in her
blood. She extracted a chisel and a file from her handbag

and began to scrape away the accumulation of earth and moss that bound the lid. She worked silently and purposefully, taking care not to let her tools hit the marble, but she was not sure she could slide the slab of stone by herself without making any noise. The first push was encouraging. The lid slid a little, almost soundlessly. With all her strength she pushed it again, but this time there was a noise . . . not from the lid, but from the cobbles behind her.

She turned quickly. There was a bright flash of many-colored lights before she collapsed into blackness.

Joyce knew she was awake because she was conscious of so many discomforts. Her head hurt, and she was lying on something that felt like stones. She took a deep breath of the fetid air and moved her hands to feel her surroundings. Panic cut through her like a knife. She was enclosed in a narrow space. She could feel the uneven surface of the marble on both sides and the bones of a skeleton beneath her. How long had she been in here? How long had she been unconscious with the heavy lid back in place above her? She wanted to scream, but a footfall on the cobbles told her that someone was still out there in the night, someone who had struck her down and put her in the tomb to die. Or had he thought she was already dead when he deposited her in the sarcophagus?

Calling the object of her entombment what it was made her breathe even harder: in Greek, *sarcophagus* meant "flesh-eater," and she saw herself already consumed. She had studied skeletons so dispassionately, she thought, but they had not been buried alive. She must try to control her breathing: it was already hot and close in here. At least this sarcophagus was of Roman marble and not the flesh-consuming limestone used by the Greeks. . . .

With difficulty she looked at the illuminated dial of her watch. She had been here only half an hour, and already there were beads of moisture on the inside of the tomb.

There was no way to judge how quickly she would use up the air. She explored the angle where the lid joined all around, and she could feel no fresh drafts coming in. There was no sound outside now. Was he still there? She began to move the bones, which felt like rocks, from beneath her and found that she fit quite neatly into the groove intended for the body. For once, she was glad she was small. Raising her legs, she put her feet firmly against the undersurface of the lid and gave a push, but the only result of the effort was that the skull rolled back, touching her on the cheek. She moved it away with a shudder.

Even with leverage, she realized she could not move the lid from inside. Her legs were trembling from the effort, and she was only using up more air. She looked at her watch again: only a few minutes had passed. They had seemed like an hour. If she could survive until morning, maybe her cries would be heard. She knew Yogis could live for several hours with a limited amount of oxygen by slowing their body metabolism in a trance state, but she had never experimented with anything like that. Instead of inducing a trance she might go to sleep. . . .

She could not find her flashlight anywhere around her: it must have dropped outside. Her purse pressed into her side as uncomfortably as the bones had done. For a moment she wanted to cry. She wanted Antonio . . . Ian. They would know what to do. She never should have come here without them. What would they think when they discovered she had disappeared? Someone would finally find the car down the road if her attacker had not thought of that, too. Yes, someone would find the car, after she was. . . . No, she would not let it happen! Only a few hours ago she had felt the sun on her half-naked body: she had been alive. Yesterday she had touched Antonio, watched his face with amusement and fondness when he sparred with Vizzini about his morals. No matter how well his life was planned, she wanted to see that face again. She refused to die: she had not even lived yet. A determination rose in her to get out of the tomb somehow, regardless of what might be waiting outside. It was not yet five o'clock, and the air was getting worse.

With the top of her aching head in one corner of the sarcophagus, she groped in her handbag for her small geology pick. She had to lie flat again and strike upward at the lid, and there was not much force behind the blow: only the sound of metal on stone was alarming. She waited before she struck again: there was still no sound outside. Chips of marble gradually began to come away, striking her in the face; she changed her position again and worked diligently at one corner of the lid to make an air hole. The harder she worked, the more urgent her need for air became. Perspiration streamed from her face, and she labored for breath. At last, a fortunate blow, or a fault in the marble displaced a large chunk, which fell outward. She saw the first gleam of dawn through the opening and heard the chirp of a bird, before she pressed her face to the opening to breathe in the cool air and the scent of weeds.

Chapter Thirteen

T he sound of men's voices in the garden made her stir in her sleep. They were speaking casually, disinterestedly, in Italian, like some of the hotel staff in the hall in the morning. Then she woke suddenly, remembering where she was. One of the men made a statement, and the other responded with "*Va bene*": they were going away! Without stopping to think, she put her mouth to the opening she had made in the corner of the tomb and called out, "Help! . . . *Aiuta! Aiuta!* I'm trapped in the tomb!"

Either they did not understand English or they did not know which tomb she meant. Their voices grew excited, and she called over and over again so they could locate her. They must be some of Das's servants, she thought: he did not have any gardeners. She did not stop yelling until she heard them trying to move the lid of the sarcophagus. With two men pushing, it opened in a few minutes, and the lid fell to the ground. Joyce shielded her eyes from the sunlight and looked up into the alarmed faces above her. Then she blinked: they were wearing the smart uniform of the carabinieri. They assisted her out of her prison with exclamations of disbelief. She could hardly stand. Her clothes were damp and dirty, and her head ached when she moved it.

Neither of them spoke English. Unable to respond to the questions they asked or to figure out what they were doing here, she appreciated the swiftness with which they made her comfortable in the back of their car. They did not phone in until they were underway. She stretched her cramped limbs and let out a sigh, too numb to think. She was safe, that was all that mattered: nothing could hurt her now. She felt a surge of affection for the trim, uniformed shoulders in front of her in the bleeping vehicle. The police were not so bad after all: sometimes they were even there when you needed them.

The two men reclaimed her after she had her eyes examined and her wound cleaned at the clinic. The Alfa-Romeo did not speed through the streets now. It eased its way through the traffic as soberly and quietly as her two rescuers in the front seat.

The panic she felt when she saw Captain Vizzini's name on the door in the clean stone hallway turned to claustrophobia when she entered his office. With file cabinets along all the walls, stacked high with magazines and newspapers, and a teletype monitor hammering information in from one corner, the office was almost as small as her tomb. The captain sat at a cluttered desk, not really reading, but scanning, the morning paper. An octagonal espresso pot rested on a hot plate on a chair beside him. He looked as though he had not slept since she had seen him the day before. His face was gray, his bruised blue eyes expressionless.

"You show up in funny places," he said without looking up from the newspaper. "Dr. Lacey . . . you yourself are an 'unusual occurrence.' Please have a chair."

But there was not an extra one to sit on, so he finally stirred himself to move the hot plate. If she had hoped for mercy for her throbbing head, it was not forthcoming: he already knew the extent of her injury, no doubt, and considered it superficial.

"The stolen car is being returned to its owner. I should have it impounded. You did not follow my orders."

"I only borrowed the car. Major St. John will know that. . . ."

"You didn't stay in Pompeii. The police there didn't realize it until early this morning. We've had an all-points bulletin out on you. You've caused everyone a lot of trouble."

"Did *you* send your men to the villa?" she asked, ready to believe all that Antonio had said of this man. "How did you know I was there?"

The captain seemed singularly down-to-earth and realistic this morning as he poured her half a cup of coffee and proffered the paper container to her.

"No," he said simply. "When I got back last evening, I found that Mr. Das had put in a request for police protection. I recognized his name from your list. It seems he, too, had one of your letters . . . and a call from three people warning him to be cautious."

He had no more than glanced at the list, she remembered. Did he have a photographic memory, too? She began to grow tense. This was a man of whom to be wary, whatever his powers. If what Antonio had read was true, he might even be able to look into her mind. She tried to blot out the image of the scroll.

"I won't ask how you got into that sarcophagus. Obviously, you didn't hit yourself on the head. And Major St. John and Signor Casale are where they should be . . . I called them awhile ago. Why did you go to the villa? What were you doing there?"

At least Antonio and St. John knew about her predicament, knew that she was all right. She decided to try to use St. John's tactics on Vizzini.

"Trespassing," she admitted. "I was looking for any illegal art I could find. If your men were there to guard Mr. Das, how did I get hit on the head? Were they sleeping in their car or something?"

He shook his head slowly. "Taking the offensive won't help you," he said. "The men weren't sent out until this morning. Rome was a busy place last night: we didn't have anyone to spare. Das was locked tightly in his house, instructed not to admit anyone. Drink your coffee . . . it's getting cold. Your friends won't be able to do anything to help you: I told them to stay where they are. After the initial shock of the call, they both reacted the same way. I think they're mad at you."

Joyce took a sip of coffee, measuring him with her eyes. The bitter liquid hit her stomach like acid: it must have been standing since the night before. Or perhaps Vizzini, who did not seem to sleep, liked his espresso strong. The condensed caffeine made her heart skip, but it cleared her head a little. He had calculated the exact dosage she could stand, by giving her only half a cup.

"How do you do it?" she asked suddenly. "How do you know what other people are thinking?"

A wry smile twisted his lips. "If I knew that, I wouldn't have to ask questions, would I? If I could do that, I'd have to sleep in a lead-lined room. You overestimate me. That article in the paper worked to my advantage. Sometimes it makes people confess to things they think I know already. But," he sighed wearily, "I'm just an ordinary . . . 'cop?' . . . who reads a lot. I haven't had time yet to read up on Etruscan urns," he added, almost hopefully, calling on her authority to fill in the gap.

"I'm not an expert on them myself," she said. "As you know, my field is ancient Greece. I suspected my statue might be Etruscan, though. I still think it could have been. All I know is from what I've observed in museums here. The Etruscans seem to have been a happy, joyous people. There's so much music and dancing on their tombs . . . and most of the statues are smiling. My statue was smiling, too."

"And they cremated their dead and buried them in urns during their earliest period," he said, getting her back to the point. It was useless to use a smokescreen against him.

"Yes," she said. "Both before and after their contact with the Greeks. The later cinerary containers were boxes, sometimes made in the shape of huts. The urn that was stolen from Willoughby Hall was pre-Hellenic. Black *bucchero*." He knew this anyway. "Lord Willoughby wants it back again, now that he knows about it."

"And how was this information provided?"

She realized at once that she had made a slip. With as much composure as she could muster, she took another drink of the terrible coffee. "A chance entry in an old ledger . . . in the library at the Hall. We ran across it when we were preparing the other objects for shipment. It was mentioned in a catalog of one of his ancestors' collections."

"Aren't you taking your duties rather seriously? I understand that you're in his employ, but . . . three people have already died, perhaps over this stupid urn. Isn't that a little out of proportion?"

"We don't know it was over the urn," Joyce said quickly. "Why should it be? Maybe there's some kind of vendetta going on in the art world . . . just like in archaeology. It's only natural that some of the murdered collectors would be in possession of my letter. I sent out a lot of them. . . ."

"When the dealer died in the Piazza di Spagna, your friends weren't with you. Where did they go?"

The question took her by surprise: she had to think a moment. "Major St. John went to have a reply to one of the letters translated. It was written in Arabic. It didn't say anything . . . just hurled a few insults at me. And Antonio . . ." Antonio had been at the library looking up information on Count Luigi and the villa: she did not want to tell the captain that.

"And Antonio?" he pursued, pouring himself more coffee.

"He had some studying to do. He's entering the institute to do graduate work in the fall. . . ."

"Which one of them was in possession of that extraordinary car during that time?"

"I don't know," she said truthfully, wondering what he was putting together now.

"And when you were in Paris on the afternoon you visited Jean-Paul Denis . . . were you all three together then?"

She had to think back again. "No. Major St. John took the car to visit someone he knows at Interpol. Monsieur Denis told us about Zee's death, you see. Antonio and I walked back to the hotel together, but he was very moody. . . . I went to my room. I didn't see them again until dinner."

"Antonio was 'moody' . . . how did he spend the rest of the afternoon?"

She shrugged. "I have no idea." Then the trend of questioning began to dawn on her. "You're not implying that one of them . . . ? That's absurd! Antonio and Ian wouldn't do a thing like that!"

"How much do you know about either of them?"

"I know that Ian was in an Army hospital when Mynheer Zee was killed. And Antonio was in Pompeii . . . just as he was last night. They're both very nice men."

"But Antonio gets moody," Vizzini said. "What do you mean by that?"

"Quiet, mostly. But he's proud, intelligent, honest. We all get moody sometimes."

"Mm. Does Major St. John get that way, too?"

She tried to recall a time in the past week when Ian had been like that, but she could not do it. And he had good reason to have fluctuations of temperament, with that bullet in his back. "He's more disciplined, I guess," she said at last. "Probably from being in the Army. He's curt at times, but otherwise he's very candid and open. He, too, is intelligent and honest. They're very kind men. And neither of them," she emphasized, "has been anything but respectful toward me."

"They sound like a pair of perfect Boy Scouts," Vizzini said sarcastically.

"You've met them. Surely you must have formed an impression, Captain Vizzini," she said almost desperately. Whatever happened, she did not want to implicate Antonio and Ian.

"What do you know about Italians?" Vizzini shot at her suddenly, and she felt helpless.

"Antonio's the only one I've known very well. I like them. I don't really understand them," she admitted. "One minute, they're kind and affectionate, and the next, I'm completely confused by them. They seem to be either playing games with words, or they're angry, or quiet . . . with no reason at all. But I like them . . . I like them very much."

"Since, by your own admission, you've known only one of them, 'they' must mean Antonio. A very attractive young man."

"Yes . . . he is. But he's"—she floundered for a better word, but had to repeat the one she had used before—"*kind*. He wouldn't harm anyone. Anyway, both Ian and Antonio were in Pompeii last night when I was attacked. You said so yourself."

"I didn't say that. I said they were there when I called. That was at"—he consulted the large official clock on the wall—"eight thirty this morning. Either of them would have had time to get back by then."

"You're wrong," she said with conviction. "There's no *reason* they'd do that. . . ."

"But there are several," he said objectively, raising his eyebrows slightly at her naiveté. "The artworks you're looking for have a certain monetary value: neither of these men has any money of his own. Antonio's had a hard time, like a lot of us; he's working to continue his education: he's ambitious. And Major St. John's completely dependent on his Army pay in a regiment where the others have personal fortunes. He won't have an extra penny until his uncle dies. . . ."

"In which case, he should kill Stanton, shouldn't he?" she asked angrily. "Why go to all the trouble of killing collectors, one by one?"

"Exactly . . . unless something more valuable than you're telling me is involved. Both of those men know more than I do, Dr. Lacey."

"An urn. A statue, if possible. That's all," Joyce said shortly, but she was uneasy again. She wondered if Ian really had been in the hospital when Zee was killed. He was so cool, so clever, and his uncle had told him about the scroll. Antonio, too, had told *her* about the scroll: that could have been a setup. She remembered the archaeologist who had been ruined by people who wanted the so-called Dorak treasure authenticated, recalled Carlo Montebello's insistence that she look at his work to see if it would pass for genuine. She had to shake her head sharply to clear the doubts away: she had almost forgotten with whom she was dealing right now.

"You're trying to divide us," she accused Vizzini quietly. "You want to turn us against one another. Did you work on them, too . . . on the telephone, against *me*?"

But Vizzini's eyes, fatigued and blank until now, sparkled with sudden amusement. "Do you think I'd do anything so . . . ingenuous? The reasons I gave that these men might do such things were purely hypothetical. You've seen too many films, Dr. Lacey."

He had her completely bewildered, but she was determined not to show it. If Antonio was able to confuse her mind sometimes, she felt that Vizzini could unhinge it. Then she remembered that he was a Sicilian, and she knew that Sicilians were clever people.

"Sicilians don't like Neapolitans," she said, as though that might explain why he was after Antonio, suspicious of everything he did.

"Really? Actually, we're very much alike. On an island, of course, characteristics may become exaggerated. I think the only Neapolitans and Sicilians who don't like each other are involved in organized crime, engaged in healthy competition. I could understand a certain amount of antipathy there: one would have to outsmart the other, wouldn't he?" He leaned forward and placed his elbows on the pile of papers on his desk; his face could not have been more open. "I like you," he said, "in spite of the fact that you're 'under suspicion' right now. Do you want to know what I think of your friends, who are 'under suspicion,' too?"

"Why should you tell me that?" she asked with distrust. "Why should you like me if you think I'm a murderer?"

He waved his hand in the air with the vivacity that seemed more natural to him than his chronic weariness. "Murderers are people, too . . . people with a small flaw, like an imperfect diamond. I've liked quite a few of them," he sighed. "It's fortunate there's no death penalty here: it would make my job very hard. In Italy you just go to prison for life, and though the conditions aren't the best, we do try to keep the rats down. But," he smiled, "you've had experience with jail yourself."

She would not let him unnerve her again; he was too much for her, and she knew it. Whatever the danger, she liked him, too. In a strange sort of way, he amused her: his mind was such a labyrinth of subtlety and practicality. He was not really threatening her with prison now; he was only making a pretense of it, knowing she would see through him. My God, I'm beginning to think like these people, she realized.

"All right," she said easily, "what *do* you think of my friends?"

He lost control of his animation, as though he welcomed the opportunity to express himself freely. His hands moved in a series of gestures that underlined every statement, and were frequently statements in themselves that said more than words. She watched his hands with fascination, trying to remember every motion.

"Major St. John's smart enough to tell most of the truth. Lying isn't 'good form' for him. I think he neither lends nor borrows, nor repeats stories about other people, and he keeps his own affairs to himself. I don't really think he's waiting for his uncle to die: he likes the old man. He doesn't like the Army, though . . . but he'll pull rank if he has to. He'll leave the Army someday. And it will be a loss for them, too . . . he's a man of action."

"I think you're right. And," Joyce asked with more caution, "what about Antonio?"

The captain shook his head, and Joyce's heart fell. "Ah, Antonio. He has it here," he said, tapping his temple; then he opened both hands as though he had been electrified. "But he's in an odd position. He's stricken with the Neapolitan curse and he doesn't know what to do about it."

Joyce was concerned. "What's that? It sounds something like Montezuma's Revenge. . . ."

For the first time Vizzini looked baffled. "What's *that*?" he echoed.

"An unpleasant illness one picks up in Mexico . . . from the water," she laughed.

"Oh," he considered. "Well, this is nothing like that . . . it's more unpleasant, I'm sure. The young man's very modern: he has his own ideas. But he's been struck by lightning and he doesn't know what to do about it."

She stared at him in silence. "Translation, please," she said at last. This time it was Vizzini who laughed, leaning back in his swivel chair.

"A Sicilian expression for something that happens in Naples, too. I told you we're a lot alike. We don't fall in love gradually like civilized Anglo-Saxons . . . it descends on us like a bolt from the sky! It usually knocks us senseless. In Sicily young men grow tense, they fall ill . . . or start fights. But in Naples!" He threw his hands into the air. "The malady starts with internal bleeding; sometimes it hemorrhages into song. It's painful to bleed, alarming to be so jealous. Love is never happy there . . . it's a curse."

"You're saying that . . . Antonio's in love?" Each word came out slowly, and each one hurt. Her mind went over all the time they had spent together, his frequent reserve, his many moods. She nearly asked "With whom?" but she maintained her Anglo-Saxon reserve.

"I'll bet," Vizzini sparkled, "that his moods began after Major St. John's arrival." He watched her with penetrating eyes: Joyce was full of confusion.

"He's not in love with *me*, if that's what you think. He hardly even looks at me." Vizzini's statement upset her, and she became suspicious of him again. "What has all this to do with anything?"

"Nothing. I like people, that's all. I'd hate to see a man like Antonio Casale . . . who is so full of life . . . spend the rest of it in prison because he's been struck by lightning over a woman who's so single-minded she doesn't care what happens to him." He crossed his hands rigidly over his chest, with fingers intertwined. "You can go, now . . .

back to Pompeii. You were watching my hands when I was talking. It might interest you to know, that you'll find most of those gestures in Greek paintings in Sicily . . . yes, they go back that far. Do you know what this means?" He bit his forefinger with an expression of anger, and she raised her eyebrows in alarm.

"No," she admitted, reluctant to hear the answer.

"It means if you leave Pompeii again, and I get my teeth on you. . . ."

"I think I understand." She rose uncertainly, and his eyes followed her to the door.

"Just so you won't be led into temptation, I'm sending two of my guardian angels to watch over you. I'm not relying on the local police again. *Capisce?* I'm not joking, you know."

He waved his arm in a gesture of dismissal and went back to scanning the newspapers again.

When the carabinieri car she was riding in pulled up in front of her hotel, neither Antonio nor Ian was there to meet her. The Ray was parked in the lot, but when she inquired for Ian at the desk, she was told he had been gone for several hours. She gained silent permission from Vizzini's two officers to go upstairs to her room. Apparently, they were not going to sit right outside her door, anyway. She showered and changed her clothes. Though she was bone-tired and depressed she wanted to see her friends, and it was time for the midday meal. She had not had anything but the half cup of corrosive coffee in Vizzini's office since the evening before. Though she was not really hungry she sat down at a table in the outdoor restaurant and ordered a bowl of soup. The carabinieri took a nearby table and were soon launched into their biggest meal of the day, while Joyce watched the busy little square outside the hotel for her friends.

Her searching eyes were soon rewarded by the sight of

Ian and Antonio leaving the excavation, deep in conversation. So much for jealousy, she thought, but she got a nervous feeling in her stomach and put her spoon aside. She was sipping fitfully at a glass of milk when they saw her and strolled, without haste, to join her. Ian's blue eyes were cold and scathing.

"Good afternoon," he said politely . . . too politely . . . as though he were addressing a casual acquaintance. "I see you brought company along with you."

He was looking at the two carabinieri, who were just out of hearing. "I couldn't help it. Captain Vizzini sent them," she said; then, tentatively, "Did you get your car back all right?"

Antonio did not greet her at all. His lowered lashes hid his eyes, but she did not like the sharp arch of his eyebrows.

"Yes, thank you," Ian said, unfolding his napkin. "I must have left the keys in the ignition. Nothing to worry about, really . . . it's only worth six thousand pounds." He turned his attention back to Antonio, who had remained silent during the brief exchange. "The thing that interested me most, I think, was the Cryptoporticus. It's the only room I saw on a subterranean level. What on earth was it used for?"

Antonio responded like a good guide, but without his customary enthusiasm. "From the paintings on the walls it must have been some kind of dining hall, larger than most. The vaulted ceiling rising from the capitals indicates it was an important room. But part of it was being used as a storage space and part as a cistern, when the eruption occurred. It was probably in the process of restoration. The remains of several masons were found there. . . ."

"Essentially, though, it was a cellar?"

Antonio's shrug was apathetic. "A cellar that had been something else and was in the process of becoming something else again. There was wine stored there, but there were masons at work. The whole design of the Crypto-porticus is unique . . . the caryatids supporting the ceiling, the painting from the *Iliad*."

Joyce listened in confusion. She could understand St. John's displeasure over the car, but they were both completely ignoring her. No one had asked if she was all right or even referred to her awful experience in Das's garden. Vizzini had mentioned they were angry, but she had not expected anything like this. She thought they were her friends. The wound on her head, which she had almost forgotten, began to throb again painfully, but she could not distinguish the feeling from anger.

"Look," she said, "I'm sorry about the car. But I had to get to that house again while we still had the chance. I don't know what's bothering you, but I can't stand this silent treatment. I knew neither of you would go with me . . . you said so yourself!"

St. John placed their dinner order. Antonio stared with fascination at his own clasped hands. "You did a very stupid thing," he said at last.

"I know that, now! How was I to know I was being followed, though? We haven't had any trouble like that for. . . ."

"Followed?" St. John said in mock surprise. "Someone was waiting in that garden, probably to get at Das. Antonio's right . . . you were a bloody idiot. And furthermore," he added, scanning her face, ". . . you look like hell. You'd better go to your room and sleep it off."

Upsetting her milk glass in her haste to leave the table, Joyce fled from under the green arbor without looking back, and took the stairs two at a time. The door to her room had hardly slammed behind her before she was face-down on her bed, sobbing and pounding her fists.

The next morning the knock on her door was so diffident that Joyce thought it was the waiter come to reclaim her tray. She had taken both supper and breakfast in her room, and she was making the bed herself. She was not yet ready to face either Ian or Antonio again after yesterday afternoon. When she opened the door slightly, she was still in her robe, and the sight of Nonno Casale standing in the hall made her check to see if it was buttoned before she threw the door wide and embraced the old man. She pulled him into the room, and he seemed both surprised and pleased. His was the first friendly face she had seen since her return yesterday; even the hotel staff was a little standoffish with the carabinieri on guard. Joyce had not seen Nonno Casale since that one disastrous visit to his home.

"Nonno!" she exclaimed, hugging him again, unaware that she was calling him "grandfather," as Antonio did. "Please . . . sit down. Would you like some coffee? It's still a little warm. . . ."

He raised his gnarled hand, shook his head with a smile. "To be in the room of a pretty girl at my age is enough," he said, and pressed his fist to his chest as though to hold his heart in place. "Too much maybe . . . at my age. Why is it, a few clothes make a woman so much more exciting . . . than those 'bikini' things?"

She laughed and pulled her robe over her knees as she took the other chair. "How did you get in to see me? There are policemen downstairs, you know."

"Only one *segugio* now. Maybe he thought I was a workman. He did not stop me. He did not look." But the smile left his face, and his dark eyes, shrewd and lively, showed concern. "Are you all right?"

The question, when it was finally asked by someone, nearly brought the tears back. "Yes," she said, rubbing her head. "A bump, that's all. But Antonio's very angry with me. . . ."

"He told me what happened last night. Angry? So that is what it is? He is hard to live with these days, that one. You could have been killed," the old man said, staring at her mournfully.

"Tell me," Joyce asked, "did the police come to your place the other day? Day before yesterday, I mean."

He nodded. "They came there. A captain of the carabinieri, they said. I was not there."

"And the signora?"

"She was minding the shop, but she said she had to go out for something. She was not there, either." His eyes narrowed thoughtfully; they reminded her of Antonio's. "Why do you ask this?"

"No reason. I just hadn't heard, that's all. Your grandson isn't speaking to me. He's giving Major St. John tours of the excavation instead. . . ."

Silence fell between them. She realized she had not given the old man a chance to say why he had come. He sat without speaking, clasping his hands on his withered thighs. At last, he took something out of his pocket and extended it to her with a shoving motion. It was a small box. Her first thought was that he had come upon some new clue to finding the scroll, and she opened it quickly: a lovely cameo lay inside, with the urn engraved in delicate white relief against the rosy-beige background of the helmet shell.

"It's beautiful," she said inadequately, "but, Nonno, I haven't found the urn. . . ."

"I made it for you. I was going to give it when all this was over. I give it to you now, instead."

"It's the most beautiful gift I've ever had," she said, deeply touched. "And you made it . . . just for me?"

"For when it was all over," he repeated. He leaned forward and patted her hand. "It was a nice dream. But it is all over now."

"What do you mean?" she said with renewed enthusiasm. "We're going to find it! I haven't given up yet. I know the police weren't supposed to get into it, but that's just for a little while. They don't know a thing! As soon as this other thing's settled, as soon as we get rid of them. . . ."

"No." His voice was firm. "It's too dangerous. Your life is more important than the scroll."

He rose heavily to his feet, as though some of the spirit had gone out of him, but he attempted to smile. "You have your urn there," he indicated the cameo. "It is enough. The scroll"—he shrugged—"it does not matter. Maybe it was just a list of earnings from a bordello, huh? Maybe it was something improper. You will not look for it again."

"I won't let you do this for me," she said. "I won't do anything dangerous again. . . ."

"For you . . . for my grandson. You are young. What does a theft so long ago really matter? It is not worth a life. No," he said stubbornly when she started to speak, "it is over. *Finite.* No more urn . . . no more scroll."

Chapter Fourteen

Joyce threw on her clothes and went looking for Ian St. John. He was nowhere downstairs, though his car was in the lot. There was a different carabiniere on guard . . . only one; they must be changing shifts, she thought. But why just one? Captain Vizzini had promised her two "guardian angels," and she knew he was a man of his word. When she asked at the desk, the formerly friendly clerk told her, with considerable reserve, that Major St. John was still in his room. She had not thought to look there; they had always met downstairs. The attitude of the clerk gave her something to frown over. Good Lord, she thought, with all this police interference, how the hotel must want them out of here! She cursed Vizzini's surveillance with all her heart.

Forgetting she was under a ban of silence, she knocked briskly at St. John's door. He answered it without a shirt; apparently he had seen no reason to get dressed, either. His tea tray was still on his night table, but his bed was neatly and efficiently made. He had just finished shaving and when he saw her he snapped the towel in his hand back into neat folds and hung it on the rack beside the washbasin. Since he had left the door open, Joyce accepted it as an invitation to enter.

"Antonio's grandfather was just here," she said. "He's called off the search for the urn. He was pretty firm about it."

"That's very ironic," St. John said with a gleam of humor in his blue eyes. "I've had a cable from my uncle . . . asking why the hell he hasn't had any results. I've been lying here trying to think of how to answer him in ten words or less. . . ."

The words gave Joyce new hope. "I'd forgotten about him! It really isn't all in Nonno's hands, now, is it? Stanton has the last word. After all, the urn belongs to him!"

"From the look of things it isn't in anyone's hands. Are the carabinieri still patrolling the halls?"

"There's only one of them now."

He laughed. "The other's probably having a rather repetitious tour of Pompeii. It's a good thing Antonio doesn't have a standard spiel: he might become self-conscious. They'll be watching him, too, you know." He glanced at her over his shoulder, and his face softened. "How are you? I was a little brusque yesterday. . . ."

"It was . . . understandable, I guess," she said, grateful to be speaking with him again. "I *was* careless with the car. I didn't realize I'd left the keys in it. I had things on my mind."

"Yes . . . cat-burgling in blue jeans. Hardly what I'd have expected of you. To hell with the car, Joyce: Stanton smashes up two of them a year. It was the only way I could say. . . . Oh, you damned little fool! When Vizzini called I thought I was going to die. Was it really very terrible in that tomb? You had no right to take such a chance. . . ."

"Why is everyone so concerned about me all of a sudden? I've been on my own for a long time." But her face was reflective when she thought about the sarcophagus. "Yes, it was pretty awful. . . ."

His smile was compassionate. "You have initiative, darling . . . and you have guts," he said, buttoning his shirt. "But you don't have much sense. Now what do you say we take a walk around the village? A few days of that should drive the other carabiniere out of his mind." He put his hand on her shoulder and gave it a squeeze as he locked the door behind them. "Been on your own! Jesus, I have to reach down to touch you! Anyone as small as you are should have someone to look after her."

As Ian became more protective Joyce found it difficult not to lean on him. The days wore by without any removal of the guard, and their situation was somewhat less than pleasant. They wondered what Captain Vizzini was doing in Rome; for all they knew, he might have reached the point of gathering evidence against them. Joyce was reluctant to write a letter to her consulate unless charges were actually brought against them, because they would remember the trouble in Greece. St. John's military status prevented him from contacting his consulate. Until Vizzini made a move they were living in limbo; and in southern Italy in August, limbo becomes very hot.

Although Antonio still stopped by to have a drink with them every evening, he did not mention the urn again. But Joyce spent most of her time in the more congenial, relaxed company of Ian St. John. They drove their carabiniere guard slowly mad by taking frequent strolls into the village, or around the countryside, without leaving the commune designated "Pompeii."

Joyce had four letters during this period, and the carabiniere, whom she had come to know by his first name, Paolo, did not bother to check any of them. His orders, apparently, were just to keep her in Pompeii, not to pry. Three of the communications were from foreign museums, answers to the inquiries she had sent: none of them had any information to offer, except for negative reports that they knew nothing of such an urn. The other letter was from her student, John Gardner, who had finally made it home to California by hitchhiking across the country; at least he was all right, and preparing for the fall semester by making repairs on his motorcycle. Everything that had happened to him in Europe had been wiped out of his mind by his meanderings across America. He was looking forward to seeing her the following month, when classes began.

That gave her something else to think about. There had been no word from the university canceling her contract. It was a rather liberal institution, and maybe the trustees were more open-minded than she had imagined. She had to make a decision very soon. She doubted that she had the funds to survive in Europe for the winter. Perhaps the decision was not in her own hands. There was still Vizzini, and she doubted that the university, liberal though it was, would swallow him or his charges.

"How do you write to your department head and tell him, 'I may be a little late for the beginning of the semester. I'm under suspicion of murder in Italy'?" Joyce asked Ian one evening, pushing a strand of hair from her forehead. "This whole thing's getting worse and worse. . . ."

Then Antonio joined them. He did not speak until he had taken a long drink of lemon soda . . . with ice . . . and when he did, it was St. John he addressed. "The custodians are getting alarmed," he said. "Two weeks of that carabiniere stalking the excavation is making them nervous. He can't walk right along with me on my tours, so he roams around, just within sight of me, inspecting everything. Rumors are spreading. First, they said something had been stolen . . . and everyone, custodians and guides, began to look everything over more carefully. Now," he laughed, "it's a bomb threat! Some lunatic's trying to blow up the ruins, and the carabiniere is there to protect the site. How long can this go on?"

"Until Vizzini's bagged someone, I guess," St. John smiled. "I've been waiting to talk to you. I thought all of us should discuss it together. I've had a rather peculiar communication."

He took a square, off-white envelope from his pocket. The bond of the paper was elegant, and it appeared to contain a card. Joyce wondered why he had not mentioned it to her earlier, when the mail had arrived.

"It's from a man named Aramidian," Ian said, extracting the printed card from the envelope passing it to Antonio. Joyce and Antonio looked at one another. "It's an invitation to an auction at Das's place. I don't know why he sent it to me, or how he even knew I was here. Does it make any sense to you?"

"A little," Joyce said. "He's a very shady-type art dealer in Rome."

"The auction's to take place on Thursday night at nine," Antonio read. "That's only three days away! He's written something by hand at the bottom. I can't make it out. . . ."

"Neither could I," St. John said. "It looks like Arabic."

"Let me see it," Joyce said. She was curious. It was the first actual reply they had had from a dealer, and it had come addressed to St. John. She puzzled over the loose handwriting a moment and decided it was in English after all. " 'There will be something of invest . . . no, *interest* . . . to your uncle here. You may . . . bring . . . a friend, if you wish.' " Her heart began to beat hard. "Ian . . . I think it's an invitation to a closed auction! Antonio, you remember. . . ."

"Yes. The kind Das spoke about. Either he's decided to sell his collection, or. . . ."

"He implied he might have to!" she cried. "He was talking about selling the sarcophagi the day we were there. He even admitted his finances weren't in very good shape."

"Or?" St. John asked, prodding Antonio to finish his idea.

"It could be a trap. Joyce was nearly killed at that house."

"The villa was put under police protection the next morning. Das wouldn't dream of holding such an auction if the carabinieri were still there."

Antonio's eyes narrowed. "He called them for protection. He could call them off again. . . ."

"Maybe he's decided his collection's too dangerous to keep," St. John considered. "If he got rid of the damned thing, he wouldn't need the police. You know, for a man who doesn't believe in death, Das is pretty cautious."

They all stared silently at the neat card on the table. Joyce was the first to stir. She glanced at the two carabinieri, who had regrouped under the arbor for a cold drink after a hot day's work. Paolo looked her way and smiled. Though he did not speak English, they had become rather friendly: he deplored her attempts at Italian and corrected her politely whenever he could. She smiled back at him: he was a nice young man on a boring job.

"There's only one thing Johnnie Aramidian might think would be of interest to you," she said to St. John. "We sent him a letter, you know. And he wants you to 'bring a friend' who can verify the object. He wants to sell the urn back to Stanton, for as much as he can get. He's a real creep. He wears a wide gold bracelet. . . ."

"I don't like it," Antonio said, and St. John himself looked uneasy.

"You think he wants me to bring you?" he asked Joyce. "Darling, for some reason you're the most popular girl in the art world these days."

She winced inwardly at the term of endearment he had

been using so naturally lately, but Antonio registered no interest or surprise. She stared hopelessly at his impassive face as he studied the card: at his long eyes hidden by his lashes, the fine, chiseled lips, the lock of dark hair falling over his faintly lined forehead. She had not noticed that the squint lines from the sun at the corners of his eyes were permanent when his face was in repose. "Aramidian has the urn," she said.

Though she lowered her voice, fearing Antonio's reaction, her statement was not received with silence. His green eyes filled with sudden, pensive animation. He had not given up entirely on finding the urn, either, she realized.

"This whole thing," Antonio said, shaking the card in his hand, "may be nothing more than it appears. If Aramidian has it, and he's selling Das's collection anyway, it's the best way to get a good price from Stanton, with St. John acting as his intermediary."

"Then . . . we're going?" Joyce asked, unable to contain her enthusiasm. "We have to get out of here to attend that auction! But . . . how can we get rid of them?" She smiled again at the friendly carabiniere, feeling a little guilty.

"I've never tried it before," St. John said, "but do you think they could be bribed?"

But Antonio only laughed. *"Gesù,* my friend, don't try it! Almost anyone else in the country, but not them! If they weren't incorruptible, they wouldn't have been around for so many years." He shook his head rapidly at the thought. "You'd be in jail in a minute. No, there must be another way for you and me to go. . . ."

" 'You and me?' " Joyce asked suspiciously. "No! I'm going, too!"

"You aren't going," Antonio said firmly, with the stern glance of his grandfather. "I can identify the urn as well as you. We aren't really sure what we're getting into."

"He's right, Joyce," St. John agreed. "We can't let you

go to that place again. I should think the very thought would frighten you half to death. Be a good girl, now, so we can discuss this thing."

"A good girl," she said sarcastically. "Don't take that tone with *me*, Major. I suppose you think it's perfectly all right for you two to leave here against Vizzini's orders and wind up in jail . . . or . . . worse. . . ." She paused, remembering Vizzini's parting words, the way he had bitten his hand in warning, and what he had said about Antonio's going to prison. Suddenly, she became very calm. "None of us is going," she said flatly. "Let's forget the whole thing. Antonio's grandfather's right."

"Nonno's right about *you*!" he said, his voice rising. He glanced at the officers and lowered it again. "Don't be a stupid female, now. This is something we must do. We can take care of ourselves. *You're staying here.*"

"Is that your last word on the subject? You're determined to go?" she asked coolly.

"Yes." The green eyes were steady, determined, and she turned to St. John.

"Yes," he said. "Hell, I want to see what's going on!"

Joyce gave a little sigh and rose from her chair.

"Where are you going?"

"I'm going to talk to Paolo," she said. "I'm going to tell him you're planning to escape."

Blue anger rose to St. John's eyes. "You're *what*?"

"I'm not going to let you go, that's all."

They stared at her in disbelief. Then St. John grabbed her hand and thrust her, most urgently, back into her chair.

"All right," he said testily, "you can come, too. We'll all go. Goddammit! How does the world keep spinning with women on the planet?"

Antonio wandered desolately into the arbor the next evening, accompanied by his carabiniere guard, Sergeant

Bruno. They were discussing cars, and the carabiniere, who was about Antonio's age, shook his head sympathetically over the eccentricities of a six-year-old Fiat.

"Next time," he waved as they parted to go to their own tables, "get a Vespa, huh? You can do the maintenance on that yourself."

With a beer before him, Antonio poured out his troubles loudly to St. John. "My damn car burned out on me on the way to work this morning! Sergeant Bruno had to call a tow truck. Do you know what that's going to cost?" He ran his hand frantically through his hair. "They took it to that garage on the Salerno road . . . you know, where all the smashed up Fiats are? The mechanic's a real bastard. Twenty thousand lire, and I won't have it back for a week! The whole wiring system's gone."

Joyce and St. John knew that the mechanic was Antonio's boyhood friend, Guiseppe, that the fuse from under the dashboard was in Antonio's pocket, and that he had poured oil on the manifold before Sergeant Bruno had breakfasted, so that it would smoke when the car heated up. But they expressed appropriate concern.

"Rotten luck," St. John said. "May I give you a lift home in the Ray?"

Antonio shook his head, an expression of envy on his face. "With a car like that, you don't have to worry. I feel like junking mine. Well, I'd better start walking. I'll see you tomorrow, I guess. *Ciao*."

Joyce knew that the engine of the Fiat was tuned like a Stradivarius: Antonio did all the work on it himself. They would not get the speed out of it that they could have had from the Ray, but it would be impossible to slip the sleek British automobile out from under the noses of the guards. By tomorrow, the day of the auction, the paint would be dry on the Fiat, and it would be parked just off the Naples–Salerno road, heading in a northerly direction.

Their only problem was to elude both carabinieri in broad daylight and make it to Rome by nine o'clock that night.

Apparently distraught over his mechanical catastrophe, Antonio moodily left the excavation at one, telling Sergeant Bruno he did not feel like working: besides, it was too damned hot. Though it was the best time of year for tourists, the heat was enough to make a guide sick when he stayed out in it all day, he said. Sergeant Bruno was more than agreeable: his jacket had perspiration stains on the light khaki. It was time to eat anyway, something light, perhaps, like a salad. Would Antonio join him? No, he would have a cool drink with his friends and go home to dine. Instead, he lingered for a meal with Joyce and St. John, while the carabinieri ate in silence, wiping the sweat from their faces with white handkerchiefs. Their military hats were nearly steaming.

Joyce began to droop as she ate. Even her hair was damp: she had seen to that before leaving her room in her new peach dress. She appeared to become ill and distressed, could not finish eating. She finally excused herself and went upstairs. Her friend Paolo rose suddenly and came over to inquire about her.

"Is the signorina ill?" he asked Antonio in Italian. Antonio, too, appeared concerned.

"It's the heat, I think. She's gone to her room to rest." Then, as the young carabiniere turned away, "Excuse me . . . it is all right if the major and I go up to his room? It's too uncomfortable here to talk."

Paolo considered the request for a moment: if they went upstairs, he and his companion could also get in out of the heat. "*Va bene.* Just let us know when you're going home, so Bruno can go with you. This is one hell of a place. In Rome, at least, there are fountains. . . ."

Joyce awaited them in St. John's room. St. John locked the door. In order to get out of the hotel without going downstairs again, they would have to climb down one story from St. John's balcony, through the thick growth of blazing bougainvillea on that side of the building. St. John paused only long enough to put on a tie and jacket; Antonio's jacket was already in the car. He had worn his best trousers this morning, and his jacket would cover the short sleeves of his white shirt.

"All right, now," St. John said, drawing in his breath. "I go first. Antonio, wait a few minutes, in case someone sees me; then hand Joyce down to me. Remember to use the bougainvillea as cover us much as possible. Wait a few minutes more . . . and then you come."

The thin, gnarled branches of the vine snagged at Joyce's dress as she hung from the balcony grasping Antonio's strong hands. Her feet groped for the security of St. John's grip, but she did not feel anything.

When it became evident that St. John could not reach her, he whispered hoarsely, "Drop her, Antonio . . . I'll catch!"

Antonio's hands released her, and St. John's arms closed around her legs. Joyce slid through his arms until they were at her waist, where he held her momentarily. A second later, Antonio thumped to the ground beside them, landing in a half crouch. St. John dropped Joyce almost immediately, and she smoothed her dress, uncertain of the expression in Antonio's eyes.

They set out toward where the car was waiting. The Fiat, pale-blue now, and shining, looked years less than its age; and for the second time in weeks Joyce enjoyed the total luxury of a seat to herself.

"That was easy," she breathed when they had lost themselves in the traffic headed toward Naples. Then she thought of the two carabinieri back at the hotel. "They won't get into trouble, will they?"

St. John said grimly from the back seat, "I wouldn't like

to be in their shoes when they have to report to Vizzini. It'll take awhile before they miss us . . . and then they won't know where we are."

"It was too easy," Antonio said, without taking his gaze from the suicidal freeway. "I said they couldn't be bought . . . but Johnnie Aramidian may have other ways."

"What do you mean?" Joyce asked.

"There *is* such a thing as organized crime, and O'Keefe even warned us that Johnnie 'might be into something else' . . ."

"Nonsense," St. John said. "Don't make extra problems for us. Our getaway was just well planned, that's all. We're clever people!"

Antonio might be right about Aramidian, Joyce thought. She had not liked the man at all. And if he had the urn, how had he been able to find it so quickly, unless he had a widespread network to help him?

He was a man to be watched.

Chapter Fifteen

A number of automobiles were already parked along the dark road when they arrived at the villa. The gate had been oiled and repaired, and the front hedges cut back. The work improved the front of the house considerably, but anything would have been an improvement, Joyce thought. She wondered whether anything had been done to the inside garden, of which she had such unpleasant memories. Was her sarcophagus still there, or was it, too, going on sale tonight?

Admittance was not as easy as they had anticipated. None of Das's servants were around, and the man who answered the door, wearing a tuxedo, inspected the invitation carefully. He noticed at once that there was one guest too many and questioned Antonio.

"Tell him," St. John said, "that I'm accompanied by an expert and my interpreter. I don't speak Italian."

But that was not enough. He left them standing in the

terra-cotta hall while he sought out Aramidian. The sight of the dealer at the door of the parlor discussing the matter made Joyce more apprehensive.

"Do you think he'll recognize me?" she asked Antonio.

"Why should he? All you did was scare hell out of him a few weeks ago," he said, looking worried, too. "Put on your glasses."

She reached in her handbag and slipped the metal-rimmed reading glasses on before Johnnie Aramidian approached them with his assistant. The dealer did not look any more respectable in his tuxedo, and Joyce noted with distaste that the wide gold bracelet was still on his wrist.

Aware that Aramidian spoke English, St. John immediately put on a pretense of haughty indignation. "This is absurd," he said. "I'm Lord Willoughby's heir: my actions have never been questioned. At your invitation, sir, I'm here on my uncle's behalf. I've a good mind to leave!"

"No," Aramidian said smoothly, "no. Your expert . . . and your interpreter . . . are welcome. If you would like to join the others"—he indicated the open parlor door—"you'll find an excellent brandy on the table. I deeply regret this . . . inconvenience." His black eyes shot a threatening glance at his unnerved assistant.

"Thank you," St. John said crisply, and marched at once toward the parlor, accompanied by his nervous entourage.

The room did not look the way it had on previous occasions. All the furniture had been removed to accommodate rows of plush-cushioned straight chairs, and a dais had been set up in front of the fireplace, with a velvet-draped table the only article upon it. Even the portrait of the smiling cavalier was gone. There were already perhaps thirty people in the room, all of them men.

Still feigning indignation, St. John accepted drinks for all three of them, and led by Joyce, who wanted to see if the sarcophagi were still in the garden, they sat next to the French windows, which were open to ventilate the warm room. A list of the objects to be auctioned had been placed on every chair, but Joyce studied the faces of the other guests before she looked at it. There was no one there she recognized. No introductions were made, and most of the men sat alone, though a few were accompanied by guests. Some of them seemed to know each other, at least by sight: an occasional remote, almost jealous nod passed between them. Apparently not everyone who had been invited had arrived, or chosen to attend. Blocks of chairs stood empty throughout the room. But perhaps it had been planned that way, Joyce thought, to leave some space between the collectors, who did not seem a very gregarious lot.

"Etruscan urn, sixth century B.C.," Antonio read from the list, and Joyce looked quickly at her own.

"It doesn't say anything about its being sealed," she whispered.

"No. If he has located it without the seal, this is all for nothing. There's a bronze statue, also 'possibly Etruscan,' being auctioned earlier," he said. "Joyce, you don't suppose. . . ?"

She shook her head. "Whoever took mine wanted it for himself. There aren't any Indian pieces listed . . . and Das isn't around. Do you suppose he just lent his villa for the night?"

"Or maybe he gave it up altogether," St. John said. "The painting's gone. He was running scared, I think. Maybe he's just vanished."

"It's crazy," she said, "but I'd feel better if he were here."

Finally, a face appeared that Joyce recognized from newspaper photographs: Alberto Grossman, New York, one-time smuggler, full-time gallery owner, accompanied by a younger man who seemed to be an assistant. It was the younger man who got their drinks while Grossman sat down heavily near the front of the room, reading the prospectus through his glasses as though he were studying a menu.

Nine o'clock passed, and the auction did not begin: something was holding it up. Antonio checked his watch twice in fifteen minutes and looked toward the door. "I don't think this is the way things are done," he said. "There must be important buyers here. They must be waiting for someone special. . . ."

"But who?" Joyce wondered. "These people are all rich . . . why keep them waiting?"

Antonio turned to St. John. "Saying you were Lord Willoughby's heir was a good touch. I don't think we'd have been admitted without it."

"It's true," St. John said carelessly. "Not that it means anything . . . after the death taxes. Besides, I hope the old blighter lives to be a hundred. You know, if Das did leave, he left the Roman tombs behind . . . see, out there in the garden?"

"I noticed," Joyce said. "Probably too heavy to transport. Count Luigi left them, too. . . ."

Their conversation was interrupted by a stir in the hall, elaborate salutations in Italian, and the fall of many feet on the fine red tiles. Everyone in the room, in varying stages of irritation over the delay, turned to look at the door.

Five men in Via Condotti clothing that perfectly fit their bodies, but not their faces, entered together and walked swiftly to one of the blocks of chairs, which apparently had been reserved for them. Joyce studied them closely as they passed, but none of them was a personage whose picture was familiar to her; in fact, most of the faces were common, almost tough, as though these men had come up the hard way. One very large man had pockmarks on his face, and the smallest among them did not bother to remove his hat. He wore the kind of dark glasses that no one can glimpse through, and the candelabra above emphasized

their irridescent sheen. Once seated, he slouched down in
his chair, with one leg crossed over the other. If there had
been room between the rows, she was sure he would have
put his Ferragamo shoes on the chair in front of him. One
of the other men had already attempted to do so. Only one
thing about the men was certain: they were all Italians, of
an unrefined class. She turned at once to Antonio. "Who
are they? They look like members of the. . . ."

"Don't even say it!" he replied. "*Gesù*, I was right! Just
keep cool . . . and remain inconspicuous." He leaned toward St. John. "Whatever they bid on . . . don't outbid
them. Not even on the urn."

When the "royalty" was finally seated, the bidding
began. A painting was put up by Aramidian, and all Joyce
caught out of the Italian description was "Marcelle" and
"Toulouse-Lautrec." On the prospectus it was listed simply
as "Impressionist painting." The bidding was too involved
for her to follow, consisting of a series of hand signs that
St. John, at least, seemed to understand. An old man in
dark clothes seemed to be bidding against the man in sunglasses, though, and Aramidian lowered his gavel and said,
"*A Signor Ummari, per.* . . ." The number of lire was
so complicated that Joyce turned again to Antonio for
assistance.

"Over five thousand dollars . . ."

St. John glanced around to make sure no one heard him.
"It's increased in value since it was . . . borrowed . . . from
the Kyoto Museum in 1968. One of Interpol's failures.
We're at the sort of auction we thought we were. . . ."

Antonio straightened and leaned forward, interested and
startled, and Joyce's glance followed his to the next item
on display, a portrait of a woman listed merely as "Renais-
sance painting."

"It's a Raphael!" he nearly exclaimed aloud. "My God,
where did they get it?"

"Right here in Italy, in 1970," St. John replied, putting

up his hand for silence. "Christ, I've bid on the damned thing! And I don't have that kind of money. . . ."

But the bidding rose steadily, and St. John kept his hands folded in his lap while it continued. Once again, the man in the hat outbid everyone else, but with no real appreciation evident in his manner. Joyce did not like him, nor any of the thugs surrounding him.

"One million," Antonio sighed.

"Lire?"

"Dollars." He looked as though he were about to cry. "Something should be done about this . . . that painting is priceless!"

She remembered what Lyman Churchman had said about the current investment in art: it was more stable than gold on the market and continued to increase in value. She was watching that kind of investment in action; it was like looking in on the stock exchange. Signor Ummari had no interest at all in what he was buying: the paintings were an investment. The only satisfaction he was achieving was in making himself appear a bigger man than he was. His complete lack of appreciation for art dispelled in her mind the last hope that he was really someone respectable, perhaps an Italian movie director. Italian directors were artists themselves.

Her mind wandered as less impressive objects went up, and some of the other collectors gathered a few crumbs. One elderly man had interested her slightly from the time they had entered the room, and she watched while he bid on some of Aramidian's Anatolian pots. He was so bald that the light from the chandelier reflected from his skull. His nationality was impossible to distinguish, but his companion, a younger, dark-haired man with soft eyes and a nose that slanted in an even line directly from his forehead, was unmistakably Greek. The nose was almost classical. But the bald man was a cautious bidder, a connoisseur. He let most of the Turkish pottery go to someone else, until a really fine, undamaged object was displayed. Then he bid almost recklessly and always got what he wanted, clapping his companion on the shoulder when he did so. His name was not mentioned at the completion of a sale.

"I wish we were closer to those two," she said. "I'd like to know who he is."

She found out, but in a way that left her shaking. The "bronze statue, possibly Etruscan," was put on the velvet-draped table, and she nearly cried out when she saw it. St. John had to hold her down.

"For Christ's sake," he said in a tight whisper, "don't blow it now."

"Bid on it," Antonio said, forgetting his former warning. "Please, for Joyce's sake . . ."

But it was Joyce herself who would not allow it. She shook her head slowly. "No," she said more calmly. "There's something wrong with it . . . the feet are facing the wrong way. It isn't mine. God, I'd like to get a better look at it, though!"

The bald man with the straight-nosed companion got red in the face and lost all caution when the bidding began. His first bid was high enough to interest the man in sunglasses, who had been polishing his nails on his jacket and studying them critically. He knew nothing about art, but obviously this statue was something of value. He made a bid, which attracted several others, including one from Alberto Grossman. The ugly little statue, so much like Joyce's that she wanted to study it more closely, smiled down on all of them. Even Aramidian seemed surprised at the turn the bids had taken on the pitted, corroded object, but he rallied swiftly. His deft fingers stroked the smiling face as he extolled the merits of the piece in both Italian and English. Joyce knew the statue was valueless, except for its history: she wished she could have it dated.

When the bidding narrowed down to the bald old man, whose neck was almost purple with agitation, and the cold, haughty Signor Ummari, she found herself being drawn into the excitement. She did not want either of them to have it, but if there was a choice, she favored the bald man over the relentless Italian: the old man, at least, seemed to like what he was buying. The completion of the sale took place too fast for her to follow it. Signor Ummari conferred briefly with one of his companions and stopped bidding. When the gavel fell forcefully, Aramidian cried out in his excitement, "Sold to Signor Karavitas for . . ." at the same time the bald man said in Greek, "At last, I have a pair!"

He turned his head slightly, and suddenly Joyce recognized him: Karavitas was the man she had met at Mrs. Amboy's masquerading as "Professor Arapkilos"! Only he had not been bald then; perhaps he had worn a wig . . . or had he shaved his head later? As upset as she was, she decided it had been a wig. Priapos Karavitas was an older man and his own hair would be white: but with a wig he had become the middle-aged Dr. Arapkilos. She slouched down in her chair. Though she was trembling with anger, she did not want him to see her here. He was the one man in the room who was sure to recognize her, and after the declaration he had just made, she was in a hazardous position. He had already gone to a lot of trouble to protect the statue he had stolen from her.

St. John brought Joyce a brandy while Antonio tried to console her during the intermission that followed the sale. Everyone was drained. Johnnie Aramidian, who had nearly gone hoarse during the bidding, paused to have a drink with Signor Ummari and his unwholesome friends. Joyce was shaking all over: she wanted to cry. Karavitas was right here—in the same room. He had admitted he had her statue, and there was nothing she could do about it.

"I'll report him to Captain Vizzini," she said with the brandy snifter trembling in her hands.

Antonio touched her shoulder gently. "You do that," he comforted her. "He'll take care of everything."

"I hope she doesn't get the chance," St. John said with asperity. "What are we going to do about him, anyway? Go back to Pompeii and say we had a night on the town? Look, we're out of our class here, in more ways than one: we don't have enough money, and I don't like the look of that Signor What's-his-name and his henchmen. What do you say we get Joyce out of here? Go back and face the music, whatever tune the captain plays. Maybe reporting the Greek will save our souls."

Joyce swallowed the brandy and cradled the glass in her hands. "No. We came to see the urn and we're going to *see* it, at least. If you don't act too eager, maybe we can afford it. You saw what happened just now. The Anatolian pots, four thousand years old, went for almost nothing. It was Karavitas who raised the bids on the statue by showing his interest." Her voice was bitter. "If we're going to jail for coming here, let's get something out of it, at least."

Half an hour later, the *bucchero* urn stood, black and dull, on the velvet-draped table. They were close enough to make out the detail, and her eyes met Antonio's briefly: they agreed, the decoration was identical to that of the urn in the Casale papers. But they couldn't tell whether or not it was still sealed. Joyce did not dare make a move out of fear of attracting the interest of the collectors, but Antonio yawned and stretched his arms behind his head: he rose and manipulated his shoulders as though they were cramped. Then, with an apologetic smile to the men seated several rows behind them, he resumed his seat.

"No clay," he reported, "but there has been some."

St. John shrugged in mild dejection and looked away from the stricken faces of his friends. "Shall I bid on it?"

"Yes . . . but nothing excessive," Joyce replied with disappointment. "If we can't have what we want, we might at least get the urn for your uncle."

The opening bid was a surprising three hundred dollars, and it rose quickly when both Grossman and Karavitas made motions; then someone raised it to a thousand, and St. John stopped bidding. As he had said, they were outclassed financially in this company. Joyce realized that several people in the room had received her letters, to say nothing of what might have been spread around the art world since. When the bidding began, there was already a good deal of interest in the black *bucchero* urn. And like a hunting dog, Signor Ummari caught the scent. When he started bidding, Joyce knew everything was over. She motioned for St. John and Antonio to stay behind and slipped out into the garden; after all that had happened tonight, she wanted to be alone. She deserved a good cry.

Tears were already in her eyes when her feet found the narrow path between the sarcophagi, and were flowing freely down her face by the time she reached the secure darkness of the far one, near the ivied wing that had contained Das's collection. The Pompeii Scroll was lost forever. Someone had opened the urn years ago, probably without realizing what was inside. There was no way to find it now.

Once beyond the light from the house, the garden was not so dark as it had seemed. The moon, on the wane now, still cast its blue light on the funereal enclosure. The moonlight turned out to be a blessing: it saved her from sitting down on what appeared at first to be a closed sarcophagus. But it was not closed. The lid had been shoved aside slightly. Conditioned by her previous experience here, her tears dried up and even her mouth went dry. This was not the tomb she had been in: that was covered again. Someone had been fooling around in the garden, had gone to all the trouble of removing the moss and soil from the third sarcophagus. Why?

She knelt to look inside, but without a flashlight could see nothing. Reluctantly, she began to grope with both hands in the dark interior. There was more than a Roman skeleton in this one, but her fingers could not interpret the objects within. Perhaps one of the gardeners had used it to store his equipment, though there had not been a gardener around in years. Only when her hands closed around a biconical, voluptuously rounded surface, did she realize what she had stumbled upon. But she couldn't be sure— until the moonlight revealed the *sealed*, dusty urn in her hands.

Count Luigi, she thought. You dear, morbid, smiling cavalier. You didn't sell *everything* before you went into the monastery. The urn, the scroll, were in her hands. She wanted to rush back to tell her friends, but she could not do that, not with the company inside. She examined the dull surface in the moonlight, wondering where she could conceal the urn for a few hours, so they could come back to get it later. Not inside the sarcophagus again, that was certain: someone had already been looking there. Behind the ivy? maybe if she put it under the heavy ivy, or in the deep weeds. . . .

The pressure between two of her ribs and another hand on the urn were simultaneous. The voice was low and deadly serious. "I'll have that, please. Make no mistake about it, this isn't a gun . . . it won't make any noise. It's an Italian switchblade. Have you ever seen one work?"

She had, as a matter of fact: the slightest pressure on the lever ejected the blade with unusual power and ferocity. She froze and tried to make out the figure of the man beside her, but it was too dark for that. She recognized the menace in his voice, but she could not release her hands from the urn: no one else was going to have it. If she tried to scream, the fierce blade would reach her heart instantly. A few hundred yards from a lighted room full of people, she would die quietly, perhaps to be shoved into a sarcophagus again.

"Give it to me!" the voice said with a shove that hurt her ribs. "Three people have already died for this . . . I've no compunctions about a fourth!"

He was going to kill her whatever she did, she realized. She did not recognize his voice, but he spoke English and he was about . . . six feet tall? He could not let her tell the police that. She still did not let go of the urn. It was just a knife in her ribs, she told herself: she knew exactly where it was in the darkness. She dropped to one side with a quick motion, holding onto the urn: the blade snapped out. She saw it flash in his hand as they struggled over the urn, felt it slash her arm as they grappled over the treasure. He was stronger than she was, and strength prevailed; the urn was wrenched out of her grasp, but not securely. It fell with a crash on the paving stones. Furious, her hand closed over the strap over her shoulder, and her handbag flew at his head. He reeled and fell. The knife clattered to the walk, and the man lay still on the ground. With a glance at the windows, Joyce dropped below the level of the high, sweet-smelling weeds and emptied her bag of everything but her wallet and passport. Meticulously scraping up the shards of pottery and fragments and flakes of papyrus, she eased them gently into her handbag. When all visible sign of them was gone, she went over the stones with her fingers, felt a tiny crumble of papyrus and sharp chips of urn she had missed. The man groaned.

Antonio appeared at the French doors. When he did not see her in the garden, he said something over his shoulder and was joined immediately by St. John. They rushed out into the garden. Joyce saw them, but before they reached her she was surrounded by Signor Ummari and his thugs: her heart nearly stopped beating. Behind them Antonio and St. John were struggling to get through, and she called to them to stay back. She rose with as much dignity as she could assume.

"If the gentleman on the ground is your friend," she said to Signor Ummari, "I'd like to report that he tried to kill me."

The knife on the walk glittered naked and sharp in the moonlight. Signor Ummari snapped his fingers, and the garden was suddenly illuminated by floodlights. The pock-marked man reached down to pick up the knife with a handkerchief as Signor Ummari removed his dark glasses wearily. There was only one pair of blue eyes like his in the world.

"Captain Vizzini!" Joyce cried, rushing to embrace him. "I've never been so glad to see anyone. . . . Get that man in there!" She pointed an accusing finger at the parlor. "Karavitas! He has my statue . . . he said that he has 'a pair' now!"

"Is he dead?" Vizzini asked of the man bending over the body on the walk. "Pleasant as this is"—he extricated himself from her arms with mild embarrassment—"we may still have a corpse on our hands, Dr. Lacey." He bent down to take the man's pulse and shook his head gravely. "You've really done it this time. . . ."

"But . . . he groaned," she said numbly. She moved to his side and looked down at him unbelievingly: "Lyman Churchman! But . . . he's such a nice man. He's the one who gave me the names of some of the collectors. . . ."

"Maybe we can call it self-defense," Vizzini considered; but at that moment Churchman groaned again.

"He's alive," Joyce said. "You knew he was alive! Damn you, Captain Vizzini, you nearly scared me to death!"

The world-weary eyes were momentarily merry. "Just a warning to stop hitting people with that lethal weapon," he said. He motioned to his men. "Take the corpse into the parlor, please: I'd like to question it. Now, where are your friends?"

When Vizzini's men had left, carrying Lyman Churchman in a kind of phalanx, Antonio stepped forward and put his arm around Joyce, but St. John looked as if he had been paralyzed.

"Lyman Churchman!" St. John exclaimed. "My family's known him for years! Why? And how did he know . . .?"

"We'll find that out, though I think I know most of the answers," Vizzini said. "In the meantime it looks as though you are all in the clear. Did you have a nice trip up from Pompeii?"

Joyce cringed, but St. John nodded with slow understanding. "You set this whole thing up. You let us escape from the hotel to be here."

"I wanted everyone together to see if I could stop these murders by precipitating one. But as you see"—Vizzini shrugged—"it went a little wrong. I didn't mean to jeopardize Dr. Lacey's safety. I only wanted to sell the fake urn and stop this business."

"But you bought the urn yourself," Antonio said. "Did you expect the murderer would go after you next . . .?"

" 'Signor Don Ummari'?" Vizzini asked with surprise. "Oh, no! I thought the freshly broken clay on the mouth of the urn would make him go after Johnnie Aramidian like a hummingbird after honey. I'd set up Johnnie. Are you all right?" he asked Joyce.

"Aside from the fact that I can hardly stand on my legs . . . yes," she said, conscious of the lightened weight of the handbag on her arm. "How did you get Aramidian to cooperate with you?"

Vizzini flashed a rare, sharp smile. "He's only in Italy on a temporary visa. Considering his background, he behaves fairly well. Oh . . . incidentally, that statue wasn't real, either."

Antonio smiled. "Only one person could have done those reproductions so well. . . ."

"Yes, Carlo Montebello. What a perfectionist he is! He's

been working day and night for over two weeks. He even insisted the clay for the *bucchero* must come from the Sarno area. . . ."

"He knew it wasn't from the north?" Joyce asked in dismay. "Only one curator recognized that. Signor Montebello made a mistake on the statue, though: it was reversed. I suspect because he did it from a photograph. . . ."

"The reversal was intentional. We reasoned that if a person had *one* statue . . . why would he want another one just like it? Unless they could be placed facing one another . . . like the duck fountains at Pompeii."

Though Joyce wanted to hear everything, she felt an increasing desperation to get away from the villa. She had never questioned Vizzini's intelligence, but she was still unsure of his psychic powers. She was sure her handbag must be giving off some kind of vibrations which he might pick up.

"We should look in on Churchman, poor devil," St. John said. "I don't know what got into him. He must have come unhinged. . . ."

"Ah, you feel as I do about murderers!" Vizzini said, taking his arm. "Questioning him is only a formality. It will be much more pleasant to stay here than be extradited to France . . . with its guillotine," he shuddered. "He's an interesting man, really. Did you know he's a book collector?"

"Yes, he's been trying to buy my uncle's library for years." St. John paused. "What has that to do with his actions?"

"I'm afraid I must reveal all," Vizzini said, glancing at Antonio. "I really don't like to . . . I'm a naturally reticent man. Signor Casale, you have the most devoted mother . . . I don't know how you can endure her, but. . . . She told me everything when I was in Pompeii the day I saw you. More than everything, I think." He looked at Joyce. "She was only concerned about your welfare, so please don't be too hard on her. I confirmed her story with your uncle," he said to St. John. "He's a chatty old man, even over the telephone. He had told Churchman about the scroll . . . before Dr. Lacey even went to see the dealer. He thought Churchman was his friend. A scroll is . . . a kind of book, you know. And one from Pompeii would be very valuable. It's a pity it is lost. At any rate, Churchman has been out of England a lot lately, and Scotland Yard found another document in his collection . . . only a scrap, really, but part of one of the Dead Sea Scrolls. He was my prime suspect, but he came early and left right away. Carlo's urn didn't interest him in the least. Either he realized it wasn't the real urn . . . somehow . . . or he was so intent on the scroll, he decided to have another go at the tombs, where he had met Dr. Lacey before and hit her on the head. If she was interested in the sarcophagi, so was he . . . and like you, he hadn't had a chance to get at them again, because the place was under guard. I must confess," he admitted with irritation, "that I had no idea he'd gotten back into that garden. . . ."

"He killed all those people just to see their collections?" St. John asked, appalled.

"What else can an illegal collector expect . . . from another illegal collector who is a fanatic about finding an item? Most of those people don't show their collections to others, you know. Of course, his friend O'Keefe had no collection. The poor man got on to Churchman somehow. Maybe he tried to enlist his aid in finding the urn. O'Keefe had known him for a long time: he probably knew something of the book collection. Then, when O'Keefe began to hear about the collectors' murders, he tried to do something to stop his colleague. . . ."

"He did," Joyce said numbly. "He put a guard on us. He was determined not to let the scroll leave Italy if it were . . . found."

Vizzini swore. "Bastard of the Holy Spirit! Why didn't you tell me sooner? I was struck at the time by the fact that only someone who knew about O'Keefe's ulcers would have killed him that way." He touched his own stomach reflectively.

Lyman Churchman was lying on the platform, still unconscious and Joyce wished St. John would stop asking questions before the man came to his senses. She did not want to be apprehended with the scroll in her handbag.

"You made us think we were suspects just to keep us out of trouble," St. John said, and the captain looked fondly at Joyce.

"In her way, Dr. Lacey's a . . . vulnerable little creature. I didn't want her to get killed. I knew you'd all go crazy and come to the auction when you got the invitation. You were pretty clever, really. If my men hadn't been watching to see how you'd do it, that burned-out Fiat would have taken them in. . . ."

"I don't feel well," Joyce said suddenly. "I think I'm going to be sick."

"Please," Vizzini said with concern, "go, then! I have all the evidence I need, short of a confession. He'll confess." He indicated Churchman and chopped his own neck with the back of his hand. "It's much nicer here than in France. I hope we meet again, my dear girl, under pleasanter conditions. Now . . . please leave this handsome parlor: I don't like your color at all."

Joyce was not feigning illness this time. She admired Captain Vizzini, but he frightened her to the point of nausea. When they were in the Fiat, she began to breathe again.

In a small voice, but with the authority of a general, Joyce ordered, "Drive directly to the airport, Antonio. Ian, how much money do you have with you? I left my traveler's checks at the hotel. . . ."

Antonio was shocked and bewildered, but St. John merely asked, "The airport? What the hell are you talking about? Why the airport?"

"Because"—she swallowed—"I have the scroll and urn in my purse. That's what Churchman was after in the garden. And Vizzini will find that out . . . soon! I want to restore them myself."

Antonio suddenly accelerated the car; he, at least, understood her feelings. "England . . . or America?" he asked.

"England, I suppose. This broken thing belongs to Stanton. We'll return it as soon as it's all together again. . . ."

"Broken?" St. John said with relief. "I was wondering how you'd got it in your purse. But what about our things at Pompeii? What about Stanton's car?"

"Are you coming, too?" she asked.

"Of course I am. Do you think I'd let you travel alone . . . with that on your person?"

Antonio drove quietly for a while. "I'll send your things along if I can. Vizzini will probably impound the car, though, when he finds out about the scroll."

Joyce had a sudden, sinking thought: they were leaving Antonio here to face Vizzini alone. And she did not want to leave him at all. "Come with us!" she urged. "Forget about our things . . . the car. Antonio, please come to England with us!"

He shook his head. "No. I belong here. The institute will be opening soon. You have a lot of work ahead of you, too. Don't worry about me. He has nothing to hold me on: I'll be all right."

St. John left to search for a counter to buy tickets in the middle of the night, while Antonio waited with Joyce. Awkwardness hung heavily between them, and they did not speak for a while. They both knew it would be a long time before they met again, if ever; Antonio finally took her hand.

"I don't know how long it will take to restore the scroll," she said to fill the silence. "I'll need the help of experts, and. . . ."

"Lord Willoughby will take care of that, I think. Joyce" —he paused—"Ian's a good man. He likes you."

She nodded miserably, with a premonition that she was not going to like what she heard next. His eyes met hers briefly, and he looked down at his shoes. "Do you realize what he's been through with us . . . with that bullet in his back? What I'm trying to tell you is that . . . in spite of everything. . . . No, that's not what I want to say. Please forgive me for behaving like an imbecile sometimes. You didn't know what I was feeling. I know I have no hold on you."

"Antonio . . ."

He took her face between his hands and kissed her very lightly on the forehead. "Good-bye, darling. Try not to freeze to death in England this winter, huh? Please . . . think about Ian."

Her emotions were thrown into complete turmoil: this night had been too much for her. Now Antonio was telling her to marry Ian. She turned her face so he would not see her expression, and did not answer until she could compose her voice.

"I know you'll be all right. You have everything planned . . . the institute, your job. You're many things, Antonio, and some of them are rather complex. But I'll say this for you . . . you're"—she reached up and kissed his lips— "wonderful. Good-bye, dear."

She walked away quickly, with her heels echoing on the marble and her heart breaking in her chest. Before she was completely out of hearing, she heard his voice call after her, "Thank you, Joyce! Nonno will be so happy!"

Chapter Sixteen

When Joyce and Ian arrived at Willoughby Hall, a telegram was waiting for her. She tore it open with trembling fingers, sure it was from Antonio: he was the only person who knew where she was. But the telegram read:

CONGRATULATIONS. YOUR TOOLS AND TOOTHBRUSH WILL BE RETURNED WHEN YOU GIVE BACK WHAT YOU HAVE. THE CAR IS IN A GARAGE IN ROME. CONSIDERING THE MAGNITUDE OF YOUR PROJECT, I GIVE YOU ONE YEAR. DURING THAT TIME, ANTONIO CASALE WILL BE KEPT UNDER SURVEILLANCE. I OWE YOU THIS MUCH FOR CHURCHMAN.

CAPTAIN GIULIO VIZZINI

Two days later, an envelope arrived from Italy with no message inside at all, only a single sheet of official stationery with a small fragment of papyrus Scotch-taped to the middle of it. Joyce spent a week, using several different chemicals, removing the tape from the scrap of scroll Vizzini had found in the garden.

The communications from Italy were infrequent after that; but whether from Vizzini or Antonio, they urged her on in her arduous, painstaking work. Though Antonio did not write often, he did not seem to be annoyed by the surveillance: he spoke mostly of his work at the institute. He often mentioned Vizzini, however: He might begin a statement, "As Vizzini says . . . ," and in response to one of her later letters, he referred to the captain simply as "Giulio," which gave her a moment of confusion. Antonio's letters were always signed "With affection," and they left her feeling empty, a void which she filled by working even harder. The continuing official interest in Antonio was hinted at strongly in Vizzini's notes.

Though the notice was short, Joyce's university freed her from her contract without any trouble; perhaps they had not expected her return, anyway. And Stanton Willoughby showed almost too much interest in the scroll from the moment of its arrival at his house: he fixed his attention on nothing else. First, he bought new guard dogs; then he went overboard in his caution and installed an electrified fence. She feared that the family gene for insatiable collecting was beginning to emerge in him.

When autumn melted into the slow fogs of winter St. John rejoined his unit and was sent to Germany. Joyce missed him more than she expected she would. He was the only real companion she had. His family, a lovely mother and younger sister, lived close enough to the Hall for Joyce to call on them sometimes, but it was not the same without Ian. They talked about him constantly, even showed her pictures of him in the family album. She knew what they were doing, and she was touched by it: they wanted her as part of their family. Ian was the only one who did not indicate such a desire, and she did not know what she would do if he ever did.

Unable to drive except with a chauffeur, disenchanted with his roses during the winter, Lord Willoughby hovered over her shoulder in the library, watching every move she made, occasionally contributing a suggestion, as though it were a sports car instead of a scroll that she was taking apart. Left alone with him and the servants, she would have lost her mind but for the complicated puzzle on the library table, which saved her.

Joyce contacted Dr. Willis-Parks to recommend an expert to advise and assist. He provided just the man she needed, an elderly professor for whom the restoration of documents had been a lifelong work. He knew papyrus inside and out, as though he had invented the frothy, beautiful plant whose stalks had first been pounded into paper. He could have removed the Scotch tape from Vizzini's contribution in a few hours' time. Under his guidance Joyce was soon able to work on her own again. On his first visit, the expert was not alone, however: Dr. Willis-Parks, long curious about the grounds of the Hall, made it his business to come along for the ride. And in the space of a single afternoon he solved Joyce's problem with Stanton. Dr. Willis-Parks was able to persuade Stanton Willoughby to share his extraordinary enthusiasm over the mound covered with bare bushes and rose hips. After that her only worry was that the two old men would end up with pneumonia from working in the garden in the rain. Dr. Willis-Parks was soon residing at the Hall, recruiting the gardeners as workmen, organizing Stanton's dig. From the appearance of their mackintoshes at the end of the day, Joyce knew the old men were not leaving the details to the gardeners, though: they were knee-deep in mud themselves. Because of their advanced ages, she did not suggest sensibly waiting until spring to start the excavation. They had

put up a tent and tarp, and they had never been so happy in
their lives. She took hot tea out to them every day.

When all the treated fragments of the scroll had been
laid out on the large table, with the windows locked and a
folding screen in front of the door to prevent drafts,
Joyce's real work began. From the pieces before her, including the almost powdered scales in small boxes, she
calculated that the scroll, though only about a foot wide,
must have been longer, and had been rolled very tightly
into the urn. It was almost Christmas before she got to this
stage, and she would have forgotten the season if she had
not received an early card from Antonio with a Renais-
sance Madonna and Child on it, and the simple greeting
"*Buon Natale*" inside. She began to wonder if she could
assemble the scroll in the time Captain Vizzini had al-
lotted. At this stage the Latin was impossible to decipher;
the letters were not all capitals like the announcements on
the walls at Pompeii. The writing was small and ran together, an individual handwriting with too many fractured
lines and serifs to give any indication of the scroll's content. She speculated that it might be a legal document,
though there had been no seal, and she wondered in dejection if it was worth all the work involved: she was tired,
using her reading glasses more often than before.

She took a break and purchased a box of Christmas
cards in the village, airmailing them to the few people
closest to her: Antonio, St. John, Nonno Casale (and the
signora), and some of her friends and students back home.
As an afterthought she addressed a card to Captain Vizzini. With his wolflike tenacity, he had been a friend, too.
He had put pressure on the Greek police to search Karavitas' house on Corfu, and her statue was now in Athens
being studied by state archaeologists. Karavitas, rich in
olive oil, had gone free, though. In response to her card she
received a rather surprising reply:

Cara mia,

Thank you for your greeting of the season. It was one of the few I received: people don't like me much. Everything here goes on as usual, even at this happy time of year: crime never ceases. In fact, the work of thieves progresses at an accelerated pace, as I sincerely hope your work does.

That Casale fellow's getting difficult to keep up with: sometimes my men can't find him at night. If he has contracted the Neapolitan Malady, no one as yet has heard him singing. Finish up soon and come back here.

Giulio Vizzini

Without pausing to pursue the intricacies of his Sicilian mind, from the affectionate greeting to his invitation, Joyce went back to work like a fury, sorting and mounting the fragments of papyrus with a specially compounded glue. At least it kept her mind off Antonio.

When spring arrived, Joyce was still leaning over the slanted easel, working diligently. Then the muddy old men made their first discovery and nearly blew the remaining flakes of papyrus away with their elated entrance into the library.

"Traces of a keel, I think," Dr. Willis-Parks cried, clutching Stanton's shoulder for support. "Too muddy to tell much yet . . . that tarp's inadequate. But if it isn't Anglo-Saxon, it's Viking, Joyce!" He held out a rotten splinter of wood in the palm of his hand. "We're taking it down to have it dated. Not that the test will distinguish between the two, of course. But it'll tell us if it's as old as I think it is, and not just some fishing craft beached by the river in recent times. . . ."

By "recent," Joyce understood him to mean anytime after A.D. 500. She took time off to celebrate with them in the evening, grateful to see them well and sound after all those months in the rain, and sharing in their happiness over the find. After dinner and coffee, Stanton Willoughby suddenly remembered something he was supposed to tell her.

"I forgot," he said. "I had a letter last week. Ian's coming home."

Ian St. John was thinner, and he seemed a little apathetic. Joyce was concerned about his appearance, and one evening she asked as carefully as possible, "Have you seen a doctor lately, Ian?"

His blue eyes crinkled at the corners. "I've seen all the doctors I care to, darling. If I never see another one, it'll suit me just fine. What do you hear from Antonio?"

"Not much," she said, suppressing a dejected sigh. "He hasn't written more than a few times . . . and one of those was a Christmas card. I've heard from Captain Vizzini more often than Antonio." She told St. John about Vizzini's harassment and even let him read the communications. He smiled thoughtfully, his eyes more on her than on the scroll she was restoring by lamplight.

"You've lost some weight," he said. "Hasn't Stanton been feeding you in my absence?"

She shrugged and adjusted her reading glasses: the work she was doing was very fine. Why was he concerned about her losing weight when he himself looked so terrible? She did not sleep well that night, and her mind was slow the next morning. So slow that it did not register, for a moment, that the last bit of papyrus was in place, and she was looking at the letter of a man who had died nineteen hundred years before.

St. John helped her sort the urn shards while they waited for a Latinist from Cambridge to confirm her translation of the scroll. The arrival of the mail became the main event of the day. When confirmation came from the scholar, an airmail envelope with green-and-red chevrons on its border arrived at the same time, and Joyce opened it first. Again, it was from Vizzini:

> *Preziosa,*
> Time is running out. Don't you even want the car back?
>
> Giulio

Joyce assembled the urn, wishing her fingers were as agile as those of the potter she had watched at Carlo Montebello's factory. She did not quite understand Vizzini's haste. According to the agreement she still had three months left to return the urn and scroll. She felt that the veiled message had something to do with Antonio, though, and that impelled her to work more quickly.

When the urn was fully restored and stood, black and somberly beautiful, on the table beside the mounted scroll, Ian finally said, "Joyce . . . you wouldn't consider marrying me, would you?"

Captain Vizzini responded to the news that the antiquities were ready for return with his usual efficiency. He called Joyce on the telephone.

"I'll have the car there in two days' time. The customs clearance has been started already, and two men from Scotland Yard will escort the boxes to the airport. The car will be there by teatime on Tuesday afternoon. Can't you even tell me what the scroll says?"

"It's a letter," Joyce smiled to herself. Revenge was sweet! "You can read it on Tuesday afternoon. *Ciao, Capitano!*"

"*Ciao, amica,*" he answered grudgingly. "I don't think you're being fair!"

Dr. Willis-Parks and Lord Stanton Willoughby were up

to their necks in their digging by the river when the Ray
swerved violently up the drive on the appointed day. The
age of their discovery also having been confirmed, the two
old men seldom left their site, even for meals. Stanton had
lost all interest in the scroll: all he cared about now was
Anglo-Saxon archaeology. The return of his car must have
meant no more than an unpleasant reminder that he could
no longer drive it, because he did not bother to come to the
house to verify that it was intact.

Joyce and Ian waited for Vizzini on the veranda, with
the tea table carefully laid. The captain was on time, right
to the minute, and they could see as the Ray passed that he
was not in uniform. Ian rose to greet their visitor, and
Joyce stepped forward with a smile. Then she saw that it
was not Vizzini at all in the driver's seat, and her heart
went wild.

Antonio smiled easily as he came up the steps, waving a
piece of paper in his hand. His eyes appraised her slowly
and affectionately, and he shook his head.

"I don't think England agrees with you . . . you're pale.
It doesn't agree with me, either!" He indicated the traffic
citation in his hand. Then he saw Ian and walked past her
to shake his hand warmly. Antonio's gaze slid quickly
away from them and wandered over the imposing front of
the Hall. "It's not much like Das's villa, is it? Well," he
added, looking at both of them, "when can I see it?"

"As soon as you've had something to eat," Joyce said
uncertainly. "You have been driving like the very devil.
Did you stop for meals along the way?"

He stuffed the traffic citation in his breast pocket. "I
have one from every country I passed through . . . a
regular collection. I stopped to eat sometimes. . . ."

"Where's the car from Scotland Yard?" Ian smiled.
"You didn't leave it in the dust like the patrol car on the
Autostrada, did you?"

"No. They stopped back there in the village to eat. That

crazy Giulio! I was just moving into my apartment yesterday morning, when he came and shoved me into the Ray. 'Take it to England,' he said. 'Have it at Willoughby Hall by four o'clock tomorrow afternoon.'" Antonio lined the citations up on the table before him: one from Switzerland, two from France, and the one he had just received. "I hope he can fix these," he said, looking worried.

"I suspect he can," Ian said, his eyes amused and thoughtful. "All in all, the captain's quite a fixer . . . Joyce, darling, the tea is overflowing into the saucer. . . ."

Actually, she had been steadying the pot with one hand against the other to accomplish the task at all. She passed the tray of sandwiches with more composure.

"An apartment?" she asked. "In Rome?"

Antonio helped himself to one of the small sandwiches. "Yes. When I finished at the institute, Giulio told me where to go to look for a job . . . and I got it! In a place where I'll be able to get something done, too. As you know, that isn't easy. He knows how to cut through red tape, that one . . . you wouldn't believe him! He seems to know everything, everyone. . . ."

"And everyone," Ian said drolly, "probably 'owes him.' "

"Probably," Antonio smiled, "but in a nice way. The Sicilian knows how to keep his mouth shut. I'm sure there are many who are indebted to him for that." He bit into the sandwich, chewed for a moment, then lifted the top slice of bread and looked at the small green leaves inside with suspicion. "What is this? I can't even taste it. . . ."

"Watercress," Joyce said. He shrugged bravely and ate another one: he was obviously very hungry. Joyce rose from the table and instructed the maid to get another tray, but to have the sandwiches sprinkled with oregano and rosemary this time. The maid was appalled, but obeyed her instructions.

"He has something big going," Antonio continued as he

ate. "I'm not sure what he's up to . . . but he'd like to have you in on it, Joyce. I told him I didn't think you'd leave here." His eyes held St. John's for a moment and moved to the sweeping green grounds, interrupted by the two old men digging by the river. "What are they doing?"

"We'll tell you about it later," Joyce said, leaning forward on her elbows with interest. "What does he need me for? All this time I've thought he was harassing you. It sounds as though you're bosom companions."

"We're friends . . . but he doesn't tell me anything. All I know is that when I accompanied him to Carlo Montebello's place a few weeks ago there were some books about fluorescent chemicals on the table . . . you know, the one in the room upstairs."

"Fluorescent chemicals?" she asked.

He shrugged broadly. "You know how thorough Montebello is! My guess is that Giulio's going after the *tombaroli* soon. If they used the right fluorescence on Carlo's 'masterpieces,' it'd only show up under a certain light. The grave robbers in Tuscany would have it all over their hands. . . ."

"What a devious mind," Ian said with admiration.

"Mine . . . or his? I'm only saying what *I* think. And of course Giulio remarked that he wished Joyce were there to help him." Antonio wiped his hands on the napkin in his lap. "Can I see it now? I've eaten. You should have told us what it says!" he reproached her. "You . . . haven't packed it already?"

"No," she smiled, "that won't take long. Everything's ready. I didn't tell the captain what it says because I wanted to get back at him for what he's done to me all these months. . . ."

"Well, it worked! He's been going out of his mind. He has a case all ready for it in the Naples Museum and he doesn't even know what the scroll says. For a while, he was

afraid it might be an amorous love letter that he couldn't
have displayed at all. Then they opened the secret room in
the museum to the public . . . all the *pornografia* . . . so he
went ahead with the display case anyway. Come, now . . ."

As Ian opened the front door his hand rested on Joyce's
shoulder. Antonio's quick eyes noted the naturalness of the
act, and he followed them slowly to the library.

The scroll, enclosed in an airtight frame, was set up on
Joyce's easel. It was an impressive display. Very few fragments were missing, though it was not easy to read. The
small letters flowed in low case and capitals, in the writing of an individual whose *s* was a long curve, running
from the top to the bottom of a line. Missing letters had
been filled in by Joyce herself, with parentheses around
them, in the parts of the papyrus that had been too powdered or lost. Instead of Antonio's acting as interpreter,
Joyce did so now:

> To Lucilius Aelius Tiburtinus
> Rome
> Lucilius, my dear friend,
>
> If the world is not ending, you will find this when
> you come looking for me. The door to the peristyle
> will no longer open, and we are alone in the cellar,
> without knowing what is happening outside. The air
> is almost gone. The lamp flickers. I shall mark the
> loose stone you know with lampblack, though you
> would probably look there anyway, knowing I keep
> my important papers there. You know everything
> about me, Lucilius, except for one last, important
> thing. Lucilius, I have found the answer for which
> we have searched so long.
>
> What a quest we set ourselves as young men, so
> many years ago: the meaning of life itself, the secret
> of happiness. First, we tried the gods and then the
> girls, and abandoned them both over chilled Falerian

wine. The philosophers did not help us, either: we
believed them all, and we believed none of them. The
key to happiness, we decided in the baths that day,
was power, wealth, all the many things that money
can buy to make a man feel superior to his neighbor.
Sometimes we became less than friends in our effort to
outdo one another. Then, when youth was gone, we
were drawn together again by our interest in our
collections.

Everything is gone, Lucilius, snatched away in a few
hours. My house, my collection, all have crumbled
around me. This graceful black urn, which you de-
sired, is all that is left: I give it to you, now, with
open hands. And with it, I hope I can give you understanding.

I stayed because I did not want to part with my
things: how ironic that is. I thought what was happening was no worse than the earthquake sixteen
years ago. But it was something different. When we
left the garden the sky was black as night and stones
were falling. The fumes were noxious. Everything is
gone, but I am happy. The answer came to me, not
from books or philosophers, but from the simple action of another human being. Yes, one person remained with me . . . my plain, virtuous wife, Albana,
whom I have almost ignored. You must remember
that I only married her for her dowry. She is sleeping
already: her face is peaceful. She has known the
secret all along.

Lucilius, life is an end in itself: things are not important. Power only covers our insufficiencies as men.
All we have done in this world is take, my friend.
Albana has given, and she has been happy. In my
concern for her in these past terrible hours, I have
known what it is to give, too. For the first time in

my life, I am really happy. The answer is not to be found in the ways we sought it. It is in the act of giving, my dear friend.

Lucilius, it is love.

The letter was unsigned, unsealed, undelivered: its author would remain forever anonymous, with less identity even than the friend who did not receive the message. If Lucilius had come back to Pompeii, as Joyce was certain he had, he had found the city buried in ash and lapilli twenty feet deep. Subsequent eruptions of the volcano had buried it even deeper, until the city itself was lost for centuries. Her eyes met Antonio's for a moment, but he looked away quickly.

"Somewhere," Antonio said softly, "in the unexcavated area, there's another Cryptoporticus. My God, I wish there were funds to speed up the excavation!" He paused and studied the scroll. " '*Amor est*,' " he quoted with a sigh; then he smiled. "Well, it's a kind of love letter, after all. You may have these things packed, now, if you like. Here are the clearance papers. I must leave again shortly."

Joyce's gaze followed him as he left the library to take the air outside on the veranda. She turned to Ian and found him watching her steadily. She attempted to smile.

"Go after him, you little fool," Ian said gently. "I understood why you couldn't give me an answer. You saved my life, isn't that enough?" She gave him a questioning look. "If it hadn't been for you, I'd have drifted on for years. In all the time I was in Germany, I couldn't find a single vice that really appealed to me: I tried almost everything, too. But all I really wanted was you! And because of you, I took the chance on that operation. I'm all right now! If I don't buy it in Stanton's car, I'll be around for a long time . . . and there are other . . . *nice* girls."

"You had the bullet removed?" she said with disbelief. "Why didn't you tell me?"

"I didn't want you to act like a nurse. I'd had enough of nurses. Joyce . . . go after him! Don't be a proud little idiot. I've never seen two people so proud in my life. If one of you doesn't unbend, *nothing* will happen!"

"But he doesn't want me. You saw. . . ."

"I knew it all along. Why do you think he was so angry when I appeared on the scene. And that day at Das's villa? He was worried about you. He thought you were really sick at first. Then, when he realized you were only pretending, he felt like a fool. He was already frustrated out of his mind by your virginal attitude, and suddenly he had competition from me. He probably thought that I had more to offer you. He loves you, don't worry about that. Have you ever come right out and admitted to yourself that you love him, too? Or . . . have you been too busy?"

"I tried not to think about it. There were other things . . . you don't understand. . . . If he liked me then, I'm not sure that he does now."

"You won't find out," he said grimly, "unless you say it first. Is that so hard to do?"

It was, not because of pride, but because she could not face a final rejection. Antonio was something sweet and beautiful in her life: she would rather have him as a friend than . . . nothing.

The men from Scotland Yard came to pack and seal the parcels under her supervision. When they were being carried to the official car, Antonio came back to the veranda to say good-bye. He shook St. John's hand first, strongly and sincerely,

"I wish you every happiness, my friend."

"I wish the same to you, Antonio," Ian said sardonically, but his smile was honest.

When he turned to Joyce, Antonio was unable to find words. He put his hands around her shoulders and touched his cheek briefly to hers.

"Good-bye," Antonio said, and started to leave.

"For Christ's sake, Joyce!" Ian boomed.

Without a chance to brace himself, Antonio nearly slipped on the gravel when she hurled herself into his arms. "Please take me with you!" she cried. "Oh, Antonio . . . I do love you so!"

His taut body was unresponsive. "What about St. John?" his deep voice said above her.

"He's all right, Antonio . . . he had the operation!"

"What are we doing, he and I . . . bouncing you back and forth like a ball?"

"I realize now why you said what you did at the airport! You were the one who was giving all along: I just took. And you didn't write for the same reason. But Ian's all right . . . he wants me to go with you. Please take me!"

"I'll have to change my plans," he said, but his arms enfolded her. "I'll even have to get a different apartment." He laughed and kissed her hair. "Once, I told you you'd have to beg . . . you do it very well." Before she could rally to his teasing, he was kissing her, and then he was serious again. "Oh, darling . . . Hurry up! Get your things together. . . ."

"It'll only take a minute. You know my duffel bag. Don't go away . . . please."

"Don't forget your handbag!" he called after her. "Giulio still has your tools. He wants to return them!"

She stopped at the door. Vizzini. He had not returned the contents of her handbag with the car, as he had promised. He had sent Antonio instead of coming himself. He had even offered her some kind of consulting job in Rome. When her interest in the scroll had lagged, he had implied that Antonio was falling in love, or seeing someone else, when . . . no doubt . . . he was actually home studying every night. Vizzini! The unmitigated nerve of the man, looking into other people's hearts, manipulating their lives!

She looked back at Antonio, standing tall and poised

against the expanse of green lawn, as innocent of the captain's schemes as she had been. He blew her a kiss and motioned for her to hurry.

She burst through the doors and took the stairs to her room two at a time, trying to get accustomed to the idea of having at last admitted how much she loved Antonio.